Trapped

Book 5 of the Jenny Watkins Mystery Series

1. Driven
2. Betrayed
3. Shattered
4. Exposed

Copyright 2014

Dedication

Once again I have a million people to thank for this book. My family—Scott Durfee, Hannah Durfee, Seneca Durfee, Evan Fish and Julia Fish—all come to mind, first and foremost. Their love and support make these books possible; I couldn't do it without them. (My eleven-year-old, Julia, was even my cover photographer this time…thanks, Jubes!)

Of course, I would have absolutely nothing without my parents. Mom and Dad, I thank you for everything you have done for me over the years. I love you both VERY MUCH.

My proofreaders are also my heroes: Bill Demarest is my fact checker…nothing gets by him. Danielle Bon Tempo is my primary editor; I thought I was good at grammar until I got a sheet from her with several pages of necessary edits. My ego has officially been deflated. ☺

My "target audience" proofreaders are also my lifesavers: Sam Travers, Stacy Vicks, Sue Durfee, Felicia Underwood and Jenny Groom—thank you so much for your honest input. You are my last barrier between pride and humiliation. I trust you will tell me, "Don't do it," if it shouldn't be done.

My friends and family, who are too numerous to name (and I am too old to try…I'll inevitably forget someone and then feel like a jerk,) have also been my inspiration. There are little bits of past conversations in these books, and I am sure you can recognize some of them. You know who you are.

Lastly, if you are reading this, I thank YOU. I cannot tell you how grateful I am for your support. Truly. I'm still amazed by the outpouring I have received.

And Cathi…tell Ron I kept up my end of the bargain. He's got to read this one.

Chapter 1

Jenny looked at the ring being offered to her, unsure of what to say. She knew the answer was supposed to be an emphatic *yes*, but she hadn't been expecting this proposal, and she'd never given any consideration to the question ahead of time. While she loved Zack, they were still very new, and she wasn't sure of their potential for longevity. This was much too big of an undertaking to jump into blindly.

As a result, "Oh my God," was all she said.

Zack smiled optimistically. "So what do you say?"

His hopeful face broke her heart. "Um...I don't know what to say," she replied, knowing that her response was not going to be *yes*.

"Listen," Zack said, softening his tone. "You don't have to answer right away. I know this is a big decision I'm springing on you, but I just want you to know where I'm coming from. I am committed to you and to this baby one-hundred percent."

A sincere and loving smile graced Jenny's lips. "Thank you, Zack. I really do appreciate that."

"And I know you said you only wanted to have legitimate children, so I wanted to make that happen for you."

Jenny laughed, in part because she'd never dreamed in a million years that would ever be an issue for her. "Thank you for that, too."

Zack continued to kneel on one knee, making Jenny nervous. "Here," she said, patting the couch. "Why don't you come up here so we can talk about this." He obliged, and Jenny continued. "I hope you're not offended when I say that I'm going to take you up on your offer to think about this for a while. I'm not saying no...I just don't feel quite ready to say yes yet, either."

"I get that," Zack replied, looking at her with a genuineness that warmed Jenny's heart. "But the ring is still here if you decide you want it later."

Glancing down at the modest solitaire ring in the box, she noted, "It's beautiful, by the way."

"I know it's not much," he said, "but I also know you're not flashy."

"No, it's perfect. Truly." Jenny once again smiled compassionately at Zack. "But let me tell you what my concern is, just so you know. I do love you; that's not the issue. My fear is that we're still in the throes of the whole *new-love* thing. Everything seems perfect now, but if my relationship with Greg is any indication, that feeling definitely wears off."

"I've got to admit," Zack said, "I've never been in a relationship long enough to reach that point." He let out a goofy chuckle. "My relationships were never more than a couple of months long, and I was always perfectly happy when the girls ended it."

Jenny winced. Zack had spent a lifetime struggling in the dating world, and now the answer to his first marriage proposal was a whopping *I don't know.* It seemed the poor guy couldn't catch a break, and she hated the fact that she was contributing to his misfortune.

Jenny released an exhale, and with it a good deal of tension left her shoulders. She looked at the man she truly did love and admitted, "My dating life hadn't been all that spectacular before I met Greg, either; that relationship is really my only basis of comparison. But, believe it or not, I was once enamored with him. I thought he was perfect in every way." She bit her lip as she stifled a giggle. "And as you know, by the end of the marriage I could see nothing but flaws when I looked at him, and now the man makes me want to vomit."

"But Greg is an asshole."

"I know that," Jenny said, feeling somewhat validated, "and that's my point. In the beginning I was so in love with him that I didn't see him for what he really was...and that scares me. I don't *think* I'm doing the same thing with you, but I need to be sure." She quieted her voice. "I just want to take a little time to think about it, that's all."

"Any idea how long?"

Jenny used a casual tone when she replied, "I don't know. A couple of years, maybe?"

"A couple of *years*?"

With a laugh and a pat on his leg she added, "Kidding."

"Good Lord, I hope so."

The smile left Jenny's face. "Honestly, I don't think I can give you a time frame, unfortunately. But I hope you realize it isn't just me I'm worried about. I don't want *you* to propose to me too soon, only to find out after it's too late that I annoy the shit out of you."

"I don't think that will ever happen."

"Remember...right now you're looking at me through rose-colored glasses, my friend."

"Yeah, but don't forget," Zack began, "we were just friends first. I don't just love you; I like you, and I don't think that's going away any time soon."

"It may not," Jenny said, sincerely hoping it never did. "It may be that I'm just being over-cautious." She took his hand and stroked it with her thumb. "But if I answer you right now, I'll be answering with my heart. I want to think about this with my brain for a while and make sure we're making the decision that's best for both of us."

"All three of us," Zack corrected.

Jenny smiled. "Yes. All three of us...you, me and our beautiful daughter."

Jenny's phone rang, and the caller surprised her. "Officer Fazzino," she said when she answered. "How are you?"

"I'm doing great, Jenny, how are you?"

"Can't complain." She pinned the phone between her ear and her shoulder as she continued to empty the dishwasher. "To what do I owe the honor?"

"Well, something interesting has come up. It's a long string of events, kind of like that whole seven-degrees-of-separation-to-Kevin-Bacon thing."

Jenny found herself giggling.

The officer continued, "A friend of mine had a cousin come up from Virginia. The cousin caught wind of the fact that a psychic had been used to solve a few murders around here and noted that a friend of hers owns a bed-and-breakfast in Virginia that is presumably haunted. The cousin wanted your contact information, but I didn't want to give out your phone number without your permission. Instead I got the phone number of the woman who owns the bed-and-breakfast, and I've been asked to pass that information along to you. She's hoping you can go down there and figure out what's happening in that house."

Making a face, Jenny said, "A *haunting*? I've never really done a haunting before."

"Is it something you think you can do?" Officer Fazzino asked.

"I have no idea," she confessed as she put away a stack of plates. "I guess I could give it a whirl, but I make no guarantees."

"Well, a whirl is the best they can ask for, now isn't it?" Officer Fazzino gave Jenny the phone number of the woman in Virginia, and Jenny concluded the phone conversation with a promise to give the woman a call.

She contemplated the phone number on the scrap of paper in her hand before dialing, unsure what to make of "a haunting." In the past she'd been the only one who could receive contact from the spirits; what would she encounter if this spirit's presence was known to everyone? Would she be completely overwhelmed? Or would she be given no more insight than anyone else?

With a strength-gathering breath she dialed the number. The woman on the other end sounded pleasant. "Heritage Inn."

"Hi, my name is Jenny Watkins, and I was given this number by Officer Danny Fazzino in Ivory Heights, Connecticut. I was told to call about a haunting that's been going on?" Jenny phrased that more like a question than a statement.

"Yes, Miss Watkins, I'm so glad you called," the woman replied enthusiastically. "I'm Jessica Thompson; I own the inn. I have to tell you, there have been some strange occurrences around this place. For years I haven't known where to turn. It wasn't until my friend told me about your ability that I realized I could potentially get some answers."

"When you say 'strange occurrences,' what exactly do you mean?"

"Slamming doors and unexplained wind gusts...inside the house," Jessica replied. "I've always told the guests that it's just because our ventilation system needs to be fixed, but I've had multiple people come out to look at it, and they all say nothing is wrong with it." She paused and her voice became noticeably shakier as she added, "There's got to be some other explanation for what's happening."

"Okay, well, I can try to see what's going on, but I have to warn you this isn't usually how things go for me. In the past I've just been minding my business and the spirits contact me; I've never really gone out in search of a spirit before."

"I'm willing to try it, even if it doesn't work. I honestly don't know what else to do. This whole concept is so foreign to me."

"Believe me, I understand that. I'm relatively new to this whole thing myself," Jenny replied kindly. "So when would you like me to come?"

"As soon as possible, actually. I've got some vacancies for the next few days; you're more than welcome to stay here free of charge, and of course I'll pay you for your trouble."

"I'm not worried about that," Jenny replied. "Let me just talk to my business partner and see if he's available for a road trip. Then I'll let you know when we'll be coming."

"Oh, I didn't realize you had a partner. Will you be needing two rooms?"

"No," Jenny said sheepishly, "we're a couple."

"That works out better, actually," Jessica replied. "I'd hate to have you by yourself if you encountered anything frightening."

"So where exactly is this place?" Zack asked as Jenny backed the car out of the driveway.

"It's in the southern part of Virginia, close to the North Carolina border. It seems like it's in the middle of nowhere—I can't imagine that many people would want to stay out there, to tell you the truth."

"Well," Zack said as he typed the address into his GPS, "sometimes the purpose of going to a bed-and-breakfast is to be out in the middle of nowhere."

"I guess you're right."

After a moment, Zack said, "It looks like the total travel time is about eight hours. Are you sure you wouldn't rather just fly?"

"A flight would probably take just as long," Jenny surmised. "We live an hour from the airport, I doubt there'd be any direct flights, and the inn is well over an hour from Richmond airport. I'd rather just drive; then we have the freedom of having our own car."

Zack glanced at her out of the corner of his eye. "You do realize you have enough money to charter a flight, right? And rent a car?"

Feeling a bit embarrassed, Jenny noted, "Yes, I do have that much money...but I won't have it very long if I keep spending it on things like private planes. Besides," she added with a smile, "I thought you liked road trips."

"I do. I also like the idea of having your car so we can high-tail it out of there when the doors start slamming for no good reason."

"*You* can high-tail it out of there," Jenny replied. "I'm going to stick around and try to figure out what the spirit wants."

"How do you know it wants something?"

"Don't they always?"

Zack thought about that for a minute. "Touche," he eventually said. "But I have to admit if I see anything...ghost-like...I'm going to be totally creeped out."

Jenny's tone was playfully argumentative. "You have always said you're jealous of my abilities to communicate with the dead, and now here you have the chance to see an anomaly for yourself—and you say it's going to *creep you out*?"

"Well, it's cool when *you* do it," he reasoned. "Me? Not so much."

Jenny laughed and shook her head. "That's the same kind of reasoning my second graders used to use."

"Well, it's totally valid."

She smiled as she drove down the road. She and Greg never used to have this kind of playful interaction; she wasn't imagining that. While she knew this relationship with Zack could never be perfect—no relationship was—at least it had the potential to keep her entertained.

Perhaps it could stand the test of time. A nervous energy tingled within her.

"Wow, this place really *is* in the middle of nowhere," Zack said. "I feel like we've been on this road forever."

The road they'd traveled since exiting the highway had wound through stretches of farmland and vast expanses of forested area. After forty-five minutes on that same road, the GPS finally directed the couple to turn right down a narrow side street. The Heritage Inn appeared very quickly on their left.

The building itself was magnificent, poised at the end of a long driveway and up a slight hill. A two-story, columned front porch extended the entire length of the house, giving the inn the distinct air of southern hospitality. The lawn was beautifully manicured with a small fountain situated between the house and the road.

"Damn," Zack said as they pulled in the driveway. "This place is nice."

"I guess now we know how this middle-of-nowhere inn stays in business."

As Jenny got out of the car, she felt a nervous energy building inside her, although she wasn't sure if those were her own nerves or if she was picking up on somebody else's emotions. Sometimes it was difficult for her to tell.

Looking up at the beautiful house, she couldn't help but wonder what history it held within its walls—and who felt so strongly about their unfinished business that they lingered inside.

The couple walked through the front door and approached an elegant mahogany desk that sat off to the right. The woman working behind it appeared to be in her early fifties with short, gray hair and glasses dangling from a chain around her neck. She regarded the couple with a friendly smile. "Hi," she said sweetly. "Welcome to the Heritage Inn. Do you have a reservation?"

"Kind of," Jenny began. "I'm Jenny Watkins, and this is my partner, Zack."

The woman stood up and clasped her hands together. "Oh, thank you so much for coming. I'm Jessica; we spoke on the phone."

Jenny extended her hand. "Pleased to meet you. It certainly is a beautiful place you have; I can see why people are willing to make the drive to stay here."

"It *is* quite a hike," Jessica replied, "but this house is steeped in history. A lot of people come out for that; others come to enjoy the peace and quiet." She leaned forward and gave Jenny a smile. "We've even been known to host a few weddings."

Zack and Jenny exchanged a knowing glance.

"Well," Jessica continued, stepping out from around the desk, "before we do anything else, let me show you to your room so you can get situated. Then, when you're ready, we can get down to business."

Jenny looked around as Jessica led the way. Two grandiose stairways curved on opposite sides of the main room, meeting in the middle on the second floor. The steps were blanketed in red carpet, adding to the elegance. Jessica led the couple up the closer set of stairs, directing them to the right once they reached the top. At the end of the hall she opened a door, exposing a room that was exquisitely decorated in period pieces.

"Wow," Jenny noted. "This looks amazing."

"Well, we tried to make it look as much like it would have looked when the house was built in the 1830s...but with all of the modern amenities, of course."

As Zack put the suitcase down, Jenny ran her hand along the quilt that adorned the bed; it appeared to be hand-stitched. The bed rails and the dressers had the sturdy look of wood, and the smooth new floors probably resembled the original flooring, only better. A fireplace graced the far wall, although Jenny concluded it was gas based on the switch positioned next to it. She wondered if a real fireplace had been there a century and a half ago.

Jessica opened another door. "And this is your bathroom. Every room has a private bath."

"That must have been a bear to accomplish," Zack noted, his former life as a home-builder shining through. "The original house had only one bathroom, and it was outside."

Jessica widened her eyes. "It wasn't easy, that's for sure. But it all came together nicely, I think."

Jenny walked through the threshold of the bathroom and saw all the modern conveniences, albeit with old-fashioned-looking fixtures. "This is simply incredible," she declared.

"Well, I'm glad you like it. This is actually our nicest room. It used to be the master bedroom when the house was first built."

A wave struck Jenny, during which time her emotions ran extremely high. Somebody in this house definitely had something to say, but she wasn't sure whom—or what.

Keeping that notion to herself, Jenny asked, "Do you mind if we take a tour of the rest of the property? I want to see all of the buildings to see if anything in particular triggers a contact."

"That's fine," Jessica said. "I'd be glad to show you. We do have other guests, so I won't be able to let you into every room, but I can certainly show you the empty rooms and walk you around the grounds."

As they walked down the hall past several closed doors, Zack posed, "How many bedrooms do you have here?"

"Seven. And as you might suspect, this was a magnificent house back when it was first built. Houses simply weren't that big back then." They approached a door that was slightly ajar, and Jessica let them in. "Here's our Carriage Room," she announced.

Jenny took several steps in and looked around. The room was smaller than hers had been, but it was still exquisitely decorated. She closed her eyes, trying to get a contact, but nothing out of the ordinary struck her.

They completed the tour of the rest of the house, and then Jessica led them outside for a walk around the property. There were several buildings on the lot, although none of them even came close to the size or elegance of the main house. The first building they entered had been converted to a modest-sized banquet facility. A stage graced the back of the large room while round tables with chairs skirted the edges, leaving an area in the middle open. She presumed that to be a dance floor.

"Back when the house was built, this was the slaves' quarters," Jessica explained. "This whole area had been a tobacco farm—tobacco plants as far as the eye could see—and the plantation owners had numerous slaves to work the farm. Now, obviously, this building serves as our banquet hall. If the weather is nice, most people prefer to have their functions outside, but when Mother Nature doesn't cooperate, we have this area as a back-up."

Jenny smiled as she looked around the room, wondering how many weddings had taken place there. The thought warmed her. Then her mind wandered back a couple of centuries and she considered how many people had been crammed into this single space, calling this tiny area home until they were sold away. The whole concept was unfathomable to her. Owning people? Buying, selling, and trading them? Keeping them in conditions barely worthy of pets? She couldn't wrap her head around it.

Perhaps the spirit haunting the main house might actually have been that of a slave, protesting the horrid conditions that he, or she, had been exposed to during this life. Jenny would need to keep that notion in mind.

Guiding the couple to a third building, Jessica said with a smile, "This building was originally used for storage, and it still is. Back then it housed the tobacco that had been harvested, but now it's just our shed, essentially."

Jenny poked her head into the building and looked around. Nothing remarkable struck her; she simply saw a riding lawn mower, countless tools hanging from the walls, and boxes throughout. She quickly decided this building was not the source of the problem.

As they headed back to the inn, Zack asked Jessica, "So what is the history of the house itself? Who has owned it?"

"Well, like I said, it was built in the 1830s, and the original owners were the Davies family. Unfortunately, they died of illness—which was not all that uncommon back then—leaving the house vacant when the Civil War broke out. Considering its size and remote location, the house was regarded as the ideal place to serve as a hospital for Confederate soldiers. While no battles were fought on this particular stretch of land, a lot of the troops who had been wounded in Richmond and areas west ended up here…or at least, those who were well enough to travel. Many couldn't make it this far…but for those who could, it was a place they could recuperate peacefully, away from the front lines."

Jenny's mind became flooded with thoughts as Zack asked, "Did any of the soldiers die here?"

"Yes, I'm afraid so," Jessica replied. "Even though these young men weren't mortally wounded on the battlefield, infection was a real problem back then. And disease. A lot of those boys who survived their original injuries came here only to die from some other cause."

And suddenly the suspect pool is huge, Jenny thought.

"In fact," Jessica continued, "there's a cemetery just on the other side of those trees. A lot of soldiers are buried out there."

Zack and Jenny glanced at each other. "Do you mind if we take a look at it?" Jenny posed.

"No, not at all," Jessica replied as they walked toward the large patch of trees. "Just follow me. Anyway, to answer your question from before, the house became empty again for a while after the war, until the Sheffield family bought it in 1872. It remained in their family for generations before they finally sold it in 1965 to another family, the Lewises. In 1997 the house went up for sale again, but by this time it needed some serious TLC. As you can imagine, a one-hundred-sixty year old house had a lot of things that needed repair and upgrading.

"And that's where I come in," Jessica added with a proud smile. "I was able to get the permits needed to convert the building to an inn. I also got it put on the registry of historical buildings in Virginia, which has really helped get the word out. With its ties to the Civil War, the inn has definitely been an attraction for history buffs. Like I said, I've been able to do a respectable business, even with it being out here in the middle of nowhere. But, honestly, I'm afraid that if people find out that it's potentially haunted, I'm going to be hard-pressed to get anybody to stay here at all."

"I would think that some people would actually be interested in staying here *because* it's haunted," Zack noted. "I'm sure there's a segment of the population who would think that was cool."

"I've considered that...but I'm afraid of the type of guests who would want to stay at a haunted inn. I certainly don't need any animal sacrifices on my property, or any other disturbing ritual that might be associated with the occult."

While Jenny listened, she noticed some small, white headstones appearing through the trees. As they became closer, the numbers seemed to multiply. By the time they arrived, Jenny was able to see about seventy grave sites.

"Here it is, obviously," Jessica said as they arrived.

Jenny squatted down to look at the writing on the headstone closest to her: *Joseph Thatcher, 1841-1861.* Jenny lowered her eyes as she realized she'd already outlived this soldier by seven years. It didn't seem right. Moving on to the next stone, she noticed the age of the victim had been twenty-three. A third headstone caused her to say, "My God. This kid was only seventeen."

"I know," Jessica said. "They were just boys. It's such a shame."

Actively pushing that thought out of her head, Jenny focused on the sensation she was feeling inside—or more accurately, the lack of sensation. Standing back up she announced, "I'm not really getting any more of a contact out here than I did in the house. In fact," she added, "if anything, it's less."

Jessica gave Jenny a sideways glance before noting, "I've never really experienced anything out here, although what goes on in the house is mostly unexplained gusts of wind. If the wind blows out here, that wouldn't seem out of the ordinary."

"Well, I don't quite feel the same energy out here."

"Energy?" Jessica asked.

Glancing up to look at Jessica, she said, "Yes. Energy. It's like I was nervous or excited about something in the main house." She looked back at the stones. "But not here."

"Isn't that normal, though?" Zack asked. "I mean, don't you usually have the feelings where the people lived—or even died—but not where they were laid to rest?"

Jenny wrapped her arms around herself as the evening chill set in. "Yes, that's true. But If I were looking at his tombstone, I would think I'd get *some* kind of inkling that I was on the right track."

Zack turned to Jessica. "Is this everyone who died here? What about the original family? Or the Sheffields? Or even some of the slaves?"

"The original family is buried in a plot a few miles from here," Jessica explained. "The same applies to the Sheffields, although it's a different cemetery. To be honest, I'm not aware of any slave burials on the property." Her voice became grim. "Unfortunately, I don't think any records were kept of that kind of thing; the slaves weren't held in high enough regard for their deaths to be documented."

Jenny closed her eyes.

"How about the soldiers?" Zack continued. "Is it possible that this isn't everybody?" He gestured toward the patch of headstones. "Could some of the Confederates who died here be buried somewhere else?"

With wide eyes, Jessica shook her head. "I don't think so. I imagine they would put all of the deceased in one place."

They all exchanged silent glances, deducing nothing. "Well, I know this is shocking," Jenny began, "but I'm getting chilly. Do you mind if we head back inside?"

"Of course not," Jessica said, and the three returned the way they had come.

Zack touched the television that hung on the wall in the Statesman Room. "This thing looks out of place, don't you think? They had tube TVs back then, not flat screens."

Jenny looked at him, desperately hoping he was joking.

"Kidding," he said with feigned defensiveness. "Jeez, I'm not that dense."

"You just said it with such conviction," Jenny replied. "It's hard to tell if you're joking sometimes."

"That's part of my comedic genius." Zack grabbed the remote and flopped onto the bed, propping pillows behind him on the headboard. Crossing his legs, he turned on the television and rested one arm behind his head.

Seeing him lie there sparked something in Jenny's mind. A brief image flashed before her eyes, only for a second. The room appeared different, looking more like the Carriage Room she'd seen on her tour. Candles burned in a chandelier from the ceiling, as well as in sticks on the nightstand. A black-haired man was lying in bed, writhing and moaning as if in horrible pain. Almost as soon as the flash appeared, it was gone.

"Wow," Jenny declared. "That was disturbing."

"What was?"

Jenny described her vision to Zack, prompting him to ask, "Are we staying in the wrong room? Should we actually be in the Carriage Room?"

She opened the suitcase and pulled out her pajamas. "It doesn't seem like it matters. Apparently, I don't have to be in that very room to get a vision from it." She slipped out of her clothes.

"Do you think it was a soldier?"

Jenny shook her head. "I can't say. The image was too fleeting."

"Well, hopefully there will be more visions to come."

Comfortable in her pajamas, Jenny climbed into bed next to Zack, feeling his warmth, looking at the fire that burned behind the glass. "I have to admit, this is really nice, despite the fact that we're here on business."

"It is nice," Zack agreed, "but I'm having a difficult time relaxing. I can't help but feel that any minute some crazed ghost carrying an axe is going to jump out and cut our heads off."

"Ghosts can't carry axes."

"They can in my mind," Zack said, "and that's all that matters." He rolled over onto his side to face Jenny. "You know what I want you to do? I want you to remind me of this when our son is a toddler and claims to be afraid of the boogey man in the closet. Even though you and I know there isn't anything in his closet, if he believes it, then it's real to him. I don't just want to dismiss it and tell him he's being silly. He's going to be genuinely scared, and I want to take it seriously."

Jenny smiled warmly. "Sure thing. When she cries because she's scared, I'll remind you of this."

Flipping onto his back, Zack said, "Do you know what this whole thing reminds me of? Scooby Doo. I seriously feel like we should have shown up in a psychedelic van with a talking dog."

"You think?"

"It especially became true when Jessica started alluding to the fact that this ghost could ruin her business." He got an evil grin on his face. "I almost said *Zoinks* when we first saw the cemetery, but somehow I didn't think Jessica would find that very funny."

"Probably not." Jenny's smile rivaled Zack's. "I do have to admit that you look a lot like Shaggy."

"You know what? I do." He seemed to contemplate that for a moment. "But you don't look like either Daphne or Thelma." He held up his hand. "Now don't be threatened by this, but I had a *huge* crush on Daphne when I was little. She was pretty hot."

"Well if I remember correctly, Fred was pretty strapping himself."

At that moment a gust of wind rushed through the room, causing the curtains to move and the flames in the fireplace to flicker.

"Holy shit," Zack said sitting up. "Did you feel that?"

"Feel it?" Jenny replied. "I did more than feel it."

Zack's eyes widened. "What does that mean?"

"I heard it." She sat up to look squarely at Zack. "As the wind blew by, I heard a name spoken in a whisper."

"What did it say?"

Jenny tucked her hair behind her ear. "It simply said, 'Andrew.'"

Chapter 2

Zack hopped out of bed in a single motion. "Holy mother of God," he proclaimed. "I'm completely freaked out about this."

"It's okay; it's gone," Jenny said calmly.

"How do you know?"

"The wave is over," she explained. "It was just a short one."

After taking a few breaths, Zack seemed to calm down.

"If it makes you feel any better, the voice didn't sound angry...or hateful...and I don't think we're in any danger." She paused for a moment before noting, "Maybe all of these wind gusts have just been him trying to communicate, but so far no one's been able to hear him."

"I guess," Zack conceded, sitting back down on the bed. He scratched his head as he added, "So all he said was 'Andrew?'"

"Yup. That was it," Jenny replied. "Did you happen to notice any Andrews on the headstones outside?"

"No, but I wasn't particularly looking for one, either. We'll have to go back out in the morning and see if we can find any."

"Andrew," Jenny muttered. "Somehow I think that was a pretty popular name back then. We might find more than one."

Zack shrugged. "At least it will give us a start."

"True."

"Hey, do you think we should go tell Jessica about this?"

Jenny glanced at the clock; it was nearly eleven. "Maybe we should wait until the morning. It's late, and I'm not sure if she's the one who's up with the birds making breakfast."

Leaning back in the bed, Zack let out a deep exhale. "I don't think I'm going to be able to sleep tonight after that."

Jenny laughed. "The funny thing is that I'm used to it by now. This contact was only different because it had wind associated with it, but other than that it's the same stuff I've been dealing with for months now. And nobody got shot or beaten up or choked or drowned in this contact...it was actually quite lovely as far as visions go."

"Well, I'm new at this, and—lovely or not—it scared the crap out of me."

Patting Zack's arm, she noted, "Hopefully we'll be able to figure out who this Andrew guy is tomorrow, we can do a little research on him, and maybe we can see what he wants. With any luck, tomorrow at this time Andrew will be a thing of the past."

"Here's one," Zack said, pointing to a headstone. "Andrew McDermott."

Jenny walked over to where he was standing. "It looks like he was twenty-four when he died." She shook her head. "He was older than a lot of these other guys, but still very young." She wrote his name and the years of his birth and death on a notepad, and they continued to read the other stones.

They were able to find one other possibility, Andrew Owens, who was twenty-two when the war claimed him. No other soldiers shared the same name.

As they walked back toward the main house, Jenny posed, "How much do you know about the Civil War?"

"Not as much as I should if I'm going to call myself an American," Zack confessed.

"Me neither. I mean, I learned briefly about it in school, but I know painfully little about specific battles and when they took place."

"It looks like research time, doesn't it?"

"Yup. Sure does." Jenny looked at her notes. "McDermott died in 1865, and Owens in 1862. I guess there were local battles around that time?"

Zack shrugged. "I have no idea."

As they headed back to the house, they encountered an older couple walking arm-in-arm out toward the graveyard. The white-haired man used a walking stick and wore a flannel shirt;

the woman was in jeans and a sweater and seemed to be relying on the man for stability as they trudged through the grounds.

"Excuse me," Zack said to them, catching Jenny by surprise.

The woman flashed a friendly smile. "Yes?"

"Y'all wouldn't happen to be history buffs, would you?"

Jenny admired Zack's ability to approach total strangers and strike up a conversation, although she found his sudden use of the word *y'all* to be a bit curious.

The woman gestured to the man accompanying her. "Roy is." She glanced at him knowingly. "I would say he's an expert."

Roy let out a hearty chuckle. "I know a thing or two about a thing or two."

Jenny smiled; they seemed like a very pleasant couple.

"Well, would you possibly be able to tell us a little bit about the battles that led those guys to be there?" Zack gestured over his shoulder toward the cemetery. "I know so much less about this than I should, and I'd like to remedy that."

"Sure thing," Roy replied, the gleam in his eye revealing his passion about Civil War history. "You want to come back there with us and I'll tell you the story?"

"That'd be great." Zack turned to Jenny with child-like zeal. "Look, we get our own personal tour guides!"

After working their way back to the cemetery, Roy pointed to some of the earlier headstones with their deaths being listed in the latter half 1862. "I'm guessing those boys were most likely victims of the Seven Days Battle. There were six separate skirmishes in that one very deadly week in late June of 1862. If memory serves, I think there were thirty-five-thousand casualties in that week alone. That's both sides together, of course."

Jenny thought back to the small town she'd grown up in; the entire population was smaller than the number of wounded soldiers in that one week of fighting. She couldn't wrap her head around it.

Zack remained much less affected. "So where did those battles take place?"

"Right around Richmond," Roy said, "on the western side. Now it's all suburbs there; it's amazing what a hundred-fifty years can do." Shifting his weight with his walking stick, he added, "I imagine a lot of the people who live there now have no idea of the horrors that took place in their own backyards."

Jenny swallowed, well aware that she just might be witness to some of those horrors first-hand over the next few days. Redirecting her mind to the issue at hand, she jotted down the information that Roy had just told them. Andrew Owens had died in July of 1862; perhaps he'd been one of those thirty-five-thousand casualties of the Seven Days Battle, living long enough to come to the hospital, only to die from complications a month later.

Roy walked over to another headstone, gesturing to it with his walking stick. "This here's from 1863. So far it's the only one I've seen from that year. That makes sense since the biggest battles around that time were in the Fredericksburg area. I can't imagine many of those boys came this far for treatment. In fact, I'm not even sure this one's due to battle; he may have died from illness. Tuberculosis and typhoid fever were rampant in those army camps. All those soldiers shared extremely tight quarters, and the living conditions were terrible...that's a breeding ground for disease. If one of those boys came down with TB, before you know it they'd all get it."

Jenny furrowed her brow and shook her head; even when they weren't in battle those soldiers were putting their lives in jeopardy. Placing her hand on her belly she hoped that somehow the world would be able to find peace within the next eighteen years.

Although she doubted it.

Roy continued his lesson, walking over to a pair of headstones dated 1864. "May and June of 1864 were particularly bloody in this part of Virginia as well. Grant's Overland Campaign started up there by Fredericksburg and worked its way down to the Richmond area, leaving over seventy-thousand casualties in its wake."

That was another unfathomable number to Jenny. Although she knew Roy hadn't gotten to the battle that had claimed Andrew McDermott yet, she decided she couldn't take it anymore. Feeling overwhelmed by the sheer magnitude of the death and destruction, she silently handed her notepad over to Zack and walked toward the woman who had accompanied Roy.

She was standing quietly on the sidelines, listening intently to the stories her husband had been sharing.

"Hi," Jenny said quietly as not to interrupt Roy. "I don't believe we were properly introduced. I'm Jenny." She stuck out her hand.

"Florence," the woman replied as she returned the gesture.

"Your husband seems to know quite a bit about the war." Quickly making a face, Jenny added, "At least, I assume he is your husband."

"Yes," Florence replied with a smile, "for fifty-two years."

Once again Jenny was awed by the size of a number. "Wow. That's amazing. Although, you don't look old enough to have been married for fifty-two years."

"Well, we were young," she replied with a laugh. "I was only nineteen when we got married."

That's how old Jenny had been when she'd met Greg, and what a mistake that turned out to be. She wondered how Florence had been able to make the right choice at such a young age. Had she really been that astute, or did she just get lucky?

Jenny diverted her gaze back to Roy, who was still spewing facts as Zack jotted down notes. "So how does he know so much about the war?"

"It's always been a hobby of his," Florence began, "but since he retired a few years ago, he's really gotten into it."

"Are you as into it as he is?"

"No," Florence said with a wave of her hand, "but I'm glad he does it."

A small smile graced Jenny's lips. "Why is that?"

"Because he was driving me crazy."

Jenny's subtle smirk turned into a full-fledged giggle.

"Things were fine until he retired," Florence continued, "and then it all fell apart." Her pleasant, soft-spoken demeanor made her comments seem even funnier to Jenny. "He spent decades looking forward to his retirement, and then when it happened, he was bored silly. It's like he was completely lost without his job to keep him busy. In order to occupy his time, he started micro-managing everything around the house. Now, mind you, I'd been running the house just fine for more than forty years by myself and he never had anything to say about it—but as soon as he retired he decided that the pantry needed to be rearranged. He'd check over my grocery list to make sure we actually needed everything that was on there. He even pulled out the refrigerator and asked me how long it had been since I'd cleaned behind it."

Jenny bit her lip.

"So I told him to get a hobby," Florence continued with a straight face. "It was either that or I hit him over the head with a frying pan. I suggested he pursue his interest in the Civil War, and that's been a blessing. He spends hours every day doing research, planning war-oriented vacations and shopping for memorabilia. In fact, he planned this whole trip. It's been a nice little getaway, and it kept him out of my hair for two good weeks while he organized it."

"Are you actually interested in this Civil War stuff, or are you just going along with it?"

"I find it interesting, yes," Florence said with a subtle nod. "Not as much as he does, but that's okay. I do enjoy these trips." She placed her delicate hand on Jenny's forearm. "It helps that he weaves in visits with the kids and grandkids. After we leave here we're going to see my new great-grandson in Alabama. He was born back in December, and we haven't met him yet." Florence beamed with pride.

"Is that your only great-grandchild?"

"Yes, he's the first one. I can't wait to see him."

"I'll bet," Jenny declared as Zack approached her. Once he arrived, Jenny focused her attention on him.

"That was fascinating," Zack said definitively. "You should have kept listening."

"I know. I didn't mean to be rude," Jenny explained. "I just couldn't bear to hear such high numbers of casualties. I think being pregnant has made me soft."

Florence placed her hand on Jenny's shoulder. "You're pregnant?"

Jenny smiled sheepishly; something about being unwed took some of the joy from the moment. "Yes, ma'am."

"Is this your first?" Florence asked.

"Yes, ma'am."

"Well, that's wonderful," Florence declared. "Being a mom is the hardest thing in the world, but just keep in mind that it's all worth it in the end."

"Don't scare the woman," Roy said curtly. "Having a baby around isn't that bad."

"That's easy for you to say," Florence retorted. "You didn't raise the kids. I did."

Mercifully, Zack turned to Roy and loudly said, "Well, thank you for sharing your knowledge about the war. I feel a whole lot smarter now."

"Glad I could help, young man."

After bidding their goodbyes to the couple, Zack and Jenny once again headed back to the house with Zack explaining, "It looks like Andrew Owens may have been a victim of that Seven Days Battle, and McDermott probably got hurt during the campaign at Appomattox."

"Appomattox," Jenny repeated with recognition in her voice. "Isn't that where the war ended?"

"Yup. Apparently it's not all that far from here. The end of the war started with the capture of Richmond, and the fighting gradually moved west to Appomattox, where Lee ultimately surrendered to Grant."

Jenny nodded. "Then it does make sense that a soldier involved in that campaign would end up here."

"Unfortunately, knowing where and when they got wounded doesn't help us figure out where they're from, or anything else about them for that matter. It's not like today where they keep records of which troops are in which area. According to Roy, it was much more makeshift than that. Kids just picked up guns and joined the Confederacy. There were records of which general was at each battle, but the forces themselves weren't well defined."

Jenny twisted her face. "I guess we'll need some other way to figure out who this Andrew is and what he wants."

Putting his arm around Jenny, Zack noted, "Then Andrew is going to have to tell you more than just his first name."

Jenny looked around with just her eyes, hoping he'd heard that.

"By the way, I am sorry I bailed on you back there," she noted. "It's just all that talk about death was getting to me. I couldn't take it anymore. I mean, I'm about to have a baby. I'm going to love it and hold it and rock it to sleep. I can't imagine in twenty years that a single gunshot will take this child away from me. And then when you consider that thirty-five thousand mothers went through that very same horror in a single week?" Jenny shook her head. "I can't even listen to that."

"I'm not sure *casualty* means *death*," Zack said.

"Not right away." Jenny pointed back toward the cemetery. "But we just witnessed proof that somebody who didn't die on the battlefield might still have died from something else directly related to the injury."

Zack didn't reply. She imagined he was unsure of what to say.

"We're a civilized society," Jenny went on as they approached the inn. "I can't believe we still rely on war to solve our problems. Couldn't we just negotiate?"

"Some people aren't up for negotiations."

"Okay, so then we arm wrestle to determine the winner. Or play chess. Why do we have to kill each other?"

Zack held the front door of the inn open so Jenny could walk through.

She continued her rant. "Don't you find it odd that if two individuals disagree and one kills the other, it's considered murder and punishable by law...but if two governments disagree and they send masses of people to kill masses of people, it's called war and it's perfectly legal?" They ascended the curved stairway to the second floor. "It's just so barbaric."

Jenny froze at the top of the stairs; instead of turning right to get back to her room, she was inclined to go left. Stepping slowly, she was led to one of the rooms she hadn't seen on her tour with Jessica because it had been occupied. Placing her palm on the door, she closed her eyes and absorbed the vision. After a few moments, a gust of wind sailed through the hallway, and with it came another message perceptible only to Jenny.

Elizabeth.

Chapter 3

"Whoa," Zack said with awe. "There was that breeze again."

Jenny lowered her palm from the door and looked at him. "It was the same whispery voice as before. He gave me another message; this time he said 'Elizabeth.'"

"I wonder who that is."

"I don't know," Jenny informed him, "but I did get a visual to go along with the message."

"Oh yeah?"

She nodded in response. "It was a woman, lying in bed, looking like she was very ill. Her face and hair were very sweaty, and she moaned as if she was in a lot of pain."

"Was she in this room?" Zack posed, gesturing to the door she'd just been touching.

"I imagine so," Jenny said, "but I've never seen the inside of the room, so I can't be sure."

Zack shook his head. "Wait a minute. If this was a hospital for recovering wounded soldiers, why was a woman lying in bed? I didn't think women fought in the Civil War."

"I don't think they did either," Jenny agreed, looking up at Zack. "Maybe we're not dealing with a soldier."

Zack and Jenny sat across from Jessica at a dining table in the lobby as Jenny sketched the image of the room from her vision. "Artistic ability sure comes in handy sometimes," she noted as she quickly completed the rough drawing of a square room with two windows surrounding a brick fireplace. Spinning it around to face Jessica, she asked, "Is this what the room to the left of the stairs looks like?"

Jessica placed her hand on her chin. "Not anymore, but it's possible that it *used to* look like that. It's been so long since we've renovated that I don't remember what any of the rooms looked like before. Give me one second." She disappeared from the table into a back room, emerging a short time later with a photo album.

"I took pictures before and after the renovation. I'm sure I'll be able to find some pictures from when I first bought the property." She flipped through some pages, mumbling to herself out loud. "It's the Plantation Room...let me see...no, I think it's after these...oh! Here it is!" She studied the album for a moment before saying, "Wow. I think this speaks for itself."

She spun the picture around, along with Jenny's sketch, and the two images looked nearly identical.

"I guess we have our answer," Zack noted. "That's definitely the same room."

"The one thing we don't know the answer to is why a woman was in that bed," Jenny said.

"Could she have been one of the nurses who took care of the soldiers?" Zack asked. "The guy outside seemed to think that some of the soldiers here weren't necessarily shot, but rather had disease. Maybe she caught something from one of them."

"It could be, I guess," Jessica said with a shrug. "I don't know how we'd find that out."

"The spirit did give me a name," Jenny noted.

"Oh really?" Jessica said.

"Apparently her name was Elizabeth."

After some deliberation, Jessica shook her head slowly. "I'm afraid that doesn't help me."

"None of the previous owners were named Elizabeth?" Jenny asked.

"The Davies were Jeremiah and Sarah, and the Sheffields were James and Ann." Jessica looked helpless. "I honestly don't know who Elizabeth and Andrew could have been."

Impatient by nature, Jenny felt her frustration surface, although she kept her tone pleasant. "In every other case I've worked there's been a living, breathing human who has had some direct contact with the deceased. Unfortunately with this case, everyone with information is long dead by now. There's nobody to ask. We don't know who these people are or what message they're trying to send, and I don't even know how we could find that out." She rested her chin in her hand.

"I could try to do some research," Jessica suggested.

Jenny smiled. "I appreciate that."

"You know," Zack began, "you could call Rod and see if he has any advice." Zack turned to Jessica and explained, "Her father is also a psychic."

Jenny mulled that over for a moment before declaring, "That's not a bad idea." She checked the time on her phone. "I may be able to catch him before he goes to work; it's still early on the west coast. Give me just one minute."

She got up from the table and dialed, indeed getting a hold of him while he was still on the road. After a short conversation, she hung up and returned back to Jessica and Zack at the table.

"So what did he have to say?" Zack asked.

"Well, he said he didn't think he could help me," Jenny confessed, "but he did direct me to somebody who can."

Zack looked curious. "And who might that be?"

Admittedly feeling a little nervous, Jenny sheepishly said, "My grandmother."

"Her name is Ingunn," Jenny began, "and she's psychic as well. Apparently over the years she's been able to contact a few spirits by actually summoning them, which is something I never knew before."

"Like a séance?" Zack asked.

"I guess." Jenny shook her head. "It's all new to me."

"This is amazing," Jessica said with awe. "Your whole family is psychic?"

"Well, not the whole family," Jenny confessed. "I actually just found out a few months ago that the man who raised me wasn't my father. It turns out my *biological* father was psychic, as was his mother, but apparently his siblings weren't. It's hit-or-miss, I guess, and I just happened to get it. But I've never met my grandmother; I've only talked to her on the phone." A smirk graced her lips. "I've got to warn you, she appears to be quite a pip."

"Does she live close by?" Jessica asked. "Will she be able to come out here?"

Jenny shook her head. "She lives in Florida."

"Well, she's welcome to stay free of charge for a while, too," Jessica replied. "It's the least I can do if she's willing to help me out."

"I'll be sure to extend the invitation to her." With a shrug of her shoulders Jenny added, "I actually hope she can come out here; it would be great to see her face…in person, that is. I've only seen pictures."

Zack's interjection seemed random. "What are you supposed to call her again?"

"Amma," Jenny clarified. "It's Icelandic for grandmother."

"She's Icelandic?" Jessica asked. "Did she ever live there?"

"As a child she did."

Jessica looked puzzled. "And now she lives in Florida? That's quite a difference in climate."

Jenny thought for a moment before noting with a laugh, "I think if I grew up in Iceland, I'd probably retire to Florida, too. Maybe I inherited my hatred of the cold from that side of the family." A sigh denoted Jenny's change of mood. "Well, I did get her phone number for a reason, so let me make this call and see if I can get to the bottom of this little mystery."

As she said those words, Jenny once again saw the similarity to a Scooby Doo episode.

Ingunn's greeting was curt when she answered the phone. "Yes?"

"Hi, Amma, it's Jenny. How are you?"

"Hello, Jenny. I guess I can't complain. How are you?"

"Doing great." After a short conversation that brought the women up to speed with each other's personal lives, she informed her grandmother about the latest investigation. "So far we've been given two names—Andrew and Elizabeth—but we can't seem to figure out who they were. There are two deceased soldiers named Andrew buried on the premises, but we have no explanation at all for who Elizabeth might be. None of the home's owners had that name; we already checked into that."

"How did you come across this spirit?"

"I was actually hired to investigate it. It's been haunting the inn, and the owner wants it gone."

"Haunting, eh? How so?"

"Well, it makes its presence known through wind gusts in the house, and so far I've been able to detect that each breeze is associated with a message. While everybody can feel the wind, so far I've been the only one who can understand the intent behind it."

"Huh," Ingunn said as if she were deep in thought.

Jenny gave her a moment to elaborate, but she said nothing more. "What is it, Amma?"

"It's just that the spirit has to feel very strongly about something in order to penetrate into the world of the living."

Goosebumps surfaced on Jenny's skin. "So you've seen this before?"

"I'm old. I've seen it all before."

"And that's exactly why I'm on the phone with you," Jenny replied with a smile. "When I talked to my father, he said you've actually been able to summon spirits in the past. I think that's what I'm going to have to do if I plan to get anywhere. If you don't mind me asking, how were you able to do that?"

"I don't think that's something I can explain over the phone. It took me years to master that skill."

"Well, would you be opposed to flying up here to Virginia for a little getaway in a haunted bed and breakfast? I can arrange for everything, and it would be my treat."

"I can't let you do that," Ingunn replied.

"Of course you can. If you don't want to come, that's perfectly fine, but if you do come, I can certainly take care of it all." Jenny's tone became jovial. "It'll be a business expense."

The change in Ingunn's demeanor was obvious through the phone. "Well, in that case, I think I could deal with a little vacation. After all, I'd love to meet my new granddaughter."

New granddaughter, Jenny thought. She was twenty-seven years old, yet this made her sound like a newborn. She smiled for more reasons than one. "That sounds great. Let me just go back to my room and get my computer; then we can figure out what's the best flight for you."

After ten minutes' time, a flight had been booked for later that evening.

"I guess we have some time to kill before her flight arrives," Jenny noted to Jessica and Zack. "What would be the best use of our afternoon?"

"If you're willing," Jessica began, "you could go into the city and do a little research. There's a ton of Civil War information to be learned in Richmond and Petersburg. Maybe you can get someone to help you find out about Andrews and Elizabeths and their connection to this property. I'd offer to do it myself..." She looked down at her lap. "But I have an inn to run."

Zack and Jenny exchanged glances. "That sounds good to me," Zack said. "It beats waiting around here for cryptic messages that may or may not come."

"I'll get my purse," Jenny added with a smile.

Soon Jenny and Zack were on the road, Jenny behind the wheel. The weather was warm, the windows were rolled down, and the radio blared through the speakers. The smell of spring was in the air, and it was one of those days where it felt good to be alive.

About fifteen minutes from the highway, Jenny felt a tug. Lowering the radio to concentrate, she shifted forward in her seat and allowed her mind to relax. At first Zack seemed confused by her actions, but when she turned left down a desolate side road he seemed to figure out what was happening.

The road itself was barely wide enough to fit two cars; the shoulder consisted of a couple of feet of grass before the dense woods began. At a seemingly random place Jenny pulled the car onto the right shoulder, turning on her hazard lights before wordlessly getting out of the car. Grateful for the boots she always kept in the trunk, she slid them on and headed out into the woods with Zack following closely behind.

A path of trampled brush seemed to already be laid out before them, although Jenny followed the guide in her mind, not the clues from the ground. Five minutes into the walk Jenny froze, tapping her finger on her chin. "It's around here somewhere."

"What is?" Zack asked.

"The thing I'm supposed to find." The couple looked around the area, which was densely covered with plants and vines.

"Uh oh," Zack said.

"What?"

"There's a shoe." He pointed a few feet off the beaten path, where Jenny glanced and saw a woman's dirty sneaker lying ominously by itself. The sight gave Jenny a chill.

Taking a few more steps into the woods, Jenny's attention became directed to a shiny object on the ground. It was a buckle. "And there," she said, "it looks like a purse."

Silence weighed down on them like a wet blanket. They continued their search for a few minutes when Zack announced, "Oh shit."

"What's the matter?"

He guided Jenny by the elbow, gesturing about fifteen feet in front of them. "Correct me if I'm wrong," he began, "but I think that's a body."

Chapter 4

The police arrived in droves. Zack and Jenny stood off in the background as the officers cordoned off the area with yellow crime scene tape. An officer with a notepad approached Zack and Jenny, flipping through several pages until he found a blank one. He then began a series of questions.

"How did you come across these bodies?"

Jenny surprised herself with the confidence in her voice. "I was led to them. I'm a psychic, and I was just driving through on route two-fifty-seven. I felt a tug that told me I needed to come out here, so I followed my instinct, and here I am."

Despite her conviction, the officer looked at her with one raised eyebrow.

"Look me up," Jenny said. "I'm all over the internet. My psychic ability has helped solve several murders. I've already worked with a few police departments; I can gladly give you the contact information of some of the officers I've helped, if that will get you to believe me."

"I think I'll take you up on that," the police officer said.

She chose to give him Danny Fazzino's number as opposed to Elijah Murphy's; she still felt badly about how that last case had unfolded, and she didn't want to poke a sleeping bear.

"Whoa," the officer in front of her said as he hung up his phone. "You really are a psychic."

"I'm glad you believe me," Jenny replied with a smile. "I'm actually in town to look into some paranormal activity that is potentially Civil War related, and while on my way to Richmond to do some research, I got this feeling that I needed to come here."

"Sarge, we got another one!" The voice came from deep inside the trees, causing Jenny, Zack, and the interviewing officer to look back in that direction.

The police officer who was apparently the sergeant traipsed over to where the voice had come from. "Jesus Christ," he muttered loudly enough for everyone to hear. "It's a friggin graveyard out here."

The interviewing officer turned back to Jenny. "So let me get this straight. You were just driving along, and you felt the need to come down this tiny little road...and walk out into the woods?"

"Yes, sir. Apparently one of these victims wanted to be found."

As the officer wrote, he said, "This is going to be a difficult one to explain."

"Well, we found them, didn't we? Isn't that all the proof you need that there's some validity to what I'm saying?" Jenny asked. "Besides, now you'll be able to put an end to some missing persons cases...that will feel good, won't it?"

The officer looked at her intently. "We don't have any missing persons cases."

The words confused Jenny initially until she considered their proximity to the highway; these people could have been from anywhere, dumped along the road by some lunatic who was just driving through.

"Sarge!" A voice came from a different area. "You're not going to believe this."

"Don't tell me you found another one," the sergeant said with disgust.

"Actually," the newest officer said, "I found two."

Members of the FBI showed up in staggering numbers. Zack and Jenny had been ushered back to their car; the entire area was now considered part of the crime scene, and the couple wasn't allowed anywhere near the activity. Through bits of overheard conversation, Jenny was able to deduce that the body count was sitting at seven, although they weren't sure how high it would eventually go.

The local police officers looked much more frazzled than the seasoned FBI agents; even without the uniforms Jenny could have easily determined their affiliation based on the expressions they wore. As she stood watching the professionals do their jobs, Jenny felt a short-lived but very distinct wave wash over her.

She hunted down the first officer she could find. "Excuse me," she said.

The overwhelmed local officer turned to look at her, although he didn't say anything.

"I just wanted to let you know that the letter T is going to prove to be important in this case."

He looked at her as if she had two heads. "The letter T?"

"Yes, sir. A capital T."

The officer continued on his way.

"You're going to need to tell that to someone else," Zack noted. "He thinks you're a nutball."

Jenny giggled, realizing how crazy she must have just sounded. "I think you're right. Where's that original guy we talked to? He believes me."

Zack and Jenny scanned the crowd until they found the man who had first interviewed them. He was behind the crime scene tape, and Jenny had a difficult time getting his attention. With enough arm-waving, however, she finally got him to notice her, and he excused himself from his current conversation to approach her.

"What can I do for you?" he asked.

"You can believe me," Jenny said.

"I do believe you."

"Well, that's good, because I have something else for you. I just got a brief flash of the letter T. Somehow that's going to prove to be important."

Opening his notepad, the officer scribbled the latest information.

"So what's the body count at now?" Zack posed.

"Right now eight, in varying stages of decay. This has been somebody's dumping ground for a long time."

Jenny shook her head.

"And none of these people are local?" Zack asked.

"I don't believe so. We don't have anybody unaccounted for at this time. But we're not that far from truck stop alley, so this would be a convenient place for someone who's just passing through to dispose of evidence."

"Truck stop alley?" Jenny asked.

"Yeah. That's what we call it. Right off the highway you've got those four truck stops, one on each corner...northbound, southbound, left, right...no matter where you're going or which direction you came from, there's a convenient place for you to stop and rest your bones." He made a guilty face before quietly adding, "Perhaps I shouldn't have worded it that way under the circumstances."

"I know what you meant," Jenny said without batting an eye. "I guess there are people streaming in and out of there at all hours of the night, too, so this guy could have easily used the cover of darkness to hide his actions."

"All four stops are twenty-four-hour," the officer said, "and they're all busy as hell."

A voice crackled through the unit on the officer's chest. "This one's got ID. A girl from Georgia."

Jenny closed her eyes, sickened by the fact that somewhere in Georgia a family was about to get the worst phone call of their lives.

The officer turned off his unit. "I guess I'd better be going back," he said. "Listen, my sergeant asked me to get your contact information, just in case we have any more questions about this. I'd like to give you my number, too...that way you can give me a call if you get any more divine insight."

Jenny exchanged information with the officer, whose name turned out to be Kevin Howell. "Honestly, if you want me to be able to come up with anything new, I'll probably need to come back when there's not quite so much commotion. I was able to get that one quick reading about the letter T, but generally speaking I need quiet in order to get a good contact."

The officer looked over Jenny's shoulder. "Shit. Already?" Jenny turned to see a news van pulling up at high speed. "How do they always catch wind of this stuff so quickly?"

"Well, I guess there goes any chance at quiet for a while, huh?" Zack noted.

"I'm sure this place will be a zoo for days," Jenny muttered disappointedly. "But listen," she said to the officer, "would it be possible for me to get a copy of that one victim's ID? Or any others that you find? My father out in Washington state is also a psychic, and he can get a lot from a photograph."

The officer shook his head. "I don't know. That's a new one for me. I'll have to ask the higher-ups to see if that's possible."

"My grandmother is also coming," Jenny continued, pulling out her phone to check the time. "In fact, I have to pick her up from the airport soon. She has the gift, too; maybe she'll be able to give you some insight."

The officer looked at her with disbelief. "You're a *family* of psychics?"

Jenny shrugged; family was too strong of a word given the circumstances. "It's a genetic trait, apparently."

"I tell you what...I'll call you after I talk to the boss."

Smiling politely, Jenny pulled her keys out of her purse. "Thanks. I look forward to helping you in any way I can."

Zack and Jenny remained quiet in the car for a long time. The only sound was the hum of the tires on the road and the occasional mechanical utterance from the GPS, which was now programmed to take them directly to the airport. The unscheduled events of the afternoon left no time for research at the library.

Eventually Zack's voice permeated the silence. "That was pretty creepy, wasn't it?"

Raising her eyebrows, Jenny replied, "Indeed."

"Well, as upsetting as it is to make such a find, hopefully this will put an end to this sick bastard's little game." He patted her leg as she drove. "Thanks to you, maybe the body count won't go any higher."

"Either that or he'll just find a new dumping ground. It'd be great if the press didn't know about it. Then the cops could just stake out the area and catch this guy in the act."

"But that would mean another body," Zack noted.

"Correct me if I'm wrong, but I believe the goal is to *prevent* this from happening again. Maybe the press getting a hold of this story will actually be helpful in that regard."

Another silence ensued; Jenny was simply too affected to discuss the topic anymore. Was that family in Georgia getting the phone call right now? She sighed and ran her fingers though her hair. This day had seemed so glorious just a few hours earlier; now she was so upset she could cry.

"I've forgotten what to call her again," Zack said as they pulled up to the airport parking lot.

"What?"

"Your grandmother. What do you call her again?"

"I call her Amma," Jenny noted. "That's Icelandic for grandmother." She shot him a playful glance out of the corner of her eye. "But she's not your grandmother. Truthfully, I'm not sure what you should call her."

"Well, you can marry me," Zack replied with a smile, "and then she will also be my grandmother...kind of."

Jenny bit her lip; the topic of marriage still made her nervous. Keeping the conversation light, she noted, "We don't have time to get married between now and the time her plane lands, so in the meantime you'll have to figure something out."

They exited the car and walked wordlessly toward the terminal. The talk of the proposal had put Jenny's brain into overdrive, and she once again began considering a notion that had plagued her before. She debated whether or not to bring it up, ultimately deciding it was something that needed to be discussed. "Can I ask you a question?"

"Sure," Zack replied. "Fire away."

She gathered her strength with a deep breath. "It's something I've been thinking about, even though it's not necessarily a pleasant topic of conversation." She clenched her fist and swallowed before continuing. "What if, God forbid, I miscarry tomorrow? Would the offer for marriage still be on the table?"

"Sure," Zack replied. "Why wouldn't it?"

Jenny made a disapproving face, although her voice returned to its playful nature. "You didn't take enough time to think about that. It was a serious question that required consideration, but you didn't give it any."

"Okay, I know what this is," Zack said, waving his finger. "I've heard about stuff like this before from my friends. This is one of those damned-if-I-do, damned-if-I-don't situations."

"What are you talking about?" The double doors slid open, and the couple walked into the airport.

"You're upset because I answered too quickly. But if I'd paused and thought about it before I said anything, you would have taken that as doubt, even if I had said yes."

Jenny considered his argument before conceding, "You're probably right."

"So either way I'm totally screwed. But I'm telling you the answer is yes, I want to marry you, baby or not."

Jenny couldn't help but smile. "But you didn't propose until you found out I was pregnant."

"But that doesn't mean I hadn't thought about it."

Nerves surged within her as she glanced at him out of the corner of her eye. "You'd really thought about it before that?"

"Sure," he said. "I'm thirty now, and things were going really well, so yeah, I'd toyed with the idea a little bit. I just figured I'd wait until your divorce was final before I asked you, because at the time there was no reason to hurry." He didn't look at her as he put his arm around her.

This moment made Jenny want to scream, *Yes, yes, yes! Yes, I'll marry you!* But she knew she couldn't allow her emotions to get the best of her. She'd been down this road before, and she'd learned first-hand just how horrible a seemingly-promising romance could become. Simply knowing that his proposal was genuine was not a reason to accept it.

But what would be? What was she going to need to see from him before she'd agree to say yes?

Distracting herself with logistical matters, Jenny searched the signs until she found Ingunn's flight, and she and Zack took seats on a bench while they waited near the baggage claim. Their conversation dealt with the fact that their relationship had consisted largely of airports and funerals, much more so than the average couple. Soon Ingunn's flight status changed from *on time* to *arrived*, prompting Zack and Jenny to stand up and move closer to the hall through which she would inevitably enter.

An elderly man being pushed in a wheelchair with a tall orange flag was the first to come through. Then a second gray-haired woman in a wheelchair emerged, after which a third orange flag came into view. "Good grief," Zack said. "That's a lot of wheelchairs for one flight."

"The plane's from Florida," Jenny noted.

Zack made a face. "Oh yeah. I guess that makes sense."

After the parade of wheelchairs came through without a spark of recognition from Jenny, a lone woman with white hair came walking around the corner, carrying a small suitcase. Her stride was determined, her pace faster than some of the younger people around her. Jenny immediately knew it was Ingunn.

With a smile Jenny approached her. "Amma! So nice to finally see you in person."

The woman set down her suitcase and studied Jenny up and down. Placing her hands on Jenny's shoulders, Ingunn whispered, "You *do* have the gift."

"Yes," she replied with a smile, "I really do have it."

The woman hugged Jenny in a surprisingly tight squeeze, causing Jenny to make a face in Zack's direction. For an older woman, Ingunn sure was strong.

Ingunn let go of the embrace, and Jenny announced, "Amma, this is my boyfriend Zack. Zack, this is my grandmother Ingunn."

Ingunn cupped Zack's face. "A handsome one, eh?" she said. "You can call me Amma, too. Everybody calls me Amma."

"Nice to meet you, Amma." Zack shot Jenny a knowing glance.

Ingunn stepped back and straightened out her clothes before picking up her suitcase again.

"Here, let me carry that for you," Zack posed with an outstretched hand.

"Nah." Ingunn made a dismissive gesture. "It's not heavy. I've got it."

Feisty, Jenny thought. Her mind immediately went back to Elanor, whose fiery personality was not enough to overcome a body that had ultimately failed her. Ingunn, it seemed, had the physical spunk to match the personality. Jenny felt a sense of pride—that was her grandmother carrying her own suitcase—but she also felt sadness that Elanor couldn't have enjoyed similar health at the same age.

Deep down inside, Jenny missed her friend dearly.

"Okay, well I guess we'll get the rest of your luggage," Zack said, snapping Jenny out of her temporary sadness.

Ingunn raised her small suitcase and patted it. "This is all I brought. I pack light."

"Alrighty, then," Zack said with an amused glance in Jenny's direction. "To the car we go."

After small talk about the quality of Ingunn's flight and the lines at Miami Airport, Jenny brought up their interesting afternoon as they pulled out of the parking lot. "I might like to stop at the crime scene on our way back, if you don't mind," Jenny concluded. "Maybe you'll be able to offer some insight that I couldn't get."

"Eight bodies?" Ingunn said. "And the letter T?"

"That's all I've been able to come up with," Jenny confessed.

Ingunn nodded. "I'll take a look."

"I don't know if you have the same issue I do," Jenny began. "I have difficulty getting readings when there's too much commotion. And as we were leaving, the media was arriving in droves. It will most likely be a circus by the time we get there."

"Get me close," Ingunn said, "but not too close. I might be able to get something."

Jenny sat back in her seat, confident that she was in very good hands. "I think I can do that."

As soon as they exited the highway and headed down route two-fifty-seven, Ingunn declared, "I'm getting something."

"Already?" Jenny asked. "The crime scene is still about fifteen minutes away."

Ingunn remained silent, which Jenny respected. As they continued down the road, Ingunn declared, "It's fading. We passed it."

"Passed it?" Jenny asked with surprise. "We haven't gotten there yet."

Ingunn shook her head. "No, we passed it."

Jenny searched for a spot to turn the car around, but the remote road offered few opportunities for a three-point-turn. Eventually she found a dirt driveway she could pull into, and soon she was headed back toward the highway.

Jenny drove slower this time, much to the dismay of the driver who had approached very quickly from behind her. The passengers of Jenny's car were silent as they got closer to truck stop alley, until Ingunn directed her to pull into the first truck stop on the right. Once in the parking lot, Jenny started to feel her own senses buzzing, leading her to a remote parking spot in the back row.

Ingunn and Jenny both got out of the car and absorbed their messages. "There's something significant here," Jenny noted softly, "but I don't feel fear."

"Agreed," Ingunn replied. "Whatever bad things happened to those people didn't happen here." She closed her eyes and kept them that way as she pointed to a parking space. "There was a small blue car there."

"I'm getting that capital T again," Jenny said. She found it intriguing that two psychics standing next to each other could receive such different messages.

Ingunn opened her eyes, indicating to the others that her vision was over. "So who do we tell about this?"

"I imagine the police are still milling around the crime scene and will be for days," Zack said. "I'm sure we can still catch them there."

"If we can get close enough," Jenny noted. "At this point it is probably pure chaos."

Chaos turned out to be an understatement. Jenny couldn't even get anywhere near the crime scene; as soon as she turned off the main road a police officer stopped her, asking her for her reason for being there.

"I found the bodies," she said, "and I have some more information for the police."

"Mmm-hmm. Sure you did," the officer said. "If you've got anything to tell the police, you can call a tip into the station. You don't need to be here."

"He's right," Ingunn said. "You don't need to be there."

Unsure what Ingunn had meant by that, Jenny decided to accept her statement at face value. "Okay," Jenny said pleasantly to the officer, "I'll just call the station later."

This time managing a three-point-turn, Jenny reversed the car and ventured back out onto the main road.

"Why don't we need to be there?" Jenny immediately asked her grandmother.

"There's too much going on," Ingunn said, waving her hand around.

"I understand," Jenny replied sincerely. They headed back to the Heritage Inn, where once again Ingunn carried her own suitcase into the building.

Jessica's desk was unoccupied as they walked in. "Let's see if we can find her for you," Jenny said to Ingunn. "If not, you can take a load off in our room for a while." Jenny clammed up uncomfortably for a moment; she had introduced Zack as her boyfriend and then just gave away the fact that they shared a room. At moments like this she wished she was married to Zack.

Ingunn seemed unfazed. She looked curiously around the room for a moment before saying, "Someone is upset."

Jenny looked at her with disbelief. "You're picking up on that?" She hadn't felt it herself.

Ingunn set her suitcase down and strode intuitively up the curved stairwell. Turning right at the top of the steps, she walked with purpose toward the Statesman Room where Jenny and Zack had been staying. The couple followed her, keeping their distance to respect her abilities.

"He resides mostly in here," Ingunn said, pointing at the door.

"We think his name is Andrew," Jenny whispered.

A gust of wind came from nowhere, causing a shiver up Jenny's spine.

"No," Ingunn said, turning to look at her granddaughter. "I'm quite certain his name is Samuel."

Chapter 5

"This is friggin unreal," Zack said with disbelief.

"Are you sure?" Jenny posed to Ingunn. "I'd gotten the name Andrew before."

"He made it very clear," Ingunn replied curtly. "His name is Samuel."

Jenny thought about her previous visions for a moment. So far the voice had said two names and showed visuals of two people in rooms other than the Statesman room. Perhaps the spirit was really named Samuel, and he was referring to two *other* people who went by Andrew and Elizabeth.

"Do we need to go back out to the cemetery and look for Samuels?" Zack asked.

Jenny considered that question before saying, "The cemetery didn't give me much other than last names that may or may not have been false leads. Maybe we should focus on the inside of the house until we figure out what's going on." She turned to Ingunn. "Did he say anything else?"

"No," Ingunn declared, walking past Zack and Jenny to head back downstairs. "It was brief."

Jenny smiled; Ingunn was certainly a no-nonsense kind of woman.

Faced with little choice but to follow, Jenny and Zack started down the steps as well. Jessica must have heard them come down because she emerged from a back room to greet them, looking pale as a sheet.

"What's the matter?" Jenny asked quickly. "Are you okay?"

"It's terrible," Jessica replied, seeming almost lost. "Have you heard about what they found off the highway?"

Jenny made a face. "I'm familiar with it, yes."

"They're up to twelve bodies now. They think most of them are runaways from up and down the east coast."

Twelve. The number sickened Jenny.

Jessica continued, "Somebody's been preying on these girls and dumping their bodies off the highway, right up the road from here." She shook her head. "This is positively awful."

"If they find that blue car, they'll find their guy," Ingunn said matter-of-factly.

Jessica glanced up at Ingunn with silent awe.

"Jessica, this is my grandmother, Ingunn," Jenny said, although she was sure the introduction was unnecessary after that comment.

"You know who did this?" Jessica whispered. She looked like she could faint.

"No, but he drove a blue car." Ingunn noticed a string hanging from her sleeve and pulled it off with a yank. "But so do a lot of other people, so it's not a lot to go on quite yet."

At a loss, Jessica simply looked back at Jenny.

"We drove past the crime scene," Jenny explained, "and we have a theory or two about who is involved."

"Don't sell yourself short," Zack said, turning to Jessica. "My girlfriend here *found* the bodies. She's the one who led the cops to them."

"You *found* them?"

Jenny nodded modestly. "Yes, I was led to them. Somebody pulled me in that direction...One of those victims obviously wanted to be found." Furrowing her brow, Jenny added to Jessica, "You don't look well. Do you need to lie down?"

"Just a seat," Jessica said, walking past the crowd to a small couch in the lobby. "And maybe a glass of water."

"I can get that," Zack suggested. "I'm the least useful person here." He disappeared off in the direction of the kitchen.

Sitting down on the sofa, Jessica announced, "Yes, that's a little better."

"I'm glad," Jenny replied. "I don't want to upset you."

"*You're* not upsetting me at all. What's happened just down the road...*that's* upsetting."

Ingunn chimed in. "Would it make you feel any better to know we have a name to go along with your presence here at the inn?"

Jessica looked confused. "I thought his name was Andrew."

"It doesn't appear that way," Jenny explained. "I think Andrew and Elizabeth were the names of the people I saw in my visions, but the spirit himself seems to have a different name."

"He goes by Samuel," Ingunn announced.

Zack returned with a glass of water. "Here you go," he said, carefully passing it over to Jessica.

She drank from it quickly. "Thank you, Zack," she whispered when she finished her sip. "That does help."

Jenny continued the conversation, asking Jessica, "Does the name Samuel mean anything to you?"

"Samuel..." Jessica repeated. Looking back and forth between Jenny and Ingunn, she declared, "I'm afraid not."

Jenny tried to mask her disappointment while she thought about who this Samuel may have been. Suddenly a notion occurred to her. "Wait a minute...what about the children?"

Jessica looked surprised. "The children?"

"Yes, the children. You have mentioned the first names of the home*owners* who had lived here in the past...but what about the children? Is it possible that Andrew, Elizabeth and Samuel were siblings who lived here with their parents?"

Zack looked at Jessica with wide eyes. "Do you have any record of what the kids were named?"

Placing her hand on her chin, Jessica seemed to think hard for a moment. "Maybe...I can certainly check on that. Come to think of it, I may even have one better." Forgetting her previous uneasiness, she hopped off of the couch and disappeared quickly into the office.

Jenny looked at her boyfriend and grandmother. "I wonder what that was about."

They didn't have to wait long to find out. Jessica returned awkwardly carrying what appeared to be a sofa-size painting wrapped in a blanket. Zack quickly noticed her struggle and took the painting off her hands, setting it down gently on the floor while Jessica removed its covering.

The image, which appeared to be from long ago, showed eight well-dressed children in various rigid poses around a couple that she presumed to be their parents. The children seemed to range in age from the mid-teens to the smallest child, who was just a toddler. Jenny's eyes scanned the picture until they fixated on one of the older daughters and what appeared to be the oldest son.

"That's them," she whispered, pointing to the two familiar faces. "Those are the people I saw in my visions."

"Yeah, but who are they?" Zack asked.

"This," Jessica said as she looked intently at Zack, "is the Davies family."

A brief silence hung over the group as the implications of this latest discovery set in. "Well, then," Ingunn began in an emotionless voice, "it looks like we may have our answer."

"Do you think Samuel is one of these children?" Jessica asked.

"I can't say for sure," Jenny began. "From what I understand of my abilities, I can only see what the spirit saw, so this *Samuel* person has to be someone who had access to Elizabeth and Andrew while they were sick. The spirit may not necessarily be one of the other children, but it could be a housekeeper or a slave or something of the sort."

"Or a doctor," Zack noted.

Jenny shrugged. "Or a doctor. But whoever this person is, they clearly have an unresolved issue that is causing them to linger."

"And it has to be a powerful one," Ingunn noted. "When spirits can make themselves known to people without the gift, that means they are very passionate about something."

Jessica looked concerned. "I wonder what that issue could be."

"I imagine it involves the two sick people," Jenny noted. "I don't know why else I'd be shown those scenes."

"Samuel cared about those people," Ingunn declared bluntly.

After some silent deliberation, Jenny noted, "I guess that makes it more plausible that Samuel was one of the siblings."

"So you're saying it's possible that this spirit is a *child*?" Jessica asked with disbelief.

"Not necessarily," Ingunn clarified. "Even if Samuel is one of those children in the picture, that doesn't mean he died as a child. It could be that he lived well into adulthood, and he's just dealing with some unrest that stems from this house."

"Well, if my visions are any explanation, he may have watched two of his siblings die here," Jenny declared. She turned to Jessica before adding, "Actually, didn't you say that the whole Davies family had died of illness? Wasn't that why the house was vacant when the Civil War broke out?"

Jessica covered her mouth with her hands and silently nodded.

With her eyes scanning the crowd, Jenny said, "Then maybe Samuel did die as a child."

"Maybe," Ingunn replied, "but maybe not. If the parents died, the surviving kids may have been sent to live with a relative. That would also cause the house to be empty."

"Would it also cause unrest?" Jenny felt a rock forming in the pit of her stomach. "I mean, losing half your family, including your parents...wouldn't that be enough to upset your soul?"

Ingunn remained emotionless as she noted, "You have to consider that dying from illness was not that uncommon in that era. If this couple had eight children who all survived into adulthood, that would have been amazing. So while I'm sure it was sad for Samuel to lose his parents and siblings, I don't know if that alone would be reason enough for him to stick around for a hundred fifty years."

Jenny had to agree that a century and a half was a long time; something truly must have gone wrong in Samuel's world if he was to linger that long. Eventually Jenny whispered, "I wonder what could be bothering him so badly."

Nobody knew the answer.

"Thanks for agreeing to meet with us," Jenny told Officer Howell in the interview room at the station. "I didn't want to just leave the information on the tip line. It probably would have been thrown into the trash heap if anyone other than you heard it."

"No, thank *you*," Officer Howell replied. "I am glad you're willing to work with me. We may have never found those bodies without your intuition leading the way. We didn't even realize anyone was missing."

Jenny assumed a sympathetic tone. "So what's the body count up to now?"

"Thirteen," he replied. "All female."

Jenny looked at her lap. For a split second, she desperately hoped she was pregnant with a boy.

"Have they identified them all?" Zack asked.

"A few, and even those are tentative. Some of the victims had identification on their person, although with the advanced state of decay we're going to have to wait for dental records or DNA analysis for confirmation. You would think that IDs in pockets would go with the bodies wearing them, but if someone is sick enough to kill women and dump them off the highway like trash, he might be willing to switch around some IDs to mess with people's heads."

"He didn't," Ingunn announced, causing Officer Howell to look up with surprise. She elaborated, "He never intended for those women to be found. If he wanted to mess with people by putting IDs with bodies that didn't match, he would have put the bodies in locations where they would have been found more easily."

Jenny got a kick out of her grandmother's blunt demeanor, but she could see where others might have been less amused by it. She wondered what Officer Howell was thinking as he cleared his throat and said, "That's our assumption as well, but we can never rely on assumption as fact. We still need to wait for confirmation."

Feeling the need to change the subject, Jenny added, "My grandmother and I both got the feeling that one of the truck stops off the highway may have something to do with this."

"Which one?" Officer Howell asked as he jotted down notes.

"I can't remember the name of it," Jenny confessed, "but it was on the southwest corner."

"Dale's," Howell stated flatly as he wrote. As soon as he said it, Jenny remembered the name to be correct.

"We were drawn to the back row in the parking lot," Ingunn explained, "where a blue car was once parked."

After Officer Howell made a note of that, he looked up and said, "Do you know what happens at the back row of a truck stop?"

Admittedly naïve about the ways of the world, Jenny replied, "No, I don't."

"A lot of truck stops house prostitution rings, and Dale's is no exception. These girls make their living by knocking on windows of trucks and providing their services to any drivers who want them. Generally speaking, the truckers who are looking for *company*," he said with finger quotes, "park in the back row; it's known as the party row."

"So these girls get into the trucks willingly," Zack determined. "That would mean no big, noticeable scene with kicking and screaming as the girls get pulled against their will into a vehicle."

"Exactly," Officer Howell said. "And these girls may get into as many as seven or eight different trucks in a night. It would be hard to tell which one was the culprit's vehicle—if that's even what we're dealing with."

Jenny made a face as she considered that the women at Dale's had more sex partners in a single night than she'd had in a lifetime.

"And not only that," Officer Howell continued, breaking Jenny away from her thought process, "but sometimes the girls get tired of where they are, so they agree to go off with these truckers and head to the next town. Essentially, if a girl gets into a cab and is never seen again, it's no big deal." He let out a disgruntled chuckle. "It happens all the time."

"Wow," Jenny said. "These are the easiest victims in the world, aren't they?"

"Prostitutes often are," Howell noted sadly. "And truck stop prostitutes are even easier. We're trying to hurry up and get some IDs on these victims so we can contact family members. We want to know how long they've been missing and if they were runaways or addicts or what. If we can get an idea of where the victims had last been seen and when, maybe we can find some kind of pattern in the perpetrator's travels. Unfortunately, this particular location makes it difficult to determine whether it was north and southbound travel or east and west. We're right off 95, obviously, which would imply north and south, but with 85 and being as close as they are, the girls can just as easily be from the west somewhere."

Howell continued, "If we had to guess, though, we would say that the culprit has ties to this area. You wouldn't be able to find that dumping ground unless you knew where to look."

"And you wouldn't get to that dumping ground in a big eighteen-wheeler, either," Ingunn said with conviction. "But you could get there in a blue car, which is what our killer did."

Howell cocked a skeptical eyebrow at Ingunn, but he humored her theory nonetheless. "You're saying it's a blue car. Do you know what kind of car?"

"A sedan," she noted. "Not sure what type."

Jenny chimed in. "Another thing I will say is that my grandmother and I both felt no fear at the truck stop. Something terrible obviously happened to these girls, but we don't think it happened there."

"So you think they may have gotten into the killer's car at the truck stop only to be assaulted elsewhere?"

"Yes, sir."

"Do you think they were assaulted at the dumping ground?" Howell posed.

Jenny thought about that for a moment. "If I had to guess, I'd say no. I didn't feel any fear there, either. I was drawn to that location, yes, but I think that was just because they wanted to be found. However," she added, "I would like the chance to go back there with my grandmother. She's never been at the scene, and she might pick up on something that I didn't. We tried to go back there the day of the discovery, but we were not allowed to even drive down the street."

"Yeah, the whole area got cordoned off," Howell said. "We weren't sure how many bodies we were going to find. Or where."

"Could you possibly take us there?" Jenny asked.

"I guess it can't hurt," Howell said. "Right now we have absolutely no suspects in mind. All we know is this guy travels a lot and has ties to the area, so that narrows it down to, what, about a thousand people?" He let out a frustrated grunt as he looked back and forth between Jenny and Ingunn. "I guess I'll get my coat."

Ingunn seemed undeterred by the brush that intermittently clogged the path before them. She marched along with purpose, arriving at the dump site with a furrowed brow. Ducking under the yellow crime scene tape she quickly noted, "No, there's definitely no fear here."

Jenny had been thinking the same thing. She looked around, noticing all of the upturned ground, which made the area look very different than the last time she'd been there. Crews had obviously been searching the area with scrutiny.

"This is a dumping ground and nothing more," Ingunn proclaimed. She squinted with confusion before simply adding, "Huh."

"What is it, Amma?" Zack asked her.

"Don't know yet," she replied, looking around intently as if trying to find something specific. She wandered off a few yards, away from the other three.

"I'm getting that letter T again," Jenny told Howell in a whisper, trying not to disrupt Ingunn's train of thought. "This time I'm actually seeing it. It's orange."

"University of Tennessee?" Zack asked.

"That's exactly what I was thinking," Howell agreed.

Jenny made a face. "Is that their mascot?"

"Their mascot? No," Zack replied, "but it is their logo."

"Same difference," Jenny whispered with a laugh. She then turned her attention to Ingunn, who still looked puzzled. "Is everything okay, Amma?"

"No, I don't think so," Ingunn said in a tone that brought a chill down Jenny's spine.

"What's wrong?"

She walked in one last slow circle before returning to the rest of the group. "There's another victim."

"We're not done canvassing the area," Howell declared. "The crews have just worked out into a wider radius so we can't see them right now, but believe me—they're still looking."

Ingunn shook her head. "Don't bother with that."

"Don't bother with what?" Howell said with surprise.

"Don't bother with widening your radius."

The officer seemed confused. "But you just said there's another victim."

"I know," Ingunn announced, "and there is." She looked up at Howell and placed her hands on her hips. "But she isn't here."

Chapter 6

"She isn't here?" Howell looked dumbfounded. "What do you mean *she isn't here*?"

"She's elsewhere," Ingunn said calmly.

"Elsewhere? Like fifty-yards-to-the-east elsewhere? Or like South Carolina elsewhere?"

"She's not here." Ingunn gestured all around her. "Not in this area."

"Jesus Christ," Howell whispered to himself. "Do you think there's only one other victim?"

"Only one that I'm being made aware of."

Howell looked at Jenny for an elaboration she couldn't make; as a result she responded only with a shrug and a shake of her head.

He turned back to Ingunn. "Do you know the name of this alleged victim we should be looking for elsewhere?"

"No, not her name. But she's fair." Ingunn waved her hand in front of her face. "She's got light hair and a pale complexion."

Howell slowly wiped both hands from his forehead to his chin. "You know what she looks like but you don't know her name or where she is?"

Ingunn shrugged. "I get what I get."

"Amma," Jenny began, "you said you can summon the spirits. Do you think you can do that now? Maybe that can get us some answers."

With a shake of the head, Ingunn simply said, "Nope."

While amused by her grandmother's bluntness again, Jenny didn't laugh. "Do you mind if I ask why you can't?"

"I don't have what I need."

"What do you need?"

Ingunn looked squarely at Jenny. "Quiet—tranquility on a spiritual level—and I don't have that here. I also need a possession of the deceased, or a photograph, and I don't have those, either."

Jenny understood, at least the part about needing serenity. When there was too much excitement surrounding an area, she also had a difficult time sustaining a reading.

"Would it help if we went somewhere else?" Howell asked. "I could potentially get my hands on a photograph of one of these girls for you."

"I doubt it. Usually when I can initiate a contact it's because there's only one spirit in an otherwise quiet space." Ingunn looked around as if she could see things that weren't there. "But in this case, there are too many victims occupying this one area. I'll never be able to single anybody out well enough to establish a meaningful contact."

Jenny closed her eyes for a moment, knowing that this crowd of spirits continued to 'occupy that one area' because they couldn't rest; their deaths had been too traumatic for them to be at peace with their fates and cross over. The notion made Jenny want to jump out of her own skin—as if dying in a horrific manner wasn't bad enough, these women then had to endure years of unrest afterward. It was as if they'd been victimized twice.

A shudder crept up her spine.

Seeming a little more patient than he had been just seconds earlier, Howell reiterated, "Okay, so we're dealing with at least one more victim, and she's got a fair complexion?"

With a single vigorous nod, Ingunn replied, "That's right."

"We've been inundated at the station," Howell confessed as he released a sigh. "Ever since this discovery has been made public, just about every family with a missing female has been calling and sending pictures, asking if their loved one was among the victims."

Inundated. The word made Jenny's previous uneasiness even worse. There shouldn't have been any missing women, let alone enough to cause the station to be *inundated* with phone calls.

She placed her hand on her pregnant belly, her faith in humanity temporarily reduced to nothing.

Howell continued, "We haven't released any names yet; we're still waiting on those positive identifications I talked about earlier. But we have requested the dental records of the women whose identifications were found at the scene. Sadly, though, there were more bodies than there were IDs. We are completely at a loss as to the identity of some of these women. And with the amount of decomposition their bodies have endured, the photographs their families send don't do us any good. Of course, we don't want to tell the families that. But I guess it's good to know we should spend a little extra time looking at the pictures of the fair-complexioned women that come in." Shaking his head, he addressed Ingunn one more time. "But you're *positive* you have no idea where this last victim is?"

"If I knew I'd tell you," she replied assuredly. Once again, Jenny couldn't help but smile at her curtness.

The officer continued to speak, although he appeared to mostly be talking to himself. "There could be bodies all up and down this Goddamn highway. This might just be his Virginia dump site. He could have one in every state for all we know."

"Well, would it help if we got closer to the interstate?" Jenny posed. "Maybe there will be more clues at the truck stop."

"It can't hurt, I guess," Howell said as he pulled his keys out of his pocket. "I'll let you lead the way."

"It was here," Ingunn informed Howell as she pointed to the same parking space they'd visited before. "A blue car in this spot will be helpful in the investigation."

The officer looked around and said, "Yeah, this is near the party row alright." After a moment he added, "Don't be obvious, but take a look at that guy in the Raiders jacket hanging out behind the building."

Jenny used just her eyes to glance behind Officer Howell at the man in question. He seemed to be studying their group, scrutinizing them so intently Jenny felt uncomfortable. She was glad to be in the presence of a cop.

"What's his deal?" Zack posed.

"That's the pimp who works this stop," Howell replied. "He goes by Adam X, with Adam and X both being street names for ecstasy. We've dealt with him more than once, for both prostitution and drugs."

"Do you think he had anything to do with this?" Jenny posed. "The killings, I mean?"

"I don't have a clue. We certainly can't rule it out at this point."

"Should we ask him if any of his…girls…are missing?" Jenny asked.

"His girls go missing all the time," Howell explained. "They get into trucks and move on to another stop."

"Does he ever get mad about that?" Zack asked. "Maybe taking his anger out on some of the other prostitutes?"

"Maybe," Howell replied, "but I doubt it. For every prostitute that drives off with a trucker, another drives in with a trucker. He doesn't particularly care about who any of these girls are; as long as he has some girls bringing in money, he doesn't care which ones…or how they're faring. I think the only thing that would make him upset would be if a john stiffed him some money or another pimp moved into his territory." Howell glanced back in Adam X's direction. "Or if I went over and started asking him questions."

Jenny's shoulders sank. "I hadn't thought of that. I guess he wouldn't be that excited to talk to you about his…employees."

Turning back to the crowd, Howell confessed, "He wouldn't say a word to the police, I guarantee it…even if he knew there were lives at stake."

A sickening blend of hate and anger began to rise to the surface of Jenny's skin. Looking back at Adam X, who had since lost his fascination with her group and had gone about his business, Jenny wondered how someone could be so self-serving and callous. She felt the uncharacteristic urge to march over to him and slap him in the face.

Zack's voice put an end to her twisted thoughts. "Can you get a subpoena or anything and make him talk?"

"Maybe, eventually," Howell said, "but not yet. We don't know if any of the victims have ties to him, first of all. We'd need some sort of evidence to link him to the crime before a judge would issue a subpoena. We obviously haven't established that yet."

A funny sensation started to brew within Jenny. Feeling the need to focus, she stepped away from the conversation and headed to a quieter area a few yards from where she'd been standing. A male voice echoed briefly between her ears, causing her to place her face in her hands.

"Hey," she heard Zack whisper from behind her, "are you okay?"

She turned to look at her concerned boyfriend. Lowering her hands to her sides she remarked, "You look like you could use a good meal."

Zack furrowed his brow and looked at her.

"That's what I heard." Jenny pointed to her head. "In my mind. I think that's how he got the girls to get into his car, even if we don't know who they were or where they came from."

"So then he appears kind," Ingunn stated.

The others looked at her, inviting her to continue.

"Harmless," she added. "Benevolent. The girls thought he was trustworthy."

"Are you getting that in a vision?" Zack asked Ingunn.

"No," she replied, "it's just common sense. Why else would they have gone with him?"

"Because they're prostitutes," Howell said, "and part of their job involves getting into strangers' vehicles."

"Based on what Jenny said, he wasn't asking them for sex," Ingunn countered. "He was offering them dinner."

Presumably contemplating what Ingunn said, Howell remained quiet.

"It seems strange to offer a prostitute a meal to get her into your car," Zack noted. "Why not just act like you want to hire her?"

"And here's another thing I don't understand," Jenny began. "Now don't get me wrong, Officer Howell. I don't mean any disrespect, but if you know these are prostitutes, and you know they're doing drugs, and you know Adam X is their pimp...why don't you just arrest them all? Then maybe these girls could get some help and resume their normal lives."

"In an ideal world, that would be happening," Howell agreed, "but the truth of the matter is we have limited resources. There are only a certain number of policemen and women to go around, and they have to patrol the entire county. Then there's the matter of proof—we know they are prostitutes, but we'd need to have concrete evidence of it before we could arrest them. That would involve a sting, which is costly. And then, after all of that, their sentences would be little more than a slap on the wrist. After a short stint in jail, they'd come out and most likely go right back to the same lifestyle." Howell looked sympathetically at Jenny. "As much as I hate to say this, we don't really do too much about this because it wouldn't be worth it. But now that there's murder involved, the ante has been upped. Going forward, there's going to be a lot more focus on truck stop prostitutes...if that's what these victims turn out to be."

"How long do you think it will take before you get positive IDs?"

Howell shrugged. "I don't know. I guarantee they're working on it as fast as they can." His eyes circulated the group. "I just hope they can get some answers before there's another victim."

Chapter 7

Jessica put dinner plates down in front of Jenny, Zack and Ingunn before quickly disappearing back into the kitchen. After taking a bite and grunting with pleasure at the delicious food, Jenny asked Ingunn, "So what is it you do in order to contact the spirits? I'm wondering if this is a skill I can one day master myself."

"I need a belonging of the deceased, first of all," she began, "or a photograph—a good one, that shows their faces. I also need quiet. Then it's a simple matter of focus. Focus, focus, focus. Honestly, it's difficult to achieve that level of concentration, which is why I usually do the channeling when I'm alone. Even the tiniest distraction can snap me out of that state. But once I get a feel that the spirit's presence is around me, I concentrate on the specific aspect I'd like information about." Ingunn took a bite of chicken, tucking it into her cheek before adding, "Then the answer pops into my head." She shrugged with one shoulder and returned her attention to her plate.

Jenny thought back to her first case, where she was able to summon a critical vision while sitting at a picnic table. Did she actually already possess that ability and she just didn't realize it? Perhaps she'd need to try that again in the future.

"So, Amma," Zack began, "this psychic ability runs in the family..."

"For some members, yes."

Zack rested his chin on his hand. "How did it start? I mean, somebody had to have it first, didn't they?"

"Mmm-hmm," Ingunn said in casual affirmation. "My great-great-grandmother."

Jenny's eyes grew wide. "You know how this started?"

"Sure. It's commonly known in my family." Glancing up at Jenny with a rare smile, she added, "In *our* family." She took another bite of meat.

"So what happened?" Jenny was ready to jump out of her skin. "How did it begin?"

"It was a boating accident, back in Iceland in 1852." Ingunn seemed just as preoccupied with her food as she did the incredible story. "My great-great-grandmother Greta was eleven then. She was fishing on a boat with her family when she and her nine-year-old brother Dyri fell into the icy water. They both disappeared under for a long time. Well, maybe not a *long* time," she conceded with a shrug, "but much too long to go without breathing. I guess it goes without saying that they managed to pull Greta back in the boat and she survived." She pointed at Jenny with her fork. "You and I wouldn't be here right now if she didn't."

Jenny felt a chill as she considered the fragile chain of events that led to her existence. One hiccup and she never would have been born.

Ingunn continued to talk about Greta. "She described the experience to her children later on; she said that she and Dyri held hands, in a spiritual sense, as their souls floated out of the water and up into the air. She was able to look down and see all of her family members frantically scrambling to get her and Dyri back in the boat. She even saw her own physical body just beneath the surface of the water, although she couldn't see her brother's. He had apparently sunk further down than she did.

"Greta said she felt at peace as her soul left her body, although she did feel sorry for her family; they all seemed so upset. She wished they wouldn't be—she and Dyri were leaving the earth together, and she was engulfed in an amazing sense of calm and serenity. If her family had known what it had felt like, they wouldn't have been sad for her.

"But then she felt the physical touch of an earthly hand on hers, and before she knew it she was being pulled back downward. She felt torn...she knew her family wanted her to return to her physical body, but she didn't want to leave Dyri alone in the spirit world. He encouraged her to go back, telling her she had her entire life to live, but she insisted she didn't want to go without him. That's when he made her a promise...if she went back, he wouldn't leave her. He assured her he would always be by her side. With that promise, she agreed to go back.

"Luckily for Greta—and you and me—the icy water seemed to slow her vitals down enough that she was able to be under the water longer than a person ordinarily would be. Once they pulled her out of the water, her family rowed her to shore and wrapped her in blankets, putting her by a fire to warm her back up again. Eventually her natural color restored, and her breathing became normal. Soon after she regained consciousness, and the first thing she did was ask for Dyri. That's when her family had to inform her that her brother hadn't survived the accident. They weren't able to get him back in the boat. His body washed up on shore a few days later.

"After she made her recovery, Greta claimed to still be able to speak to Dyri. Her parents tolerated it at first, believing she was just saying that to make herself feel better about the accident. After a while, though, her parents became upset with her when she continued to make the claim. They kept telling her that Dyri was dead, and there was no way she could still hear him—she needed to snap out of her little fantasy world and accept the facts."

With obvious awe in her voice, Jenny said, "But she *could* hear him, couldn't she?"

"She could," Ingunn agreed with a nod. "But it wasn't until her uncle passed away a few years later that her parents actually believed her. Her mother's brother, Viktor, died of illness, and apparently his spirit lingered and communicated with Greta. One day while visiting her mother's childhood home, Greta shared the story of how her Uncle Viktor had fallen out of a tree as a boy. He'd been climbing with Greta's mother, and he let go with his hands in an attempt to be funny. Apparently that had backfired. He fell from several feet up, landing hard on the ground, hurting his wrist quite badly...But that had been the kids' favorite climbing tree, so they decided to tell their mother that he'd tripped over a rock instead. They didn't want their mother telling them to stay out of the tree.

"When Greta told the story, her mother was shocked. There was no way Greta could have known that; they had never told anybody about how Viktor had really gotten hurt. When her mother asked Greta how she knew, Greta simply replied that her Uncle Viktor had told her; his spirit was with them at that very moment, and he was whispering it to her. From then on her parents actually believed she had the ability to communicate with the deceased and that her claims about Dyri had actually been true."

Jenny was too flabbergasted to speak. She was glad Zack had the ability to ask the questions she wanted answered. "So what did they do about it?"

Ingunn looked expressionlessly at Zack. "Nothing. They didn't want anybody to know. They feared what would happen to her if people found out. She just continued to receive contacts from Dyri and Viktor, and her family said nothing to anyone."

"But then this trait got passed on to her children?" Zack asked.

"One of them," Ingunn replied, popping some broccoli into her mouth. "At a young age, Greta's second daughter began talking about Dyri. Greta hadn't talked about her brother to her children, so she figured that any information her daughter disclosed must have come from Dyri himself. It was apparent that her daughter had inherited the trait."

"But how did it become genetic?" Zack asked. "I understand how Greta could have it, having been so close to death, but how did it pass on?"

"That, I don't know," Ingunn confessed with a finger in the air. "But it seems when Greta was in the water, hovering somewhere between life and death, something inside of her changed. And apparently, that something can be passed down from generation to generation."

"So how many people in your family have it?" Zack asked. Jenny was still too stunned to speak.

"It's hard to say," Ingunn deduced. "When you go back that many generations, the family tree develops a lot of branches. In our immediate family, it's just me, Roddan and Jenny. I have a cousin with it, and I think one of her kids may have gotten it too. I don't remember, honestly. She is still in Iceland and I rarely talk to her." Ingunn looked around the table. "Do they have any salt?"

Zack got up and retrieved a salt shaker from an empty neighboring table. Upon sitting back down, he asked, "Is most of your family still in Iceland?"

Ingunn poured salt onto her baked potato. Without looking up she announced, "Yup. Everyone but me."

"How did you come to be in America?"

She glanced at Zack with an emotionless face. "I may not look like it now, but I was once a free spirit. I decided I wanted a change, so I came to the states."

"How old were you when you came?" Zack was still doing all the talking.

"Nineteen."

"Did you know anyone here?"

"Nope."

"Wasn't that difficult?"

Ingunn shrugged. "Maybe a little."

A smirk appeared on Zack's face. He clearly got just as much of a kick out of Ingunn as Jenny did.

The conversation continued, and Ingunn explained how she met and married Jerry Epperly, a mortician from North Carolina. Ingunn had used her gift to provide solace to the families who had come to Jerry for his services, although she had done it in a subtle enough way that she didn't disclose her gift. Unaware that she had a secret weapon at her disposal, the relatives of the deceased used to marvel at how Ingunn always knew just what to say. She credited herself—and her gift—with helping to make her husband's funeral home the most successful in the area.

Once the meal and the conversation were over, Ingunn wiped her mouth with her napkin and sighed with contentment. "So," she began, "I guess it's about time I go have a conversation with this Samuel fellow, don't you think?"

Jenny's eyes widened. "You're going to do that now?"

"No sense wasting time." Ingunn scooted her chair out from the table and headed back toward the kitchen.

"Where are you going?" Jenny stood up as well, although Zack continued to eat.

"To get another look at that painting." She didn't look back at Jenny as she added, "If it turns out Samuel is one of those children, I can use that to summon him."

Jenny scurried quickly to follow Ingunn back into the kitchen where Jessica was washing up some dishes. Jessica looked at her visitors with obvious surprise; Jenny figured it wasn't every day that guests marched with such conviction into the kitchen while she cleaned up dinner.

Ingunn spoke immediately. "I'd like to see that painting again."

Quickly overcoming her moment of shock, Jessica pulled her hands out of the sink and vigorously shook off the excess water. Reaching for a towel she began to wipe her hands dry as she spoke. "I put it back in my office, but you can come take a look at it." She placed the towel back on the rack and gestured toward the exit. "Follow me, ladies."

She led them into a room that apparently served as both an office and a giant closet; while there was a desk in one corner of the room, boxes, spare furniture and cleaning supplies littered the rest. The painting loomed ominously in the corner; it had been propped up against the wall rather than hung, and it remained free of the blanket. The large family wearing stiff expressions all seemed to be looking at Jenny, which at the moment made her feel tremendously uneasy.

An inexplicable gust of wind soared briefly through the room. Jessica's eyes grew wide as she looked back and forth between Ingunn and Jenny, clearly aware the breeze had supernatural origins.

Ingunn pointed her finger at the painting, specifically to a young boy who appeared to be about six years old in the picture. He was dressed in an uncomfortable-looking shirt buttoned all the way to the top, and his dark hair was parted on the side, plastered to his head. "This one," Ingunn said assuredly. "This is the boy who goes by Samuel."

Jessica looked at Ingunn with awe. "How do you know that?"

Ingunn never looked away from the painting. "He just told me."

"I think this painting will do quite nicely; I should be able to get a contact from it," Ingunn announced. "Now I just need quiet."

"Well, I can certainly provide you with that," Jessica replied as she scrambled to get out of the room. She appeared to still be frazzled by the events that had just unfolded.

Jenny began to follow suit when Ingunn said, "No, Jenny, not you. I want you here for this."

Surprised by the pronouncement, Jenny remarked, "I thought you preferred to work alone."

"I do," Ingunn replied, "but I want you to take part in it." She walked over to the window and drew the curtains closed. "I'm not getting any younger; I need someone to carry this on after I'm gone."

Excitement grew within Jenny, although it was accompanied by fear. This was a very big responsibility being handed down to her; she only hoped she was worthy.

Ingunn searched around the room until she found a box of tissues. Pulling a few out, she wadded them in her hand and used them as a buffer as she unscrewed three of the five light bulbs in the chandelier. She looked around the room approvingly before sliding a chair in front of the sofa-size painting. Taking a seat, she looked at Jenny. "You need a chair."

Jenny had found herself so awestruck by the process that she'd become a mere spectator. Realizing she needed to be a participant, she quickly retrieved a second chair and slid it next to her grandmother's.

Ingunn kept her eyes fixated on the painting. "You can't be tense," she said, "and I can feel your tension from here."

Now that her attention had been called to it, Jenny could indeed feel anxiety surging through her body. With a deep sigh she rolled her head back and forth, lowering her shoulders in a concerted attempt at relaxation. Despite her efforts, she wasn't sure how successful she was.

"Let all thought leave your body," Ingunn instructed. "Just be. And then when you feel the purity and the emptiness, begin the focus." Ingunn looked at Jenny and pointed to Samuel's image. "Look at him. Look only at him. He is the only thing that exists in the world. There is no you. There is no me. There is nothing material. There is only Samuel."

Jenny nodded subtly with understanding, but she was unsure she could achieve that level of focus.

"You're nervous," Ingunn noted. "This will never work if you're nervous." She reached out her hand and patted Jenny's shoulder. "What makes you think you can't do this, eh?"

A very legitimate question. Why did Jenny doubt herself all the time? At that moment something inside of her changed. She sat straighter, held her head higher and looked squarely at the painting. "I can do this," she said with confidence. "Just tell me what to do after I fixate on him."

"He'll appear," Ingunn replied. "You won't see him, but you'll feel him, just like you can feel when someone's watching you. At that moment, you ask what he wants."

"Out loud or in my head?" Jenny asked.

"Either. Hopefully he'll reply," Ingunn declared.

"Hopefully?"

Ingunn shrugged. "We can't control them. We can only encourage them."

Jenny blew out a breath as she tried to mentally prepare herself for the challenge. "Okay, so are we ready to go?"

"I'm ready whenever you are."

Both women turned silently to the picture. Jenny studied Samuel's face with scrutiny as the rest of the room seemed to disappear from sight. She focused on the contours of his face, which seemed to come alive off the canvas. She felt as if she'd known him. She could hear his laughter. She could see his joy. He had been a happy child, easy-going and carefree. He had liked his life. He had wanted for nothing.

And now she could feel him watching her.

Chapter 8

Jenny spoke softly. "What is it you want, Samuel?"

While Jenny heard no words, a feeling washed over her. Samuel missed his family, and he wanted to be reunited with them.

"They've crossed over," Jenny explained quietly. "If you want to be with them, you need to cross too."

She felt frustration. That clearly hadn't been the answer Samuel had been looking for. With a sensation that felt like all the air being sucked out of the room, Jenny experienced a withdrawal that forced her to snap back into the moment.

Before Jenny had the chance to fully grasp what was going on, Ingunn flatly stated, "You angered him."

"I-I-I'm sorry. I didn't mean to. I don't even know what I said to upset him."

"It's nothing you did wrong," Ingunn replied as she stood up. "It happens sometimes." She began to push her chair back to its original location.

Deducing that the contact session was over, Jenny did the same. "What else should I have said?" she asked. "If he wants to be with his family again, doesn't he need to cross over?"

The light bulbs had cooled enough for Ingunn to touch them with her bare hands. They lit back up as she screwed each one in, making the room seem remarkably less eerie. "I guess that wasn't what he meant."

"I guess not," Jenny noted. "I'm not sure how else he wants us to help him reunite with his family, though. He lived a hundred sixty years ago. We can't change anything that had to do with his life."

Ingunn walked past Jenny as she headed for the door. "I'm quite sure he doesn't want us to."

Jenny furrowed her brow. "What does that mean?"

Ingunn paused as her hand touched the doorknob. She turned back around to face Jenny as she said, "There's something else he wants us to do. Something within our control." She opened the door and added, "We just need to figure out what that is."

Jenny burst into the Statesman room to find Zack relaxing on the bed with the remote in his hand. He had changed into the flannel pants he always slept in, and an open beer rested on the nightstand.

"You'll never believe what happened," Jenny proclaimed as she sat on the edge of the bed. She told the entire story to Zack in little more than one breath.

"Wow, that's amazing," Zack replied as he took a sip of his beer. "I wonder what upset him so badly."

"I don't know," Jenny said with an excited shrug. "I guess we need to find out. But first," she added with a raised finger, "I need to use the little girls' room." Hopping off the bed, Jenny looked down to see all of Zack's clothes from the day scattered on the floor. The image briefly gave her pause; then she continued on her way.

She felt quite troubled as she entered the bathroom. Images of Zack's old apartment flashed in her mind—the place had been so cluttered it was difficult to maneuver in there. Granted, the basement he lived in now wasn't quite so messy, but he also hadn't lived there that long. She imagined it was only a matter of time before disarray took over that space, too. If she accepted his proposal and they lived together as husband and wife, was that how he would treat *their* house? Would she spend the rest of her life picking up after him? Would she ultimately resent him for it? Would they end up one of those old couples that did nothing but bicker?

Would they end up divorced?

She placed her head in her hands, knowing that her thought process was spiraling out of control. She wished there was a way to discern how much of this train of thought was genuine and how much was due to pregnancy hormones—or even a disproportionate fear of failing at marriage again. Should clothes on the floor really have been that upsetting? They were just clothes, after all. However, she knew one of her biggest mistakes in her previous marriage had been keeping too quiet; she failed to mention all of the things that bothered her, and for that reason they continued to happen.

But was this even worth mentioning?

Since it was troubling her so badly, she decided she'd at least send out a feeler. Finishing up in the bathroom, she returned to her seat on the edge of the bed. "You look comfy," she mentioned to Zack. Then she gestured to the pile on the floor. "I guess you were so eager to get into bed that you didn't put your clothes away."

He didn't look away from the television. With a half-hearted shrug, he said, "I figure there's no hurry; we're going to be here for days. We won't need to pack up for a while." He took another sip of beer.

Jenny's spirits sank; that was not the answer she'd been hoping to hear. She wordlessly got off the bed and took a seat in a nearby chair, opening her laptop. While she went through the motions of checking her email, she felt her insides stewing. Glancing at Zack with just her eyes, she noticed he seemed completely unaware that she was upset. She wondered how he could be so oblivious to something that, to her, seemed so painfully obvious.

You're pregnant. You're hormonal. There's a good chance you're overreacting, Jenny thought to herself. *Sleep on this, and bring it up again in the morning if it's still troubling you.* Although Jenny logically knew that was the correct thing to do, she still felt irritated, seriously doubting that the morning would make her feel any differently.

Noticing her inbox was filled with nothing but junk, Jenny leaned back in the chair and reconsidered the episode with Samuel. He had clearly been upset by her response, although she had no idea why. He wanted her to do something, and helping him cross was not the answer. She wished he would be more direct and simply tell her what he wanted her to do instead of being cryptic and getting upset when she guessed wrong.

Suddenly Jenny noticed the parallels between Samuel's unsuccessful contact and Zack's clothes on the floor. Like Samuel had done to her, Jenny had gotten upset with Zack because he didn't automatically know what she wanted. If she wanted him to pick up his clothes, she needed to expressly tell him that. Simply getting angry about it wasn't fair, especially if she had given him no indication that's what she wanted.

With that thought the anger left Jenny's body, and she relaxed into her chair. While she didn't feel like getting into it at the moment, she knew the answer to her dilemma was simple—communication—just like her friend Susan had told her several months earlier over lunch.

As Jenny enjoyed the inner peace she'd just found, she began to feel a tug. Mechanically standing up and reaching for her purse, she briefly said to Zack, "Let's go."

With that Zack hopped off the bed and slipped into his shoes. He followed Jenny out the door to the Statesman Room and down the curved stairwell. They wordlessly went outside and got into Jenny's car, which she started and headed down the driveway. She turned toward Route two-fifty-seven, but once she reached the main thoroughfare she took a right instead of a left, leading her further down the road than she'd ever been. After only a couple of miles, she pulled the car over into a small church parking lot. Silently getting out of the car, she headed toward the small cemetery in the back, arriving with determination at the largest headstone of the bunch, which was marked with the names *Jeremiah and Sarah Davies*.

"Holy shit," Zack remarked, "this is the family."

The years of their births and deaths were listed below the names. Jeremiah had been born in 1808 and had died in 1844; his wife Sarah had been born two years later but died the same year.

"They were young," Jenny proclaimed compassionately as she sunk down to look at the headstones at eye level. "He was thirty-six and she was thirty-four."

"Wow," Zack said, "and they managed to have eight kids? That's crazy."

"Well, there was no birth control back then," Jenny noted. "I think big families were pretty common."

"They both died the same year. I wonder if it was at the same time."

"I don't know," Jenny said. "I wish it had specific dates." She glanced at the headstone next to her, noting it was smaller but also read the name Davies. "This one is named William," she announced. "He was born in 1832 and also died in 1844."

"Good Lord," Zack added as he took a few steps away, "here's another one. This is Elizabeth's grave. She was fourteen when she died in forty-four."

Jenny stood and walked over to Zack. "Apparently that was the girl from my vision. She looked very ill when I saw her. I guess she didn't make it." Jenny hung her head despite the fact she had suspected that already.

"Who was the other person you saw?" Zack posed.

"Andrew."

"Well there he is." Zack pointed to another headstone, brandishing the dates 1828-1843. "It appears he lived to be fifteen."

"And it looks like he died before the others," Jenny noted. "Maybe that's why I saw him first in my visions; he could have been the first one to succumb to…whatever it was."

"Oh God," Zack said as he read another epitaph. "Do yourself a favor and don't look at this one."

Heeding his advice and keeping her eyes averted, Jenny asked, "Is it the baby?"

"Well, a three-year-old. She died in 1844, too."

"Jesus," Jenny whispered under her breath. "Something took out this entire family."

"Well, maybe not the entire family," Zack added. "Are you noticing what I'm noticing?"

She looked at him quizzically. "No, what are you talking about?"

"Count them," he replied. "There's the mother, the father, and seven children."

"Only seven?" Jenny posed.

"Yup. And I'll give you three guesses which one's missing."

"Maybe he's just in a different area," Jenny deduced as she looked at the other headstones in the small cemetery. After reading them all, however, she had to acknowledge that Samuel simply wasn't there.

"Could it be that he was the lone survivor of this thing that killed the rest of his family?" Zack asked.

Jenny wiped her hands down her face. "I supposed it's possible. And based on the fact that he's not here, I imagine it's probable. But that means this poor kid watched his entire family die. Based on their ages in the painting, I'm figuring Samuel was what, about seven or eight when that happened?" Jenny shook her head. "That poor kid."

"No wonder why his spirit has unrest."

"And I guess that's what he meant when he said he wanted to reunite with his family. Maybe he's just upset that everyone left him alone on this earth."

Zack looked at Jenny as he pointed to the ground. "Or maybe he's upset that he's not *here*."

"You think he wants to be buried here? That's what's bothering him?"

With a shrug Zack replied, "It could be."

Jenny noted the layer of gray that covered the area as sun began to set; their time to explore would soon have to come to an end. "He may have grown into adulthood and was laid to rest with his own wife and children. In that case, I doubt he'd want to be here."

"Is there any way we can find that information out?" Zack asked.

Jenny's cheeks puffed out as she slowly exhaled. "I have absolutely no idea."

Jenny lay perfectly still in bed as the morning light made its way through the cracks in the curtains. Zack managed to sleep soundly next to her, invoking an overwhelming sense of jealousy. She breathed deeply with her eyes closed, desperately trying to rid herself of her intense desire to vomit. She knew if she moved even one muscle she would instantly be sick; she only hoped that staying still long enough would make the urge go away.

Zack rolled over clumsily in his sleep, causing the entire bed to shake. Unfortunately, that was all the motion Jenny needed to put her over the top. She immediately got out of bed, speed-walking to the bathroom, eventually kneeling in front of the toilet as a cold sweat encompassed her body. Sadly, after much effort and a series of disgusting noises, she was only able to vomit a little bit of bile.

Straightening out her posture, she wiped her hand down her sweaty face. Out of the corner of her eye she saw Zack leaning against the doorway. Although she realized it was most likely her own noises that had woken him, she wasn't entirely sure she wanted an audience at that moment.

"Are you okay?" he asked.

In a move that at any other moment would have been terribly upsetting, Jenny leaned her elbow on the rim of the toilet and placed her head in her hand. "I will be. I think."

"Do you have the flu?"

Jenny shook her head feebly. "I don't feel feverish. Honestly, I think it's just morning sickness."

"Huh," Zack said, sounding as if he was contemplating something. "I'll be right back."

In Zack's absence, Jenny battled several more rounds of nausea. Every time she thought she was feeling well enough to stand up and go about her day, her body let her know she was mistaken. As a result, she continued to sit on the floor, leaning up against the wall near the toilet, wondering if the marriage proposal was still on the table considering what Zack had just witnessed.

A few minutes later, he reappeared with a plate of toast and a glass of apple juice. "Hey," he said softly, "I found Jessica, and she told me she'd had bad morning sickness, too. She said that a little bit of food can sometimes do the trick. I'm not sure if you're up to eating, but this might make you feel better if you can stomach it." He sat across from Jenny on the bathroom floor and leaned against opposite wall.

Jenny managed a smile despite the fact that she felt like she'd been hit by a truck. "You're my hero, you know that?" She reached out to grab a piece of toast.

Zack pulled the plate away. "Okay, you've been gripping the toilet with that hand. I can either wash your hand for you or feed you the toast, but I'm going to be a little grossed out if you touch the toilet and then touch the toast and then eat it."

Jenny rolled her eyes as she pulled some toilet paper off the roll. She wrapped it around her hand, using it as a mitten as she took the toast off the plate. Although she wasn't sure food would actually make her feel better, she was pretty sure she couldn't feel much worse. She took a small bite and chewed slowly, washing it down with a sip of apple juice.

The food went down smoothly. Encouraged, Jenny pointed at Zack with her toast and weakly said, "It's your daughter that's doing this to me you know."

"As if," he replied.

"Seriously," Jenny replied, "it's estrogen overload, I guarantee it. It's totally a girl making me sick."

"Actually, Jessica told me it may be low blood sugar. She recommended you eat something right before bed and keep some crackers on the nightstand for when you wake up. And that makes sense, you see, because all of your nutrients are being used to make our son all big and strong. I'm sure it takes a lot of energy to make those manly Larrabee muscles." Zack flexed his biceps.

Jenny curled her lip but didn't respond. After a few more bites of toast, she noted, "I actually feel like a human being again." She smiled at Zack sincerely. "Thank you."

He shrugged. "I did this to you. Getting you toast is the least I can do."

Her face looked defeated. "You've seen me vomit."

"I've seen most of my friends vomit, just for a different reason."

Jenny managed a laugh. "I'm glad you're such a good sport about this."

"Well, I don't mind that you were puking," he replied, "but I do have to pee. Is there any way you can scoot over so I can have a turn at the bowl?"

Finally managing to stand up without being overcome with nausea, Jenny said, "It's all yours, chief. Have at it."

He looked at her with a smile. "Don't mind if I do."

"Is it okay if I sit down?" Jessica asked as Zack and Jenny finished up their pancake breakfast.

"Absolutely," Zack replied, gesturing to an empty chair. "It'll give me another chance to thank you for this morning. The toast really did the trick for her."

"Yes," Jenny said emphatically, "it sure did."

Jessica scooted her seat in so she was sitting at the table with Zack and Jenny. "I had terrible morning sickness with my youngest," she explained. "I found the only thing that helped me was making sure my stomach was never too empty or too full. As long as I ate little bits throughout the day—and night—I did okay."

"Was your youngest a boy or a girl?" Jenny asked.

"A girl."

Jenny made wide eyes at Zack, who in return shook his head confidently.

"But the reason I'm here," Jessica added, "is to let you know they've identified some of the victims off the highway, in case you hadn't heard already."

Jenny's mood instantly became serious. "No, we hadn't heard. Who were they?"

"Well, they've only released three of the names. One was a girl from Georgia, although I can't remember her name. Apparently she was a runaway; she was determined to make a singing career for herself in New York City. Obviously she never made it."

"Do they know how long she'd been missing?"

"Almost two years, but her body was pretty badly decomposed. She may not have lived very long after running away." Jessica looked sincerely troubled. "It looks like she hitched a ride with the wrong person."

"What about the other victims?" Zack asked.

"One woman was from South Carolina. She apparently battled demons for a while before going missing, and the other was a known prostitute from New Jersey."

"So it looks like our killer travels up and down I95," Jenny concluded.

"Not necessarily," Zack replied. "Remember what Officer Howell said—these women could have easily caught a ride with a trucker to Dale's. Maybe those *girls* traveled north and south, but the killer is an east-west traveler...or even a local."

"Then there's the matter of that other victim Amma brought up." Jenny turned to Jessica. "Did they mention finding any other bodies?"

Jessica shook her head. "The article didn't say anything about any other victims, but that may have changed." She flashed a worried look at Jenny. "You really think there's *another* victim?"

"My grandmother seems to think so," Jenny replied.

"Let me check my computer," Jessica said as she stood up from the table. "I'll see what the latest is."

Zack looked sincerely at Jenny. "Are you feeling better?"

Jenny nodded with a smile. "Not one-hundred percent, but a lot better than this morning."

"That's good," Zack remarked. "Just think…only eight more months to go."

"Great. You know, I could have done without that reminder."

Jessica returned to the table with a laptop. She sat down with the computer facing outward so Zack and Jenny could look at it. "This is the article I read this morning," she said, referencing the screen. "These are the pictures of the girls they found. Somehow it's so much sadder when you can associate faces to the victims."

Jenny looked at the pictures of the girls, and while it broke her heart to see their promising faces, a surge of excitement generated within her. "Bingo," she said as she looked at Zack. Pointing at the laptop she added, "Maybe we can get Rod—I mean, my Pop—to look at these." Jenny had temporarily forgotten she'd agreed to a more affectionate term for her biological father. "He might be able to get a reading from these photos."

"Certainly can't hurt," Zack noted.

Jessica spun the computer back around. "Let me see if there are any more recent articles." After some typing she lowered her brow. "I'm not seeing anything new. These are the same stories I saw last time."

"Well, photographs should be helpful. My father has psychic ability, but it's different than mine. If he can look at a picture of victim and get a feel for what the spirits are currently thinking…" Jenny's eyes circulated around the table. "…maybe the spirits themselves can let us know something new."

Chapter 9

"I think I can do that for you," Rod said. "You say the link is in my inbox?"

"It should be," Jenny replied. "I sent it just a minute ago."

"Okay, well, let me take a look at those for you. I'll call you in a few."

"Thanks, Pop. I know you're at work…are you sure you won't get in trouble for this?"

"There's a murderer on the loose," Rod replied. "I think that's more important that this paperwork I'm looking at."

With a giggle Jenny bid her father goodbye and began the painful process of waiting for his return phone call. To distract herself, she turned to Zack and said, "What do you think would be the most productive use of our time today?"

"I think we should definitely focus on the murders," he replied. "I know Jessica called us out here to help solve her haunting issue, but Samuel can't hurt anybody. Unfortunately that isn't true with the other case."

"They've dubbed him the Highway Killer," Jenny noted. "I read that in the article Jessica showed us."

"Well, our *Highway Killer* might strike again. Although, it must freak him out a little bit to know they've found his dumping ground."

"I hope so," Jenny said. "Maybe that will encourage him to take a little break from the killing."

"Or maybe he'll just find a new dumping ground."

"I like my theory better."

"I do too, actually," Zack replied. "I think we should head to the other truck stops today. So far we've only focused on Dale's, but there just as easily could have been abductions from the others."

Jenny nodded with approval. "I like that idea. I'll go knock on Amma's door and see if she's up for a little road trip. It'll give me something to do so I don't go crazy waiting for Pop's response."

She walked down the hall and summoned her grandmother, who indicated she'd be more than willing to investigate the other rest areas. As they all headed out the door of the inn, Jenny's cell phone rang, inciting a chill up her spine.

She looked at the screen and saw it was indeed Rod calling. "Hello?" she said with anticipation.

"Hi, Jenny. I purposely didn't read the article you sent me because I didn't want my perception to be clouded. I don't know the details of the case, so if I spend time stating the obvious, please forgive me."

"You're forgiven."

"When I channeled the first girl, I felt a huge sense of regret."

"Wait...which girl was that?" Jenny asked. The description Rod gave was that of the Georgia girl who had run away to become a singer.

"Regret was her primary emotion," Rod continued." She believed the whole situation could have been avoided if she'd made better choices. I also got the feeling that there was a prolonged period of suffering at the end for her."

Jenny thought back to the lives of these truck stop prostitutes. That could have indeed been considered a prolonged period of suffering.

"But there was also a blank," Rod continued.

"A blank?"

"Yes," Rod replied, "I've never experienced anything quite like it. It's like there was a blip in her existence. A void where there was nothing for a short period of time."

"That's strange," Jenny noted.

"Indeed," Rod agreed. "Anyway, the second and third girls I channeled expressed both worry and fear as their dominant states. I can't help but feel that whatever happened to these girls is still a viable threat—not to them, obviously, but to others."

"Their killer is still on the loose," Jenny informed him. "At least, as far as we know he is."

"I think that's a good assumption," Rod replied. "If he was in jail on some unrelated charge, I don't think the girls would be as upset as they are. There'd be some solace in their souls. But their anxiety levels were extraordinarily high—I think this guy might be planning his next attack."

"Great," Jenny muttered with a sigh.

"I think it goes without saying that I want you to be careful," Rod said. "I don't want you to be his next victim."

"I don't think I'm in any danger," Jenny assured him.

"Correct me if I'm wrong, but haven't you said similar things to me in the past?"

"Okay, we needn't bring that up," Jenny stated as she got into the car, although she had to admit a false sense of security had landed her in trouble before. "I'm not this guy's typical victim. He seems to prey on prostitutes and runaways…girls that wouldn't be missed." She hated the sound of those words as they came out of her mouth, so she elaborated. "Or at least girls whose absences wouldn't cause alarm." She liked that phrasing better.

"Still, be careful. I'm a little bit concerned by just how worried the girls were," Rod said. "I hope they're not worried about you."

Jenny placed the phone against her shoulder as she started the car. "I don't think they are," she replied, "but I'll be careful anyway."

The truck stop was abuzz with activity. Police officers in full uniform were conducting interviews with truck stop employees as well as young women who appeared to be prostitutes. Jenny turned to her grandmother as she parked the car. "I guess getting a decent reading is out of the question."

Ingunn looked around. "Agreed. No readings today."

"Do you think Howell is here?" Zack posed. "Maybe we can at least touch base with him and this trip won't be a total waste of time."

"Only one way to find out." Jenny pulled her phone out of her purse and dialed Officer Howell's number. He was indeed at a truck stop, just not the same one as Jenny's gang. "Do you mind if we pay you a visit?" Jenny asked Howell over the phone.

"Not at all," he replied. "In fact, I have some updates for you. I'll meet you near the entrance."

As Jenny pulled her car into the other truck stop, they were approached by Officer Howell. She parked in the first available spot, and they all got out to greet him.

"So what's new?" Jenny asked as she shielded her eyes from the bright sun.

"Well, we've been interviewing people who frequent all four of these truck stops, showing them pictures of the girls that have been identified. So far the only girl who has looked familiar to them was Regina Putetti."

Jenny felt a hint of shame that the name didn't ring an immediate bell. She usually liked to know her victims more personally than she had in this case. "Which girl is that?"

"The one from New Jersey. She was a truck stop prostitute for a long time, and her last stint that we know of was here."

"*Here,*" Zack repeated as he pointed to the pavement at his feet. "Do you mean this particular truck stop or just this area?"

"This area," Howell explained. "She made her living at Dale's, actually."

Jenny glanced in Ingunn's direction, but her grandmother continued to look intently at Officer Howell.

"Might she have gotten into a blue car one night at Dale's? Maybe when a kind-looking man offered her a meal?" Jenny asked.

Officer Howell shook his head. "We may never know for sure, unless the driver of that car tells us so. But first we have to figure out who that is." He looked pessimistically at Jenny. "And then we need to get him to confess. And give details. Accurate ones. It's a bit of a tall order."

"So where did the other girls come from?" Ingunn asked.

Howell shrugged. "We don't know that yet. I mean, we know where they're from originally, but we don't know where they were last seen. Or when. We've been contacting friends and family members, trying to determine exactly when these girls went missing. There are also police officers working up and down I95, conducting truck stop interviews, seeing if any of the victims look familiar."

"Have they gotten anywhere?" Jenny asked.

"Not that I know of," Howell confessed, "but that's not to say there hasn't been progress. An inter-state investigation is an FBI matter, and they certainly don't report their findings to me. But I have been made aware of something you all might find interesting."

None of the group spoke, silently inviting him to continue.

"We got a call from a jurisdiction down in North Carolina. They had found a body in a remote location just off the highway earlier in the year. It, too, was near a truck stop."

"Is that case related to this one?" Jenny asked.

"It's too soon to tell," Howell concluded, "but they do have an ID on that victim, and although I wasn't shown a picture of her..." He turned to Ingunn before he continued, "it seems her complexion was quite fair."

While Jenny felt herself react to the news, she noticed Ingunn remained unfazed.

"Do they have any suspects in her murder?" Zack asked.

"Honestly, I don't know too many details about that case; I've been too focused on this one. The one thing I do know is that we need to get the autopsy results back on these women. If it is the same perpetrator as the North Carolina murder, he would have probably used the same method to kill all of his victims." Officer Howell wiped his face with his hands, the gravity of his statement clearly hitting him hard at that moment. Regaining his composure, he added, "I only hope there's enough evidence to determine a cause of death in the Virginia cases. Some of the bodies had been there a while; the elements may make it impossible to figure out exactly what happened to these girls."

"Do you know when the autopsy results will come out?" Jenny asked.

"I'm afraid I don't."

Jenny silently contemplated the choices before her. Clearly there was too much going on for either of them to get a reading. She turned to Zack and Ingunn and said, "Maybe we should just go back to the inn and do a little research on this North Carolina case. If we can send a picture of this girl to Pop, he might be able to give us a little insight."

"That sounds like a good idea," Zack agreed.

"We should be done with the majority of our interviews later today," Howell remarked. "If you want to come back tomorrow to try to...get a contact...you should have quiet." He seemed unsure how to phrase exactly what Jenny and Ingunn did. "Well, maybe quiet is an overstatement; you'll just have your run-of-the-mill truck stop chaos. Hopefully that will be quiet enough."

After thanking the officer, Zack, Jenny and Ingunn returned to the inn. Upon walking into the lobby, Jenny noticed the couple who had given them the Civil War information sitting at a table playing checkers. She waved hello, and they did the same with large, friendly smiles. They seemed like such nice people; if only Jenny could have remembered their names.

Zack headed to the Statesman room to retrieve his laptop while Jenny and Ingunn sat at a dining table. "So," Jenny began, "do you have any intuition about this North Carolina case?"

"Not yet," Ingunn said flatly.

A gust of wind whipped briefly through the lobby. In the midst of the breeze, Jenny was overcome by a horrible feeling of intense fever engulfing her; every joint in her body ached. Horrible pain surged through her stomach, almost causing her to double over. Had the feeling lasted any longer, she probably would have collapsed to the floor. Mercifully the sensation vanished quickly, and she was restored to full health.

She looked at Ingunn with wide eyes. "Did you feel that?"

"Yes," Ingunn replied, actually showing signs of being disturbed. "It looks like our little Samuel didn't escape the illness that claimed his family after all."

"It was awful," Jenny concluded. Zack had returned, and the three of them were sitting at the table. "It was the worst I'd ever felt, illness-wise." She had to acknowledge her own morning sickness paled in comparison; she'd need to remember that and try to avoid complaining the next time it happened.

Zack looked concerned. "I'm glad the sensation was short-lived."

"Me too," Jenny said emphatically, pointing over to the couple playing checkers. "I remember that guy saying that disease took out a lot of the Civil War soldiers, but I can't remember what diseases he mentioned." Her shoulders sank. "I also can't remember his name." She wondered if being scatterbrained was another symptom of pregnancy.

"He seemed like a nice enough guy," Zack noted, "and it was obvious he liked to talk about this stuff. You should just go over and ask him."

"Ask him for what?" Jenny posed. "Information about diseases or his name?"

"Both," Zack replied.

As Zack set up his laptop, Jenny waited for the game of checkers to come to its end. As the couple started to get up from the table, Jenny approached them with a smile. "Hello again."

"Hello, young lady," the man said with exaggerated excitement. "Are you enjoying your vacation?"

"Absolutely," Jenny replied; while that wasn't entirely true, she decided complete disclosure was unnecessary. "I hope you are too."

"We're retired," he chuckled. "Our lives are one big vacation."

"That sounds fantastic," Jenny said sincerely. "I hope you don't mind, but I was wondering if I could ask you a few more questions about the Civil War era." With a wince she added, "Although I have to confess that I don't remember your names."

"Well, good," the woman replied pleasantly. "That will make me feel better when I ask for your name again." The couple re-introduced themselves as Roy and Florence—names which sounded familiar once Jenny heard them.

"So, what is it you'd like to know?" Roy asked.

"If you'll excuse me," Florence said to Jenny with a knowing wink, "there's a book in my room with my name on it." Remembering that Florence liked to have Roy out of her hair from time to time, Jenny returned the wink and bid farewell to Florence, who went on to enjoy her solitude.

Jenny and Roy sat down on the couch in the lobby. "I wanted to know a little more about the diseases that claimed some of the soldiers back then."

Roy didn't bother to ask why. "Well, there are a few. One of the more common ones was dysentery."

"I don't even know what that is," Jenny confessed.

"Actually, I think you do—you just know it by a different name. You know that Norovirus that hits people on cruise ships? That's a form of dysentery."

Jenny's eyes widened. "That can be fatal?"

"Not so much anymore," Roy declared, "but back then was a different story. Today if you get it, you rest comfortably in your bed and take medicine. If you have it bad enough, you go to the hospital and get IV fluid. During the Civil War, those soldiers had very little in the way of shelter; even in the dead of winter, they lived in tents. A lot of the food they ate was rotten, and their access to medicine was quite limited. Those conditions are not exactly conducive to recovery, and prolonged stomach issues can lead to severe dehydration...to the point of being fatal."

"What were the symptoms of it?"

"Diarrhea, mostly. Sometimes a fever."

That sounded like it could have been what Jenny had briefly experienced; perhaps that was the disease that had plagued Samuel's family. She made a face as she considered the implications of what Roy was saying. The thought of feeling like that for an extended period time was horrible enough, but to feel that way while sleeping outside in sub-freezing temperatures was unfathomable. Jenny's heart bled for the soldiers.

Roy continued to recite facts. "Typhoid fever was also a pretty common disease back then, and the symptoms were pretty similar to dysentery. Typhoid came with a rash and delirium, though, and a much higher fever. About a quarter of the deaths among soldiers were attributed to typhoid, not battle."

"It was *that* contagious?"

"Sadly, yes. It was because of the poor sanitation they had back then. They didn't know what we know today, and their latrine was often too close to the food and water supply. They were literally consuming the bacteria that caused typhoid."

Jenny curled her lip as a wave of nausea resurfaced. "What about for regular families?" she posed, trying to stick to the matter at hand. "Or even upper-class families like the one that originally lived here? Would typhoid or dysentery have been a problem for them?"

Roy looked at Jenny with a knowing smile. "Money didn't make the family more knowledgeable about sanitation."

She felt her nerves surge. "So even the wealthy were susceptible?"

"Absolutely. They may have thought it would be convenient to have both the outhouse and the well close to the house. If, however, the two were too close to each other, you've got contaminated drinking water and a very sick family."

Jenny thought about that for a moment. "But a wealthy family wouldn't have had to sleep outside in a tent...they would have had a bed and a fireplace, and they may have been able to afford a doctor. Would that have mattered?"

"Maybe," Roy replied. "It depends on the severity of the illness—and the type for that matter. If a person got cholera, they could have been dead in a matter of hours."

"Hours? That's insane," Jenny noted. "And what caused cholera?"

"The same thing that caused dysentery and typhoid."

Jenny shook her head, marveling at how much misery she'd been spared due to advances in science. "Well, thank you," she said kindly. "This has been very informative."

"Glad I could help," Roy replied as he stood. "If there's anything else you'd like to know, please ask."

"Thank you, I will." The two shook hands, and Roy headed off to go upstairs and join his wife.

Jenny returned to the table and spoke with her eyebrows raised. "Well, I can't say *exactly* what happened, but I have a good idea of what caused the demise of the Davies family."

Zack and Ingunn looked up. "Oh yeah?" Zack asked.

"I'm thinking it was dysentery, cholera or typhoid," Jenny replied. "Those are all stomach conditions caused by poor sanitation, and apparently they weren't all that uncommon back then." Placing her hand on her belly, she added, "And my stomach hurt like crazy for that split second—it would certainly make sense that a stomach ailment was the problem."

"I felt it too," Ingunn confirmed. "It does sound right."

Zack let out a little laugh, which was not the reaction Jenny was expecting. "What's funny?"

Shaking his head in acknowledgement that his statement was ridiculous, Zack explained, "I'm just thinking about typhoid.

There was this guy Pete on my dad's construction crew who was sick all the time—I mean *all the time*. We used to call him Typhoid Pete." He lowered his eyebrows. "Although, if typhoid is a stomach bug, we had it all wrong; Pete mostly just coughed and sneezed a lot." After another moment he added, "And if typhoid took out entire families, I guess it's not all that funny of a joke, either."

Jenny wiped her eyes—there was never a dull moment with Zack around. "Well, we don't know for sure if it took out this *entire* family. The jury's still out as to whether it actually killed Samuel or not." She glanced over Zack's shoulder to look at his computer screen. "So, have you two made any headway on the North Carolina case?"

"If I had to guess," Zack said, "I would say it's unrelated."

"Oh yeah?" Jenny remarked. "What makes you say that?"

"This girl was a college student home for summer break. Yes, she partied, but she wasn't a truck stop prostitute or a runaway."

"He wouldn't have chosen her," Ingunn said plainly. She gestured her head in Jenny's direction. "Show her the picture."

Zack called up a photograph of the victim. She was indeed quite pale with blond hair, but she wore a smile that distinctly showed optimism. "This was taken on her twentieth birthday, just days before she went missing."

"Look at the nails," Ingunn said.

Assuming she meant fingernails, Jenny took note of the beautiful French manicure that this fair young woman wore.

Ingunn continued, "He would have never taken a girl with those nails. A girl like that would be missed. He clearly prefers to deal with girls that can disappear easily and not be reported to the police."

Zack chimed in, "Even if she was high as a kite and wandering aimlessly around a truck stop offering her services to drivers, we think this guy would have known she wasn't one of the strung out girls that worked for the truck stop pimp."

Jenny digested the information, feeling a strange mixture of disappointment and relief. The more victims this guy had, the more likely he was to leave some evidence behind. Although, if he had another dump site in a different state, he could have had dozens all up and down the east coast. His death toll could have been staggering. She deduced that this was ultimately good news. "But if this fair woman isn't our other victim," she noted, "who is?"

The silence that engulfed the table was deafening.

Jenny added to her question. "And what now? We're not going to get any information from the truck stops today; they're much too busy. But I don't want to sit around and do nothing, either."

"Visit other truck stops," Ingunn said.

Zack looked at her. "Other truck stops?"

With a nod she replied, "Up and down the highway. See if we get anything."

That tactic had worked before; Jenny once had to travel to Connecticut to get information about a Georgia murder. She glanced over in Zack's direction. "So what do you think?"

"I think it sounds like a good idea."

"Me too," Jenny said. "Just let me grab a little bit to eat and we can be on our way."

As Jenny nibbled on her sandwich, Zack continued to do some more research. "It looks like they've created a profile of the Highway Killer," he announced.

Jenny's eyes widened. "So who is it we're looking for?"

"A Caucasian male between twenty-five and forty years old. He should be a contributing member of society, nondescript, and a bit socially awkward, according to this." Zack pointed at his laptop screen.

"And harmless-looking," Ingunn noted.

Jenny figured that's what *nondescript* had meant, but she didn't dare correct her grandmother. "I guess they didn't supply a name and address," Jenny said.

Zack continued to look at the screen. "No, they weren't quite that detailed. They do note that he has to have ties to the area, but I think they've said that before."

"Unfortunately that means he could have lived here decades ago," Jenny said. "Or he could simply have a relative that lives here. That information won't necessarily help us find this guy; it will only help confirm if a suspect is viable."

Zack's fingers continued to roam the keyboard. "Oh—they've identified another victim through dental records."

Jenny closed her eyes as she prepared to learn about yet another life taken too soon. She always hated seeing their faces, but she felt as if she owed the victims that much. "Who is it?"

After reading silently for a moment, Zack announced, "Her name's Shelby Ryerson. She's from Florida, originally. She was last seen at home three years ago before she boarded a bus. She was going to travel the country, but she had no particular plans, apparently. She was just going to wing it."

He spun the computer around to reveal a curly-haired young woman with green eyes and freckles. Like the others, she smiled in her picture. Like the others, she had no idea what fate had in store for her.

Jenny rubbed her temples with a sigh. "How old was she?"

Zack returned the computer to its original position. After a pause he said, "Twenty-one when she left home. She'd be twenty-four now."

"Did they happen to mention how long she appeared to be at the dump site?"

"The article said there were *skeletal remains*," Zack announced. "I imagine it had been a while."

"How long does it take for remains to become skeletal?" Jenny asked.

"Not long in the woods," Ingunn concluded.

Jenny assumed Zack was looking for a more formal response when he started typing again. "It looks like there's no concrete answer to that question. It apparently depends on the time of year, amount of exposure to the elements and wildlife...that kind of thing."

"I guess we can narrow her time of death down to *sometime before this week,*" Jenny stated, placing her chin in her hand.

"So how's that sandwich coming along?" Ingunn asked abruptly.

Jenny held up what was left of her lunch. "Just about done. Are you guys ready to hit the road?"

Ingunn stood up from her chair. "I'll get my coat."

"You've been awfully quiet back there," Jenny said as their car continued to roll down I95 in North Carolina.

From the back seat, Zack didn't look up from his laptop. "I'm playing."

Once again, Zack managed to make her smile. "I'm actually going to be glad to stop at this one," Jenny remarked, referring to the truck stop advertised for the next exit. "I genuinely have to use it."

She pulled the car off the highway and found the truck stop to be easily accessible. As she had done with the three other stops they'd visited along the highway, she headed toward the back row of the parking area. Just as Jenny started to get a funny feeling inside her, Ingunn patted her leg.

"You too, huh Amma?"

"There's definitely something," Ingunn noted.

Jenny felt the eyes upon her as she exited the car. She wasn't sure if she was being sized-up for sexual potential or if the intent was more to intimidate, but a man leaning against the building was definitely eyeing her up and down. Undeterred, she closed her eyes and tried to absorb any message she could perceive.

Here. Why don't you come on in? I'll get you something to eat.

She heard the words as clearly as if someone right in front of her had spoken them. There was kindness in the voice of the speaker—harmlessness, as Ingunn had suspected. He almost seemed to have a fatherly quality to his tone.

Feeling the contact was over, Jenny opened one eye and glanced over at Ingunn, who appeared to still be having a reading. Jenny remained silent and motionless until Ingunn breathed deeply and resumed her natural posture. "So what did you get?" Jenny asked.

"A little blue car," Ingunn replied, "with something significant about the license plate."

"What about you?" Zack asked of Jenny.

"He was offering the girl a meal again. He sounded friendly."

Zack turned to Ingunn. "You said there was something noteworthy about the license plate. Do you know what that something is?"

"If I could have gotten that good of a glimpse, I'd have read the tag and this whole thing would be over."

Zack and Jenny both giggled.

"All I know," Ingunn continued, "is that when the car is found, the plate will have something special about it."

Jenny glanced back toward the man leaning against the building, noting he wasn't looking at her anymore. That made her feel better as she stated, "Well, I have to hit the rest room. Anyone care to join me?"

"Yeah, I want to go in." Zack walked back to the car and tucked his laptop under his arm before they headed inside. Jenny found that behavior to be odd, although she determined he just didn't want his computer to be stolen.

Jenny concluded that the restroom wasn't the worst she'd ever been in, which was a nice relief. When she headed back out, she saw Zack at the restaurant counter with his laptop open, showing an image to the wait staff.

She approached to find the waitresses squinting and pointing at the screen. "Yes," one of them said as Jenny got close enough to hear, "that one definitely looks familiar."

Another waitress nodded in agreement. "Yup. That's Colleen, without a doubt."

"When was the last time you saw her?" Zack asked as Jenny stood next to him.

The waitresses looked at each other as one spoke. "What was it, about six months ago?" The other waitress nodded in confirmation.

Zack turned his computer back around, revealing multiple pictures of the same girl, only with different hair styles, cuts and colors. Jenny recognized the girl to be Shelby Ryerson, the latest of the victims to be identified. Making a face, Jenny asked, "Are you sure her name was Colleen?"

"That's what she went by," the waitress confirmed.

Jenny was still stumped by the discrepancy. "Did she tell you her last name?"

The woman shook her head. "The working girls never do."

"So what's the deal with her?" the other waitress posed.

Zack broke the news. "Her body was one of a dozen that was found off the highway in Virginia."

"I'd heard about that!" the woman exclaimed before her face grew sad. "Colleen was one of them?"

Lowering his eyes, Zack replied, "It appears that way."

"What a shame," the other waitress said. "She was always such a nice girl. There was something different about her than the others. Most of the girls that work back here are so strung out they're difficult to talk to—they're almost like bodies with no souls. But Colleen just always had such nice manners...it seemed she was raised differently than the rest. I always felt that she didn't belong here."

"I'd even told her that," the other confirmed. "I used to say she should go back home and get some help, but she used to tell me that heroin had gotten the best of her. The sad thing is she knew it was ultimately going to be the death of her—she just hoped the end would be quick and painless."

Jenny scratched her head uncomfortably; she suspected that Colleen's death had been neither.

"Do you have any idea who she might have left with?" Zack asked.

Both women shook their heads with certainty. "No. There are so many people coming in and out of here, and it's not like we saw her every day. We can't pinpoint exactly when she left here for good, and even if we could, it wouldn't tell us anything."

Jenny felt her spirits sink. "Okay, well, thank you for your help."

"Thank *you* for trying to find justice for Colleen."

Zack took down the women's names and phone numbers for future reference before heading through the exit doors.

"Wow," Jenny remarked, "I'm quite impressed! I had no idea that *playing* meant you were putting different hair styles on our victims. That was very smart thinking."

"I figured those pictures from the articles were taken when the girls still lived at home. I was sure they'd look quite different after spending some time prostituting. If we wanted anyone from a truck stop to recognize them, we'd need to doctor their appearances a little bit."

"But how did you do it?"

"I'm savvy."

Jenny rolled her eyes. "I'm serious."

"The other night when you and Amma were summoning Samuel, I downloaded a program that allowed me to try different hair styles on pictures of faces. The program was offered by a salon, and it was designed to let women actually see themselves with certain haircuts before they got them, but I thought it would be useful here. I downloaded pictures of the victims, Photoshopped out their real hair, and added different styles and colors. I actually made their faces appear thinner, too…more gaunt. I figured prostitution and drug addiction would have that effect on them."

Jenny stopped in her tracks. "Holy shit."

"What is it?"

She squinted to get a better idea of whether she was actually witnessing what she thought she was. Unfortunately her suspicions appeared to be confirmed. "I think Amma is talking to the pimp."

Chapter 10

"Oh my God," Zack said as they quickened their pace. "What is she thinking?"

When Zack and Jenny got within earshot of the conversation, Jenny heard Ingunn say, "Don't let it happen."

The conversation didn't sound like it was troubled in any way; the pimp actually looked mildly amused by Ingunn's determination.

"Hi," Zack said to the man, "I see you met Amma."

The man raised his head in acknowledgement. With a sinister smile, he said out of the side of his mouth, "Yeah, I met her."

Zack stepped forward, although he looked visibly uncomfortable. "So, what's going on?"

Ingunn clearly didn't share in the discomfort. "I'm telling him to warn his girls against men in blue cars who offer them food."

In a voice that would have intimidated most people, the man said, "She said some sick bastard is killing my girls."

Suddenly Jenny understood Ingunn's angle. "Yes," Jenny agreed emphatically. "He took your girl Colleen, and he needs to be stopped." She pointed to Zack's laptop. "Show him the picture."

Zack opened his laptop, which seemed to take three lifetimes to load. The pictures of Colleen with various hairstyles were still on the screen, and Zack clumsily pointed to the image the waitresses had recognized. "This girl," Zack said. "She was found off the highway in Virginia...well, her body was, anyway."

The man studied the picture. "Yeah, I remember her." Without emotion he added, "She got killed?"

"Yes," Jenny said quickly, "and she may have been taken from this very truck stop."

The man remained quiet, looking as if he were challenging the trio to say more.

"Don't let it happen again," Ingunn repeated, pointing her finger at the man. "Tell your girls to avoid this man."

A slight smile graced the pimp's lips. "Yes ma'am." He looked at Ingunn with a blend of curiosity and respect.

"I don't suppose you'd be willing to call the police if you see him?" Jenny asked.

The pimp studied her with disbelief. "What do you think?"

Jenny smiled. "I think that was a stupid question. But if I give you my number, would you be willing to call *me* if you see him? Maybe you can try to get a plate number or something?" The man didn't react, prompting Jenny to continue. "He's taking your girls, which means he's taking your money, and he needs to be stopped."

After some thought, the man coolly gestured his head in Jenny's direction. "Give me the number."

Reaching into her purse, Jenny scribbled her number down on the back of a receipt. She handed it over to the man, and with a quick goodbye Zack and Jenny guided Ingunn back to the car.

"What on earth possessed you to go over to him?" Jenny demanded of her grandmother as soon as they were out of earshot.

"He needed to know."

Jenny was still upset. "Don't you think you should have waited for Zack before you approached him? He could have been dangerous."

"He wouldn't have hurt me," Ingunn countered. "He's too street-smart for that."

"He's a pimp," Jenny declared. "He hurts women on a daily basis."

"Not women my age." They all opened their respective car doors. Once inside, Ingunn continued. "He would never have hurt an old lady in broad daylight. The worst he would have done would be to ignore me—which he didn't, once I told him someone was stealing from him."

"You know," Jenny conceded, "as much as I hate to look at it that way, I have to admit that was a good tactic."

"He's a selfish man," Ingunn explained. "He doesn't care about the girls' well-being. But he does care about his money, and every time one of the girls from this stop goes missing it's less money in his pocket." She clicked her seatbelt into place. "I figured that would be the only way to get him to talk."

"Well done," Zack chimed in from the back. "It looks like he's not the only one who's street-smart."

"I still don't get it," Jenny posed as she drove the car back toward the Heritage Inn. "Why would the man offer them food instead of just propositioning them? It seems so unnecessary. Considering their career, you'd think they'd be willing to get in his car if he just showed them some cash."

"Maybe he wanted to come off as kind," Zack proposed. "You know, get the girls to let their guard down. I would imagine that the girls would have some sort of defense mechanism in place whenever they get into a guy's car. These men are strangers, after all. Maybe this tactic of his made him appear different."

"The girls weren't afraid of him," Ingunn noted. "I didn't feel any fear at all at the truck stop—either truck stop."

"And I didn't feel any fear at the dump site either," Jenny added. "Whatever's happening to these girls is happening somewhere else." She strummed her fingers on the steering wheel. "If only we knew where that was."

"Jenny, do you remember Lashonda Williams?" Zack asked, referring to a victim in a previous case.

"Of course I do."

"Okay, when Lashonda first got into Orlowski's car at the dollar store parking lot, she didn't feel afraid...she thought she was just waiting for her roommate to come get her. But then when Orlowski started driving, Lashonda suddenly became frightened. Isn't that right?"

"Yes, that's right." Jenny was unsure where Zack was going with this.

"But you say at the truck stops you didn't feel fear. No fear at all."

"There was no fear," Ingunn stated flatly.

"So even when the killer started to drive off with the girls in the car, there was no fear?"

Jenny hadn't considered that before. "No," she replied, "I guess not."

"The girls were apparently willing to leave with him," Zack declared. "Do you think he offered them a nice place to sleep, too, in addition to the meal?"

Jenny shrugged. "It's possible." After more consideration she added, "Although, if that's the case, then why aren't the girls telling us that? Both victims have made it known that the man offered them food; they've never said anything about being offered a place to stay. If that was the man's ploy to lure them someplace unsafe, I think they would have mentioned it specifically."

"He could have drugged them," Ingunn declared.

Something inside Jenny's brain flicked like a switch. "Oh my God," she said. "That's it! That's got to be it. He must be putting something in their food."

Ingunn spoke calmly, "Or their drink."

Zack seemed to be formulating thoughts as he spoke. "Maybe the girls know that. Maybe their food—or drink—tasted funny, or they got loopy immediately after eating it, and they knew something was up. But once it started to take effect, there was nothing they could do about it. They were at his mercy. But that's why they're making a point of mentioning the food now...they're trying to let you know it was tainted."

Jenny waved her finger in the air. "I remember what my Pop told me. He said when he channeled their spirits, one of the victims showed a blip in time—a period where there was nothing. He said he'd never seen anything like it. Maybe that missing piece of time was when she was drugged."

Silence took over as they considered this newest theory.

Ingunn's voice shattered the silence. "Have they determined the cause of death yet?"

Jenny shook her head. "I don't know. Maybe Officer Howell can tell us."

After more quiet, Ingunn added, "If he did drug them, did he kill them while they were still passed out? Or did he wait for them to wake up first?"

A sickening rock formed in the pit of Jenny's stomach. Her voice lowered to a near whisper. "I remember something else Pop told me." She swallowed before continuing. "He said the victim had experienced a prolonged period of suffering at the end. At the time I thought he meant her life as a prostitute, but..." Jenny couldn't bring herself to complete the sentence.

"We've got to find out where this guy brings his victims. I bet there's evidence there," Zack announced. "Do you think it's near the dump site?"

"I would assume so," Jenny replied. "Although, I guess it's possible he lives somewhere else and just drives through Virginia for work or whatever."

"He must do a fair amount of driving," Ingunn concluded. "Now we know he's abducted women from both Dale's and now this place in North Carolina, and those are only two that we know of."

"And the dump site is pretty close to the highway," Jenny remarked. "It could be a matter of easy-off, easy-on—quick and dirty body dumping with no witnesses."

"I guess the murder site really could be anywhere," Zack concluded with defeat in his voice.

"The boy is right, though," Ingunn said, gesturing to Zack in the back seat with her thumb. "We do need to find this location, and we need to find it quickly." She glanced over at Jenny. "Something tells me there's a young woman with a fair complexion whose life depends on it."

"That's right," Jenny said over the phone as she paced the lobby of the Heritage Inn. "Zack modified the pictures of Shelby Ryerson, making her face thinner and her hair shorter, and the waitresses identified her as a prostitute named Colleen."

"Colleen," Officer Howell replied slowly, as if he were writing the name down. "That's good information."

"Why would she change her name?" Jenny asked.

"A lot of the girls do it," Howell explained. "I think it's a defense mechanism. They pretend like they're living someone else's life when they turn tricks. It wasn't Shelby, middle-class girl from Florida, sleeping with strangers for drug money; Shelby wouldn't do such a thing. Colleen, however, was a different story."

Jenny closed her eyes. "Well, Shelby also made it clear to me that a man offered her a meal. We're thinking he might put something in the food to knock them out because we didn't feel any fear at either abduction site. It appears he was able to leave the truck stop with each of the girls without invoking any emotion."

"That doesn't mean they were drugged," Howell countered. "At least not by him. They might have been heavily drugged by their own doing. Or they might have just decided to leave with him and hit another truck stop for a while. Those girls are often quite mobile, remember."

"We didn't feel any fear at the dump site either," Jenny added, ignoring Howell's last comment. "I think they were already dead when they were left there, which would mean the murders happened somewhere else."

Howell sounded unimpressed. "It's possible."

"And if that's the case, that other victim my grandmother spoke of might still be alive. My father had specifically mentioned that the spirits were highly upset, indicating that the killer was still very much a danger. Perhaps he has someone in his custody right now...somebody that can be saved if we work quickly enough."

"Do you have any evidence of this?" Howell asked. "Any *tangible* evidence?"

Jenny hung her head. "No."

"Do you have any idea where this guy might be bringing his victims?"

"No."

"Were you given any indication of who this guy is? Or what he looks like?"

Jenny's voice reflected her defeat. "No."

Howell's tone softened as if he recognized Jenny's mood shift. "Listen, I know you're working very hard on this case, and I really appreciate it. That legwork you did today was extremely helpful, and it was excellent thinking to modify Shelby's picture like that."

"Zack did it," Jenny replied in a near whisper.

"Well, Zack did great, then. And I assure you, here at the force we are already working on this case as if every second counts. Even if he doesn't have a woman in custody right now, he might be planning his next attack. Shit, he might be *executing* his next attack as we speak. The information you provide us is helpful, and we'll definitely consider it, but unfortunately we need cold hard facts to drive this investigation. Right now the only fact we know for sure is that thirteen women are dead—fourteen, if that North Carolina victim turns out to be related."

Jenny nodded with understanding. "Okay. I'll work on getting you some facts."

"That'd be great," Howell said. "If any of your leads turn into evidence, I'd love to hear about it."

"You'll be the first to know." Jenny concluded her call and turned to Zack and Ingunn. "He seemed less impressed with this information than we were."

"Well, his goal is to catch the guy," Zack said, walking over to Jenny and putting his arm around her. "And while our news was telling, it didn't get him any closer to his goal."

Jenny leaned into Zack, comforted by his touch. "I just hope we're wrong about the woman with the fair complexion."

"There's definitely a woman," Ingunn replied. "She's fair and she's a victim. If she isn't alive with him right now, then she's dead."

Jenny wondered which was better.

Wiping her eyes to get that thought out of her head, Jenny said, "Okay, Officer Howell asked us for facts. How can we get him those facts?"

After a long silence and an exchange of glances, Zack noted, "Maybe our North Carolina pimp friend will come through."

Jenny faked a smile. "Let's hope."

Chapter 11

"I found a website here," Zack said as he reclined on the bed. "You won't believe it."

Jenny walked out of the bathroom and stepped over Zack's clothes, which still remained on the floor. Taking a seat on the edge of the bed she posed, "What is it?"

"It's a site that allows you to type in a name, a state, and an approximate year for birth and death, and it tells you where the person's grave is."

"For real?"

"Yeah, it's crazy." Zack spun the computer around to face Jenny. "Look, it even has pictures."

Jenny squinted as she examined the screen, noting the image of Andrew Davies' grave in the upper corner of the webpage. "Holy shit," she remarked. "That's amazing. That cemetery is so small. Someone actually took the time to photograph those headstones and post them on this website?"

"Apparently so," Zack remarked, turning the computer around to face him again. "I guess it has to do with the whole genealogy craze that people have gotten into. When you find out who your ancestors are, it would only make sense that you might want to go visit them."

"So what does it say about Samuel?"

"That's just it," Zack replied. "It doesn't say anything."

"It doesn't say *anything*?"

"Nope. There's no record of him being buried anywhere."

"Are you sure you have the birth and death years right?"

"I've tried a bunch of different combinations," Zack explained. "I determined he must have been born around 1836, but I've gone a few years in each direction. I started with death dates in 1843, and I allowed him to live to be a hundred and ten. No matter what I punch in, he's nowhere to be found."

"What about different states?" Jenny posed. "Is it possible he had to move to a different part of the country when his family died? Maybe he went to live with an aunt or something."

"I can check that out." Zack began typing. "But it might take a while."

"We've got time," Jenny replied. "What we don't have are answers. Maybe figuring out where he's buried will give us some insight into what his life looked like after the illness." She let out a vigorous yawn. "Good grief," she added. "I *cannot* shake the sleepies."

"Take a nap," Zack said, patting the bed beside him.

"You know, I think I might," Jenny replied. "I can't keep my eyes open." She slipped out of her jeans, folding them and putting them on the chair near the bed. Next she pulled her arms out of her sleeves, one at a time, and removed her bra from under her shirt. She pushed her arms back through her sleeves and placed her bra neatly on top of her jeans.

"That's quite impressive," Zack noted.

"What is?"

"The ability to take off your bra without taking off your shirt."

"It's not impressive," Jenny informed him. "I think every woman in America has the same talent."

"I still think it's awesome. I mean, I can't take off my underwear without removing my pants."

Jenny giggled. "It's different mechanics." She pulled back the covers and climbed into bed, instantly feeling the comfort of the sheets surrounding her. Contentment surged through her body. "I am so incredibly happy right now; I can't even begin to tell you about it."

Zack smiled and patted her arm. "Well, good. Get some sleep. You've got to conserve your energy so you can make our son's super-big penis."

"You know, I feel so good right now I'm not even going to let that comment disturb me." She rolled onto her side and sighed deeply. For a few minutes she could hear Zack's fingers tap the keyboard, but before long she was sound asleep.

Jenny stretched out her muscles and blinked her eyes open, instinctively reaching for the crackers she kept on the nightstand.

"You're awake," Zack said. "Can I just tell you how incredibly freaky that was?"

Jenny took a bite of cracker as she pushed herself up to a nearly seated position. "How freaky *what* was?"

"The wind," he replied. "I assume you were dreaming about Samuel?"

"Yeah." Jenny furrowed her brow as she recalled her dream. "How did you know that?"

"There was a slight breeze, but only around you. It wasn't like the other times when a giant gust blew through the entire room. This time is was just enough to make your hair move a tiny bit, almost like someone was blowing on it." Zack shook his head. "It lasted a long time. It was creepy."

"Well, he definitely communicated with me; that's for sure."

"What did you dream about?"

"I was lying in a bed in this room," Jenny recalled, pointing to the opposite wall. "But the bed was over there, and the room was decorated in colonial-style furnishings. I didn't feel well, but somehow it wasn't as bad as the first time. It was almost like I was detached or delirious or something." Jenny took another bite of her cracker and turned to Zack. "But there was a woman…"

"A woman? Was it Samuel's mother?"

She shook her head. "No. She must have been a slave woman, based on the color of her skin. She sat next to the bed. She was singing."

"Singing?"

"Yes," Jenny replied with awe. "She had the most beautiful voice, and even though I was too sick to express it, the sound provided me with a lot of comfort—by that I mean she provided Samuel with a lot of comfort. I tell you, that woman had the voice of an angel." She held up her arm, displaying her goose bumps. "I still have the chills thinking about how beautiful she sounded."

"What was she singing?"

"I don't know. It was a song I'd never heard before. It went *Poor mourner's got a home at last,* and then something about *no harm* and *go tell Elijah.* I'd sing it, but there's no way I'd do it any justice. I couldn't even come close to singing it like she did."

Zack began typing on his laptop, which was still on his lap—the same place it had been when Jenny had fallen asleep. After a short time he said, "It looks like there's a song called *Poor Mourner's Got a Home At Last.*"

Jenny laughed. "I guess that's an appropriate name. I've got to say, you found that pretty fast."

"You forget I'm savvy. Here, listen to it and tell me if it's the same song." Zack clicked the play button and the familiar tune filled the room.

"That's it," Jenny said, closing her eyes. "That's the song."

Zack kept the song playing as he typed. Eventually he pressed the mute button. "Check out the lyrics. It goes *Oh mourner, mourner; ain't you tired of mourning; bow down on your knees and join the band with the angels.*"

"Oh my God, I could cry," Jenny said sincerely. "That kind of supports our theory, don't you think?"

"What theory?"

"That Samuel was the last surviving member of the Davies family. The words say *Ain't you tired of mourning?*" Jenny leaned over onto one elbow. "If he watched every member of his family die, don't you think he'd be tired of mourning? And why else would this woman be encouraging him to join the band with the angels? She wanted him to be with the rest of his family." She shook her head quickly and repeated, "I could seriously cry."

"I guess that does make sense."

"And," Jenny continued, "why would a slave be sitting by his bedside if someone from his family was still alive? Wouldn't his parents have held that vigil if they were able to? Or a sibling?" She scooted herself further upright. "And why was he in here? Jessica said this was the master bedroom. The other kids were in different bedrooms when they were sick, presumably their own. I would think Samuel would have been in his own bedroom, too, if his parents were still alive to use this one."

"Why would he use this bedroom, even if his parents were gone?"

"Maybe the bed was more comfortable. Or the fireplace was bigger in here." Jenny grew sadder when she added, "Or maybe simply being in his parents' bed brought him comfort. He was just a child, after all."

"Here's a thought," Zack added. "If Samuel was just a kid, and his parents did die, wouldn't that have given the slaves the ability to escape if they wanted? A sick eight-year-old boy wouldn't have been able to prevent them from running off."

The tears that had been threatening Jenny's eyes made it to the surface. "Maybe this woman could have run off if she wanted to, but she didn't have it in her. There was a kindness in her face that I just can't explain. She looked at Samuel lovingly as she sang." She wiped her tears as she glanced at Zack. "I get the feeling that she wouldn't have been able to walk away from a deathly ill child, no matter what the circumstances."

"That's amazing," Zack replied.

Jenny spoke in a whisper. "That *is* amazing. And you know the saddest thing? Look how this kind and gentle woman was forced to spend her life."

Zack didn't say anything as he shook his head.

Despite the mild nausea, Jenny threw the covers off of her and put her feet on the floor. "I know what I have to do," she said with determination.

"And what is that?"

Reaching for her clothes on the chair, Jenny replied, "I have to go to a craft store."

Jenny returned with painting supplies and set up shop by a window in the lobby. Ideally she would have worked outside in the natural sunlight, but the temperatures were still a little too chilly for that. Light shining through the window would have to serve as a second best. Closing her eyes to envision the woman with the amazing voice, Jenny recalled the features she would try to capture on canvas. She wished the painting would have been able to reflect the beauty of this woman's voice; Jenny knew a simple two-dimensional image wouldn't do her justice.

Zack came down to the lobby shortly after Jenny got started. "Will it bother you if I talk to you while you paint?" he posed.

"Nah," Jenny said, "but I won't look at you when I respond."

"I'm used to that," he replied. "That's how most of my ex-girlfriends conversed with me. So, I searched every state within reason and found no results for Samuel Davies' grave."

Jenny fixated on her pencil as it touched the canvas. "Huh. That's a shame."

"I'm beginning to think he was never formally buried."

With that Jenny looked at Zack. "Never buried? What do you mean *never buried?*"

"I think he was buried," he replied, "just not formally so. If he died from this disease that took out the rest of his family—and he died last—who would have been there to bury him?"

Jenny thought about that for a moment. "This woman that I'm painting right now."

"Exactly. And I don't think she'd have the means to give him the type of burial the rest of his family received, and certainly not at the same place."

With her blood frozen in her veins, Jenny replied, "Do you think he's buried somewhere around here? Like on the property?"

"I think it's possible," Zack replied. "Where else would a slave bury somebody?"

"My goodness," Jenny whispered. "If that's true, no wonder his spirit lingers."

"I'll tell you what," Zack said. "You keep working on that, and I'll start doing a little research on slave burials."

Jenny nodded slightly. "Sounds good."

She flashed him a quick glance and a smile, but she noticed he wasn't looking at her. His gaze was fixed beyond her and through the window. He squinted as if to get a better look at something over her shoulder before blurting, "Holy shit."

Chapter 12

"What is it?" she asked, quickly looking out the window in the direction Zack had stared.

"It's a dog."

Spotting the wretched animal Zack was referring to, Jenny hung her head in relief. "Okay, seriously, we're in a haunted house. You can't look off into the distance and say *holy shit* like that. I nearly soiled myself."

"Sorry," he replied, "I just didn't expect to see a dog roaming around out there."

Regaining some of her composure, Jenny looked back through the window and took a better peek at the dog, who appeared to be an emaciated and dirty black lab mix that gazed longingly in the direction of the inn. Immediately her heart softened. "Awww. Poor thing. It looks hungry."

Without another word Zack and Jenny both headed toward the back door of the inn, opening it slowly as not to frighten the animal away. It acted unfazed by their appearance. "He seems socialized," Zack noted. He took a few steps toward the dog and squatted down, extending his hand. After a few kissing sounds, he gently said, "Come here, buddy. I won't hurt you."

With its tail between its legs, the dog slowly approached. After allowing it a few sniffs, Zack used his extended hand to scratch its head—a gesture which was well received by the animal.

"He has a tag," Jenny said. "What does it say?"

Zack tilted the bone-shaped tag toward him. "It says his name is Baxter, and there's a phone number."

"We should call it," Jenny said. "They must be missing him."

"My phone is inside," Zack confessed. "You?"

"Mine too. You keep Baxter here and I'll get my phone. I'll see if Jessica has any food for him, too, while I'm in there." Jenny scampered back into the inn and headed straight for the kitchen, where Jessica was working with another cook to prepare the evening meal. "Excuse me, Jessica," Jenny began in an apologetic tone, "I'm sorry to bother you."

Jessica smiled pleasantly. "It's no bother. What can I help you with?"

"Do you have any...meat?"

"Meat?" She looked puzzled. "Are you having a craving?"

With a laugh Jenny replied, "No, not a craving. There's just a dog outside and the poor thing looks like it hasn't eaten in ages."

A blend of frustration and concern graced Jessica's face. "Is it Baxter again?"

Again? "You know Baxter?"

"Yes, I know Baxter," Jessica replied as she headed for the refrigerator. "He's shown up here several times already." She pulled out some ground beef and prepared to brown it as she spoke. "I always give him a little bit of food and bring him home, but he inevitably shows back up again, looking hungry and neglected every time."

Jenny was so glad she stopped in the kitchen before finding her phone. "How many times has he shown up?"

Jessica fired up the stove. "This is probably the fourth or fifth time now."

"Here," Jenny said, extending her hand toward the skillet of raw meat. "I can do this. You've got a dinner to prepare."

"Oh, it's no bother."

"Truly," Jenny said. "I'd rather be useful."

With a smile Jessica conceded, and Jenny took over the ground beef duty.

As she waited for the pan to sizzle, a million thoughts swirled around Jenny's head. "Is there a vet around here?" she finally posed.

"A vet? I'm sure there is one in town, about twenty minutes to the west."

Jenny stirred the meat and thought some more. "How about a pet store? Or even a general department store?"

Jessica shifted her eyes in Jenny's direction, her slight smile indicating she understood where the conversation was going. "There are a few discount superstores in town."

Jenny returned the smile. "And about that shed in the back…"

Jenny walked outside with a bowl full of ground beef. Baxter immediately began to jump when he saw it; apparently this was what he had come for. She put the bowl down on the grass and marveled at how quickly its contents disappeared.

"Did you bring your phone?" Zack asked.

Jenny looked lovingly at Baxter. "Nope."

"Did you forget?"

"Nope."

"What do you mean, *nope*?"

"I mean, I didn't forget."

Zack clearly didn't understand. "Aren't you going to call his owners?"

Jenny reached out her hand and scratched the dog's head. Once she had Baxter's trust, she squeezed the clasp that held his collar together, detaching it, allowing the collar to fall to the ground. "Oh, look. We can't call his owners. He has no tags."

Zack stared at her with awe. "Jennifer Watkins, you aren't seriously thinking about stealing this dog…"

"No, I'm not thinking about stealing this dog." She cupped Baxter's face in her hands as he licked her chin. "I'm definitely stealing this dog. And by the way, I wouldn't consider it stealing. If we stole him, that would mean we went onto their property and took him, and that's not what happened. Jessica says this dog is a repeat customer. Baxter continues to find his way here because his owners aren't keeping a proper eye on him, and apparently they're not taking good care of him, either. If he was well cared-for he wouldn't keep coming back in this condition. So, yes, while I do plan to take this dog home with me, I do not consider it stealing. I believe in this case his owners have simply relinquished him due to their lack of care." She looked at Zack and batted her eyes.

"You know, it gets me kind of hot when you talk this way."

Jenny laughed out loud. "Does the word *relinquish* do something for you?"

This time Zack laughed. "No. I just love the way you are all sweet and innocent, but then you can turn around and break the rules and totally justify it."

"Well, this *is* justified. Besides, when else have I broken the rules?" Jenny kept her gaze, and both hands, on the dog.

"Um, you broke into a house?" Zack reminded her.

"That was to keep a kid out of jail."

"You totally lied to a guy's face to get him to confess a secret to you."

"Who," Jenny asked, "Archer?"

"Yes, Archer."

"He was hindering an investigation."

Zack couldn't contain his laughter. "See? This is what I'm talking about."

Jenny spoke with conviction. "I believe every one of my actions was totally reasonable under the circumstances."

"And now you're taking someone's dog."

Jenny turned to Zack, still cupping Baxter's face. "Look at him," she said. "You can see every one of his ribs. He's covered in burrs and probably fleas and ticks. Can you honestly tell me that you think the right thing to do is call his owners and bring him back to the people who allowed this to happen in the first place?"

"Absolutely not," Zack said with a smile, putting his arm around Jenny, "and I just love that you don't either. Although, if we do keep this dog, that *really* makes this whole thing look like a Scooby-Doo episode."

"So where is he now?" Ingunn asked at the dinner table, referring to the dog.

"Zack brought him to the vet. He wasn't able to make a formal appointment for Baxter until tomorrow afternoon, but the vet said he could at least go in, get the dog weighed and start him on flea and tick medicine. He needs to be on that stuff as soon as possible."

"That's good," Ingunn replied. "Where will the dog stay until you go home?"

"The shed out back. While it's hard to say for sure because he's black, I think it's safe to assume he has fleas. The last thing I want to do is bring him in the house...or the inn, in this case. Jessica doesn't need an infestation. So for now Zack is buying Baxter a comfy bed, some toys and a bag of food so he can be comfortable out there in the shed until we go back to Tennessee. It's a good thing the weather is mild; that shed isn't climate controlled. If it was summer or winter I'm not sure what we'd do with him, to tell you the truth."

Ingunn raised her finger. "I'm glad you're keeping the dog. Dogs are good protection."

Jenny flashed her grandmother a smile that wasn't returned. "Zack was harassing me about it—jokingly, of course—telling me I'm *stealing* him."

"You are stealing him," Ingunn confirmed.

"Amma," Jenny said with semi-feigned offense, "I thought you just said you were glad I'm keeping him."

"I am," Ingunn replied as she shook more pepper on her steak, "but that doesn't mean you're not stealing. You are taking something that you know belongs to someone else. That's stealing."

Jenny lowered her shoulders. "You make it sound so...*wrong*."

"No, not wrong," Ingunn said with a shake of her head. "Illegal, but not wrong."

Jenny smirked at her grandmother. "Aren't they the same thing?"

Ingunn once again shook her head. "Not necessarily. Suppose I collapse, right now. What would you do? You'd bring me to the hospital, right?"

Confused, Jenny nodded. "That's right."

"On the way to the hospital, if you hit a parked car, would you pull over and try to find the car's owner? No. You'd keep driving to the hospital. Then, the next day you'd figure out who owns the car so you could pay for the damages. See? Leaving the scene of an accident is illegal, but in this case it wouldn't be wrong. It would be wrong to let me die in your passenger seat while you knocked on doors to see who owned the dented car." She took a large bite of her steak.

Admittedly relieved by her grandmother's approval, Jenny laughed. "I said something similar to Zack last night, but I tried to explain why that made it *not stealing.*" She made finger quotes.

"Oh, it's stealing," Ingunn said definitively. "Make no mistake about it. It's just not wrong in this case."

"I'm glad I have that clear," Jenny said with a laugh. "Oh, Amma, please don't let me forget...we need to save a plate for Zack when he gets back. No doubt he'll be starving." After thinking about it a moment, she added, "He's always starving."

"He's a growing boy."

Afraid to let herself get too full, Jenny slid her plate forward and rested her elbows on the table. "I took a nap this afternoon," she began, "and I had a very interesting dream...or actually *vision* might be a more appropriate word."

Ingunn didn't look up. "Oh yeah?"

"Yes. I was Samuel, sick in my bed, and I was being sung to by a slave woman."

Ingunn shifted her eyes toward Jenny's sketch, which still sat on the easel on the other side of the room. "Is that the woman you're drawing?"

"Eventually it will be a painting, but yes, that is her. I just wanted to make sure I had captured the outline of her image before I stopped for dinner. I can go back and put the color in later. But anyway, Zack and I have a theory about her. We think Samuel may have died last, and this woman stayed to take care of him. We decided that if their owners had all died—except Samuel, of course—that would have been the perfect opportunity for the slaves to escape...but this woman didn't. She stayed to provide Samuel with some comfort."

"Noble," Ingunn commented.

Jenny's eyes shifted solemnly toward the table. "Yes. Very. That's why I wanted to immortalize her in a painting. I feel like people need to know about her."

"Also noble," Ingunn added, although Jenny felt her actions paled in comparison to those of the woman she was painting.

After a polite smile, Jenny added, "Zack and I theorize that Samuel may have died from his illness and is buried somewhere on the property. That probably would have been the only means this woman would have had to lay him to rest, and it would be a rational explanation as to why he lingers. It also explains why he relayed the message that he wants to be reunited with his family, but then he got mad when I told him to cross over. That wasn't what he meant. He wants to be *physically* reunited with his family at the cemetery."

Ingunn nodded with understanding, although she didn't comment.

"If we are correct, I'd like to find Samuel and give him a proper burial with the rest of the Davies crew, although I haven't a clue about how we would go about doing that."

"I might have some insight," Ingunn said with a wink. "Remember how my husband made his living?"

Jenny had indeed forgotten. "Ah, yes. We have a ringer on our team." A sobering thought occurred to Jenny. Changing her tone to be much more serious, she asked, "Amma, can you tell me a little bit about my grandfather?" The only thing Jenny knew was that he had been a mortician and he had passed away a long time ago.

"Sure," Ingunn said unemotionally. "What would you like to know?"

With a shrug Jenny said, "I don't know. What was he like?"

Ingunn smiled briefly before speaking. "Jerry was an interesting man. There were two distinct sides to him: the professional, mortician side, and the off-duty, family-man side. At home he was very light-hearted and fun. He had quite a sense of humor, that's for sure. He was always laughing and joking and carrying on."

Jenny thought back to her childhood with three brothers in the house; it sounded similar.

"But then he'd get the phone call, and it's like a switch got flicked. Suddenly he was all business. But he was a good mortician; I realize not everyone could do it."

"Did you guys have a good marriage?" Jenny asked.

"We did, for the most part."

Jenny smiled. "For the most part?"

"Well, every marriage has its ups and downs, and we were certainly no exception, but the good definitely outweighed the bad."

With defeat in her voice, Jenny admitted, "I guess you probably know that my first marriage didn't work out so well."

"Yes, your father told me you were divorced."

Separated, Jenny thought, but considering she was pregnant and sharing a room with her boyfriend, she figured she should just let that one go. "Yeah, and let me tell you that was a very hard decision to make. Like you said, all marriages have their ups and downs, so it was difficult to tell if I was just having a *down* or if the marriage needed to end."

"There's a difference between being annoyed and being unhappy. Jerry annoyed me plenty, but I wasn't unhappy with him."

With a laugh Jenny said, "I spoke with the other couple that is staying here, and the wife said she's wanted to hit her husband over the head with a frying pan from time to time—but they've been married for decades, and she did seem happy."

Ingunn looked squarely at her granddaughter. "There is not a married woman alive that hasn't have the urge to hit her husband over the head with a frying pan. But I'm sure the husbands have a legitimate gripe or two themselves. The difference is that in good marriages the irritation blows over. In bad marriages, it stays."

Jenny thought back to her marriage to Greg; contempt was her primary emotion toward the end. A small feeling of validation surged through her before she posed, "But how do you prevent it from reaching that point? My ex-husband didn't *always* infuriate me...it wasn't until near the end that I found him intolerable."

Ingunn considered the question before answering. "Well, I guess the first thing you have to do is choose carefully. Make sure the person you marry is your friend, because ultimately that's what carries you through the long haul. But I would also suggest that you remember that you're flawed, too. I don't care who you are, living with you isn't always a walk in the park either...but if the guy's willing to put up with your annoying habits, you should find it in yourself to do the same."

Once again, Jenny felt validated. She didn't leave her first husband because of his annoying habits; she left because she was being mistreated, and that was indeed a very legitimate reason to go. Despite his clothes on the floor and his endless potential for future irritation, Zack didn't seem capable of mistreating her. Perhaps this conversation was tipping the scales in favor of accepting the proposal.

Her grandmother, however, had become widowed at a relatively young age. She hadn't spent decades with her husband; would she have been singing the same tune if Jerry were still alive? Or would she have grown so tired of his irritating habits that she'd have left him by now?

Jenny dropped the mental debate for more concrete matters. Her grandfather had died young—for her own benefit and that of her unborn child, she probably should have known why. "Do you mind if I ask what happened to your husband? I know he passed away a long time ago."

"Cancer," Ingunn said flatly. "Lung cancer. He smoked."

Jenny hoped she wasn't overstepping her bounds when she continued with the questions. "Knowing that you have this gift, did he cross over? Or did he—or *does* he—still linger?"

Shaking her head she announced, "He crossed. He knew he was dying for a long time, so he said everything he needed to say during this lifetime. There were no unresolved issues for him. And I told him to cross, back when he was still alive. There is something wonderful on that other side, even though I don't know exactly what it is. I didn't want him to waste any time sticking around here, especially since the end was so miserable for him. After watching him suffer, I wanted him to finally be free."

"You'll see him again," Jenny said softly.

Ingunn remained remarkably unemotional. "I know I will."

A question that had been circling in the back of Jenny's brain for months finally made it to the surface. "Amma, if psychic ability runs in the family, and I was born with it, then why didn't I have my first experience until I was twenty-six?"

Ingunn shrugged with one shoulder. "For most of us, we know we are psychic from the time we can talk. If a baby is born with the gift, the other psychic family members can tell right away. The ability is then honed in the child. I imagine if you had no one around to teach you, it would have taken longer to master the skill." She looked up at Jenny with just her eyes. "But can you honestly tell me you never had *any* psychic experiences prior to age twenty-six?"

Jenny thought back for a moment before confessing, "You know, there were some incidents where I thought I heard a voice of some kind, but every time I just figured it was my mind playing tricks on me. I always had a vivid imagination as a kid; it wasn't unreasonable to think I was fabricating it."

"Well, you weren't."

Jenny felt strangely violated. "But what do you think was different about Steve, my first true contact? Why was I so convinced he was real when I could dismiss the others?"

"Was he strong-willed, this Steve character?"

With a smirk Jenny conceded, "Yes. Very."

Ingunn nodded as she raised a hand. "Well, there you have it. That first one has to be very determined in order for you to decipher the message; then after that it becomes effortless. It's like the floodgates open—once you access that part of your brain, it remains available. From there it only gets better."

"Pop said he still has to make an effort—he has to purposely channel the spirit."

"Yes, that is true," Ingunn agreed, "but he can channel the spirit much more easily than he could at first. And speaking of your Pop, he called me earlier. He said he tried to call you but you weren't answering your phone."

"I didn't have it with me," Jenny confessed. "So what did he have to say?"

"He said the girls aren't worried anymore."

Jenny looked at her grandmother with awe, wondering why this hadn't come up earlier. "The girls aren't *worried* anymore?"

Ingunn regarded Jenny with confusion, as if she was unsure how her message could have been unclear. "That's right."

"The girls from the dumpsite?" Jenny asked.

"Yes."

"They're not worried?"

"They're not worried."

A thousand thoughts cluttered Jenny's mind as she tried to figure out what it all meant. She had assumed their previous worry had stemmed from the unknown, fair-complexioned victim Ingunn had described—the one that might still have been very much alive. But if the spirits weren't worried anymore... "Do you think that means the fair woman is dead?"

"I can't say for sure." Ingunn's eyes met Jenny's. "But that would be my guess."

Chapter 13

Baxter ran happily around the shed as Zack and Jenny sat on the concrete floor, Zack revealing the highlights of the visit into town. "The vet said he weighs around forty-five pounds, but he should probably be about ten pounds heavier than that. They gave me only one dose of flea and tick stuff because if he gains enough weight this month, he might require a stronger dosage next time."

"So he's got the medicine in him?" Jenny asked as the dog stopped to scratch his neck with his foot.

Zack nodded. "I gave it to him right away. I also bought some stuff at the store. Let's see," he said as he pulled merchandise out of a bag, "I got a leash and a dog bowl. Ooh…here's his new tag." He held up the new identification, which said BAXTER with Zack's phone number. "I wasn't sure what chewy things he'd prefer, so I got a few squeaky toys, some nylon bones, and a couple of bully sticks." He held a bully stick up with two fingers, barely touching it as it dangled toward the ground. "Do you know what these things are made of?"

"No idea."

"It's a bull's penis," Zack declared with a mixture of humor, awe and disgust. "A dried-out bull penis. The woman at the pet store told me that dogs love these things."

Jenny curled her lip. "I'll let you give that to him."

"The vet also said he appears to be full-grown, so I bought this dog food for adults." Zack gestured to the large bag of food he'd set down against the wall. "I hope Baxter likes it."

"He's a dog," Jenny said, "and he looks like he hasn't eaten in a month. I get the feeling he's going to like whatever food you give him." With an evil grin she added, "Kind of like you."

Zack lowered his eyebrows but didn't respond.

"Did you get him a bed?" Jenny asked.

"That's still in the car," Zack replied. "It's kind of big, so I couldn't carry it with all this other stuff."

Jenny looked lovingly at Zack. "You're a big sap, you know that? You're totally spoiling this dog."

"After what he's been through, he deserves it, don't you think?"

With a smile she said, "I couldn't agree more."

"Oh," Zack admitted with a wince, "I almost forgot. I do have a confession to make."

Jenny felt her demeanor instantly become serious. "And what is that?"

"I kind of got a speeding ticket on the way there."

"A speeding ticket?" Disappointment surged within Jenny's bones. "In my car?"

"Yeah. I'm actually pretty lucky. It could have been considered reckless driving, but the guy had mercy on me because I was from out of state."

"Just how fast were you going?"

"Seventy in a forty-five."

Jenny hung her head. "Are you serious?"

"Well, the road was so flat and straight, it was easy to go fast. The speed limit was fifty-five for a long time, so seventy wouldn't have been that bad, but then the speed limit got lower because the road went through this little town. I didn't notice the change or I would have slowed down. But like I said, the cop was nice. He said I was only doing fifty-nine, so it's just a ticket. I don't have to go to court or anything."

Somehow Jenny didn't share in the joy of that news. "Okay, from now on I'll do the driving...*all* the driving." Out of fear of saying something regrettable, she turned her attention to the dog. "Come here, buddy. Do you want one of your new toys?"

Baxter stopped scratching and padded over to the selection of goodies laid out in front of him, sniffing each one before picking up the bully stick and heading to the corner of the shed. He lay down, crossing one paw over the other with the stick in between, and began chewing vigorously.

"My dick hurts just watching that," Zack announced.

Ordinarily Jenny may have laughed at that comment, but her current train of thought was preventing her from seeing any humor in the situation. Zack's irresponsibility and immaturity were shining through in grandiose style, and yet she was pregnant with his child. She found herself doubting his ability to be a good father. Or a good husband.

But a marriage proposal was on the table.

With a sigh she said, "We have to figure this out."

"Figure what out?"

"This," Jenny replied, gesturing to the very happy dog. "Baxter. Is he going to live upstairs with me or downstairs with you?" With that comment Jenny was trying to emphasize their separate living quarters, which for the moment she intended to keep.

Zack shrugged. "Can't he do both?"

"But that would mean leaving the basement door open. Either that or we'd have to keep opening and shutting it every time he wanted to switch. It seems like that would get annoying."

"Or we could just get married and both live upstairs," Zack said as he flashed his famous toothy grin in her direction.

The smile that normally melted Jenny's heart was ineffective this time; the speeding ticket had dampened her mood too much. Glancing toward her lap she whispered, "I'm not ready to agree to that yet."

He patted her on the leg and said, "Okay, then. Maybe we can just install a dog door so he can go up and down as he pleases."

Admittedly, Jenny liked that idea better, but she was still troubled. "But what are we going to do when we get called out of town? You know as well as I do that we often have to leave at a moment's notice. Who is going to take care of Baxter then?"

"Our house is in the epitome of suburbia; I'm sure we'll be able to find a neighbor with a teenager who'd be willing to earn a few extra bucks by dog sitting. The yard is fenced in, too, so it wouldn't be hard; someone would just have to let him out a few times and make sure he's fed." He smiled at Jenny, looking at her curiously. "What's this all about? Why so nervous all of a sudden?"

Once again Jenny found herself reluctant to say what was really bothering her; she wanted to make sure her doubts were legitimate and enduring before she opened that can of worms. Instead of confessing the truth, she simply shrugged and kept the nature of the discussion focused on the dog. "It's just a big commitment, and I guess it's occurring to me that we didn't think this through."

Zack repositioned himself so that he was hugging his knees. "I've been thinking about it a lot, actually...not because of the dog, obviously, but because of the baby. It's going to be a lot harder to find somebody to take care of the baby when we get called out of town in the middle of the night. The dog can be left unattended for a few hours before we get someone over. But after the baby is born...what if you get a pull at three in the morning? If you take the time to call a babysitter and wait for her to arrive, you'll lose the contact. And I certainly don't want you to head out alone while I stay home with the baby; the last time you went out by yourself you almost ended up dead."

Jenny closed her eyes. She knew these were notions she would eventually have to face, but she hadn't allowed herself to think about them yet. Admittedly, that was uncharacteristic for her; she was usually an incessant planner, but these decisions were so frightening that she tucked them away for a later date. Although, it seemed that Zack had already tackled the issues, causing Jenny to question which one of them was actually the irresponsible one in the relationship.

"So I was thinking," Zack continued, "I remember you saying your mother was having a tough time living in the house she'd shared with your father—that everywhere she turned there was a reminder that he was gone. I thought maybe she'd like to come live with us...in the downstairs apartment. That way if we do need to go out without advanced notice, there will be another adult in the house to take care of the baby. We can just let your mother know that she's in charge until we get back."

While the idea sounded good to Jenny, she immediately saw the hole in the theory. "But that would mean you and I would be living together upstairs."

"Well, yeah..." Zack replied, looking at her optimistically.

She rubbed her eyes. "I'm not sure my mother would agree to that," she found herself saying, even though she was the one who was reluctant to say yes. "There are a lot of memories in my mother's house—good ones—that she may not want to move away from. She even mentioned once that the basement door still has height markings from our childhood. We may find that she's unwilling to leave that."

Jenny's phone rang; when she glanced at the caller, she noticed it was Howell. "Hang on," she said, "this may be important." She answered the phone with, "Hello, Officer Howell. Anything new?"

"Hi, Jenny. Not sure yet. There's been a new development, but we still don't know if it's related to the case or not."

"Oh yeah? What's that?"

"A woman was left at a gas station off the highway just over the North Carolina border last night."

Jenny felt her blood run cold.

Howell continued, "The difference is she was alive. But I'll give you three guesses as to what she looked like."

"She was fair," Jenny said in a near whisper.

"As fair as they get," Howell confirmed, "and the story she tells is unbelievable."

Chapter 14

Jenny put her phone on speaker before Howell continued. "A clerk who worked the morning shift at the gas station found her sitting up against the building, cold and confused, so he called the police. At first they figured she was just coming off a high or something—it was fairly obvious from her appearance that she was an addict, and she couldn't tell the local police how she'd gotten there. But she kept insisting she'd been held hostage for a few days."

"Hostage?" Jenny felt compelled to interrupt.

"I know," Howell said, "it's crazy. They didn't believe her at first because her story was so incredible, but she was adamant. Then they remembered the finding just off the highway here in Virginia, and they thought maybe the cases were related."

"Did she say what happened?"

"It was like you described. She was working as a truck-stop prostitute when a man pulled up and offered her a meal. She remembered he was dressed in a shirt and tie, which made him appear different than most of the guys who proposition her. Plus he didn't seem to be looking for sex—he said all he wanted to do was feed her since she looked so emaciated. He told her he'd go into the truck stop and place an order for her, to go, and he'd bring it back out to her. She said she requested a burger, fries and a Coke.

"When he came back out," Howell continued, "he said she could sit in his car and eat. She told him that would actually be helpful since her pimp would not have been happy seeing her standing around eating instead of working. She got in his car and they pulled to a remote parking spot. She said the food tasted perfectly normal, but the next thing she remembered was waking up in a dark room chained to a wall."

"Dear God," Jenny replied.

"She could feel soundproofing on the walls of the room, but she screamed anyway. It obviously didn't do any good. The only person who ever came to her was the person who was holding her captive."

"I don't think I want to know this," Jenny asked, "but what happened to her while she was there?"

"What you'd expect. They swabbed for semen, but they didn't find any. I guess he was smart enough to wait before letting her go."

"According to the profilers, we may be dealing with a man who has no criminal record anyway," Zack noted. "DNA may not have helped."

The disappointment in Howell's voice was noticeable. "But at least it would have confirmed we had the right suspect if we ever found him."

Jenny rubbed her temples as she formulated her thoughts. "Okay...this guy must have spiked her drink, and she woke up chained to a wall. Did she say how long she was there?"

"She has no idea. The room was completely dark except for when the man came in, so she had no way of knowing if it was day or night."

"Did she get a good look at the man when he visited her?"

"In fact she did, which indicates he initially had no intention of keeping her alive. She's been working with a sketch artist to create a composite. Unfortunately, she's somewhat difficult to work with. It appears she was a meth addict, and she hasn't had any for a while now. They've got her on other drugs to help her come down from the meth, and those are messing with her mind a little bit. Sadly, she's just about the worst witness we could ask for."

Jenny couldn't help but fixate on one aspect. "So why do you think he let her go alive?"

"Fear, I imagine," Howell stated. "His dumping ground had been uncovered, and he probably was keeping the woman in a location that would implicate him. I think he may have panicked and set her free in case we came looking for him. He certainly wouldn't want to have a captive in his custody if we knocked on his door."

"But wouldn't a sound-proof room with shackles be evidence against the guy, whether or not there was a woman in there?" Zack asked.

"Not necessarily. Kinky sex isn't against the law, as long as it's consensual," Howell replied. "At least, that's the position the defense attorney would take."

Jenny remained focused. "Does this woman have any idea how long she was in the car before she was dropped off at the gas station?"

"Unfortunately, no," Howell replied. "She was told to drink some soda while she was being held in the room, and the next thing she knew she was at the gas station. They tested her for different drugs that could induce unconsciousness or amnesia, and she tested positive for having Rohypnol in her system. You probably know it as Roofies. The effect of that usually lasts four to six hours, or so they tell me, but that means he could have come from two-hundred miles in any direction. That doesn't exactly narrow it down for us."

"Where was she abducted from?" Jenny asked.

"Central North Carolina, about an hour from where she was found. Once again, if she was given Rohypnol at the truck stop, he could have taken her to Virginia or South Carolina before she regained awareness."

"If you figure out where some of the other women were taken from and draw two-hundred-mile circles around each location," Jenny said, "maybe there will be only one specific spot where the circles overlap. Then you can figure out where his hideout must be."

Zack looked impressed by Jenny's comment.

"We've thought of that," Howell remarked, immediately bursting Jenny's bubble. "But we have no way of knowing where these women were taken from, and we don't know how long each woman has been missing. Even if the other prostitutes at the truck stop can recognize one of the victims and can give us an exact time of disappearance, which is doubtful, we wouldn't know for sure if the perp took her from that spot or if she just hopped a ride with a trucker. We would need to formulate timelines as to when each of these girls was last seen in order to determine exactly where the abductions took place, and I don't think strung-out prostitutes are going to be able to give us accurate enough data. The last thing we want to do is base an investigation on false information."

"Maybe we could do it," Jenny said. "I'm sure my grandmother and I could determine where some of the abductions took place. We may not know which girl it was, but we could definitely get a feel for whether or not the killer propositioned anybody at a particular truck stop." Jenny shrugged one shoulder. "For some of the girls, at least."

Howell remained quiet for some time. "I would love to say yes to that," he replied. "You've been right about so much already. But I'm not sure the higher-ups are going to be willing to base an investigation on the testimony of psychics. No offense."

"None taken," Jenny assured him. "But we could still do it and at least let *you* know what we find."

Another long pause. "If you could, that'd be great. I'll take any insight I can get."

As Jenny's paintbrush filled in the lines on her canvas, Zack approached through the front door of the lobby. He marched immediately over to her with a smile on his face, remarking, "I just bought a compass." He proudly pulled it out of the bag he was carrying, reminding Jenny of the countless circles she'd drawn in geometry class. "I'm totally badass with these things."

She looked at him curiously. "Badass? Do you stab people with them?"

"No, I do not *stab people*." Zack took a seat on the couch near Jenny's easel. "It's just after all those years in the construction business, I'm completely awesome at using one. You should see me make a perpendicular bisector."

Jenny remained quiet, unsure of what to say.

Zack produced the maps he'd also purchased. "Okay, before I can demonstrate my circle-making expertise, I want you to help me decide how big to make the radius. How far should we go from each abduction site?"

Sitting back in her chair, Jenny sighed as she thought. "Howell said the amnesia effects of Roofies last four to six hours, isn't that right?"

"That's what he said."

"We might want to verify that," Jenny noted, "just to be safe. And I'm assuming that Roofies knock these girls out?"

"I'm honestly not sure what they do," Zack said. "Let me get my laptop and I'll check." After a short moment he reappeared and set up shop on the table in the lobby. While he was gone, Jenny was able to add a little more color to the slave woman's face. "Okay," Zack said as he read, "it looks like it acts as a sedative that causes amnesia."

"Sedative," Jenny repeated. "How *sedate* do the girls get?"

"This article doesn't say," Zack eventually concluded, "but I imagine sedate enough to not make a scene when he drives away with her."

"Or to make a scene when he arrives at his destination," Jenny thought out loud. "I'm sure he'll want her to still be loopy when he gets her to his little torture chamber." She shuddered at the thought.

"So what do you think, then...he'd try to keep it under four hours?" Zack posed. "I'm sure he'd rather err on the side of caution."

"That's what I'm thinking."

"And four hours on the highway would equate to two-hundred forty miles, give or take."

"Let's go with that," Jenny replied. "I think that's probably generous because he must take into account that he could hit traffic. I also think he must not spend the entire time on the highway unless his hideout is right off an exit. But I'd rather make the circles too big than too small. I don't want to miss an area of overlap because we underestimated the distances."

Zack unfolded his map and adjusted the compass to equate to two-hundred-forty miles. "Okay," he said, "the first abduction that we know of is from Dale's, which is right...here." He put the metal into the map and drew a circle. "That limits us to Maryland, Virginia, West Virginia, North Carolina and a tiny bit of South Carolina. The Atlantic Ocean eliminates a good chunk of the east." After making the other two circles based on the North Carolina abductions, Maryland became eliminated from the list.

"We still have a long day ahead of us tomorrow," Jenny noted with a yawn. "We need to go further south than we did last time, and we need to go north—and west for that matter." She frowned. "And even east. I'm sure there are a lot of truck stops in our target area."

Zack typed furiously on his laptop. "I bet I can tell you exactly how many." A few moments later he pointed to his screen and said, "Yup. This website tells you all of the truck stops along any particular highway. It even lets you filter by certain attributes, like *has a restaurant* and *open twenty-four hours*."

"That's cool," Jenny said sincerely. "That will be very helpful."

"I'll make a list of all of the stops we need to visit, although I may disagree with you about heading east and west. I think we should focus on north and south now that we know he's had a few abductions along I95."

With a stretch Jenny said, "Good point. I still had better get to bed. Even without the east-west, we've got a long day tomorrow, and our daughter sucks the energy right out of me."

"I feel like we've been driving forever," Jenny said as her hands gripped the steering wheel.

"Well, it has been about three hours," Zack noted from the back seat. "Are you doing okay up there?"

"Yeah," Jenny replied, "I just have to admit it will be nice to get out and stretch my legs."

"The truck stop should be coming up soon," Zack said. "It's off the next exit."

The trio remained silent as Jenny pulled off the highway and found a parking spot near the back. After exiting the car, Jenny and Ingunn tried to get a feel for any hints of abduction. After a moment Ingunn declared, "There's nothing here."

"I'm not getting anything either," Jenny agreed, "but I do need to go in and grab a little bite to eat. My stomach isn't feeling the greatest. I hope you all don't mind."

"Me?" Zack asked. "Mind getting food? Never."

As they approached the front door of the restaurant, Jenny gasped at what she saw. A flyer featuring a composite sketch of a dark-haired man was taped to the glass, complete with the caption, "Have you seen this man?"

The image of his face immediately brought Jenny back to a small, square room, illuminated by a single light bulb hanging from the center of the ceiling. Gray soundproofing covered the walls, and Jenny could feel her hands cuffed next to her head. The man from the composite sketch walked toward her, smiling, saying in a deep voice, "Hello, my pet."

The flashback was fleeting but powerful. "Whoa," Jenny said, gripping on to Zack's arm.

"Is everything okay?" he asked.

Jenny nodded. "I just need a pen and paper. I have a picture to draw."

Jenny sat in the booth, continuing to sketch the image of the room, her empty plate in the center of the table. The soundproofing was proving to be time-consuming to replicate.

"If you want," Zack offered, "I can drive us to the next truck stop while you finish your picture on the road."

Jenny glanced up at him with just her eyes. "You, chief, are not allowed to drive my car." She refocused her attention to the picture.

Zack checked the time. "I have a vet appointment for Baxter this afternoon. I want to make sure we're back in time to take him."

"He's got his medicine in him," Jenny noted while she sketched, "so he's getting treated for fleas and ticks already. He's got food in his belly. And you set up his lead so he can go in and out of the shed, right? And access his bed?"

"Yeah," Zack replied.

"Then he should be good, no? I would think we could even wait and take him to a vet down in Tennessee for his official check-up if we need to." She looked at Zack, whose expression reflected his sadness, causing Jenny's heart to soften. She reached out her hand and placed it on top of Zack's. "If you want, we can call Jessica and ask her to go out and check on him."

"I'd like that," Zack replied with the smile of a child. "Do you happen to have her number?"

Jenny pulled her phone out of her purse and handed it over. "She's a contact." She continued to draw as Zack made the phone call.

He hung up with a smile. "Jessica says that Baxter is sound asleep on his bed. I have to admit I feel better."

"Good, I'm glad," Jenny said sincerely. As Zack called the vet to reschedule the appointment, Jenny found herself troubled by a notion in her own head. While she considered not mentioning it, ultimately she decided to bring it up after Zack got off the phone. "It's more than a little sad that Baxter is being treated better than these women got treated while in this psychopath's custody," she said. "At least the dog has a long lead and a comfortable bed. I'm under the impression the women were shackled to the wall."

"You said he called you—meaning the victim—*my pet*, right?" Zack recalled. "Do you think that was more of a literal word than a term of endearment? Like he actually regarded these women as his pets?"

Jenny's pencil stopped moving as her eyes rose to meet Zack's. "Probably. And that's almost too disturbing to think about."

"You know what else is disturbing?" Zack posed. "I haven't seen Amma in about twenty minutes. Do you think she's outside scolding the pimp again?"

"Oh, God, I hope not."

Zack looked over his shoulder toward the door of the restaurant. "If she is, my money's on Amma. She's one tough lady."

"Maybe you'd better go try to find her," Jenny suggested. "If that is what she's doing, that poor pimp might need a little help."

While Zack was gone, Jenny finished up her sketch and took a picture of it with her phone. With a quick text, she sent the picture to Howell, explaining that she believed that this was what the killer's hideout looked like. Just after she hit send, Zack approached with Ingunn by his side. "I found her."

"I wasn't lost," Ingunn proclaimed.

Jenny couldn't help but smile.

Ingunn continued, "I was trying to figure out where we should go next."

"We have a list," Jenny informed her. "Zack researched all the truck stops along the highway."

"That list is too long," Ingunn said.

"I know it's long," Jenny agreed. "But I'm finished with my drawing, so we can get going…"

"That's not what I mean," Ingunn replied. "I'm not worried about running out of time. What I'm suggesting is that some of the stops on that list are unnecessary."

Zack and Jenny waited silently for an elaboration.

"All of the women seem to have been kidnapped from truck stops that are among many at the same exit." She gestured around her with her hand. "We've visited stops like this—that are alone—and we always get nothing. It seems like a waste of time."

Jenny thought about that for a moment before asking, "So do you think he, like, shops around the different truck stops before choosing a victim?"

Ingunn shrugged. "Maybe those stops are just more likely to have prostitutes."

Zack had already pulled his list out of his pocket. "It looks like the next truck stop group is about fifty miles south of here." He glanced at the ladies. "What do you think?"

Jenny put her purse strap over her shoulder. "I think it's time to get back on the road."

"That was a good call, Amma," Zack said from the back seat as they finally headed back toward the inn. "Both of our new contacts occurred at a truck stop that was one of many off the same exit. I'm not sure how you figured that out so early on."

"There was a pattern," she proclaimed.

"A pattern that I hadn't picked up on," Zack added, "but getting a reading at a truck stop that far south eliminates a good chunk of northern Virginia, and the reading near DC takes southern North Carolina off the map. I'll have to wait until we get home to draw my official, perfectly-round circles, but it appears his hideout is somewhere between Fredericksburg and Raleigh."

"I think we need to let Howell know this," Jenny said as she picked up her phone. "Call Howell," she directed robotically as she kept one hand on the wheel and both eyes on the road; the phone obeyed.

After a few rings Howell picked up. "Hi, Jenny. I'm glad you called; I was just getting ready to call you, in fact."

"Oh yeah?"

"I showed the picture you sent me to our survivor, and she immediately recognized the room as being the place she was held captive."

Jenny wondered why news that didn't surprise her still invoked such nerves. "Well, you can tell her that it was her composite sketch that inspired that vision. As soon as I saw the guy's face on that flyer, I got a distinct visual of the room." Jenny swallowed and softly added, "That God-awful room."

"So you have no indication where that place might be?" Howell posed.

"Not specifically. We just had a couple of contacts, though—one at a truck stop in southern North Carolina and one just south of DC. The visions were just like the others; we could definitely sense that a guy offered up a warm meal, so we feel fairly confident that they were related to this case. The contacts were far away from each other, too, so that narrows down where the hideout might be...on *our* map, anyway. I realize this information doesn't affect the official police map."

"And where do you think it could be?"

"Somewhere between Fredericksburg and Raleigh. But my grandmother had another interesting observation." Jenny disclosed Ingunn's theory about the truck stops in groups.

Howell sounded as if he was writing as he spoke. "Well, thank you for the insight. Hopefully this will help speed things up."

"I hope so, too." She paused before adding, "Do you think he'll strike again soon?"

"Well, we're treating it like he will, but, to be honest, I'm personally inclined to think he won't. I believe he dropped off that one victim—alive and in a different state—because he was scared. He knows we're on to him now, so I think he'll lay low for a while."

"Good," Jenny said as relief washed over her. "Maybe we'll be able to connect the dots before anyone else gets hurt."

"That's the plan."

Jenny rubbed her tired eyes as she pulled the car off the highway. She was grateful to finally have reached their exit; this had been a very long day for her, and she wondered how her grandmother had managed spend this much time in the car without complaining. "You doing okay, Amma?"

"I'm okay," Ingunn replied. "I'm a tough old bird."

"I'm certainly ready to be home," Jenny said. "Or at least back at the inn. I'm exhausted."

They remained silent for a few minutes before they drove past the narrow road that led to the dump site. Ingunn placed her hand on Jenny's arm and said, "Go back."

"Go back?" Jenny asked. "To where, the dump site?"

Ingunn, clearly on to something, only nodded. The prospect of turning around on a dark, windy road invoked some fear in Jenny, but she managed to do it anyway. She drove the car back and took the left that would bring them to the site.

A police car sat on the side of the road, making Jenny wonder what was happening. She pulled over and Ingunn wordlessly got out of the car. The officer inside the cruiser did the same, approaching Ingunn.

Knowing that her grandmother needed to be uninterrupted, Jenny hopped out of the driver's seat and intercepted the officer. "Hi," she said quickly but quietly. "My grandmother is a psychic working on the case."

The officer looked over Jenny's shoulder at Ingunn and then looked back at her. "She needs to stay out of those woods." He spoke louder than Jenny had wanted him to. "That's a crime scene."

"Okay," Jenny said, "I'll make sure she doesn't..."

"Something has happened," Ingunn announced, causing Jenny's blood to run cold.

Jenny directed her attention from the officer to her grandmother. "What?"

"I don't know," Ingunn replied, "but the spirits are upset."

Jenny looked at the police officer and felt fear run through her body. Was he the killer? Were the girls upset because the man responsible for their horrible deaths was standing right there? While he seemed an unlikely suspect,

Jenny's previous cases had taught her that no one was above consideration.

"Come on, Amma," Jenny said with urgency, fearing they were in the presence of a murderer. "Why don't we get back in the car and go to the inn?"

Ingunn shooed her hand, indicating her unwillingness to honor Jenny's request. Instead she took a few steps closer to the woods.

"You can't go in there, ma'am," the officer said.

Ingunn went no further, but she remained frozen in place for quite some time. "Yes. Something definitely has happened." Turning back around, she added, "And it isn't good."

Chapter 15

"I feel like I owe you an apology," Jenny said as Jessica put a plate of French toast in front of her.

"An apology?" Jessica asked. "For what?"

"Well, you asked me to come out and investigate your inn, and I've spent just as much time, if not more, working on the abduction case."

"My goodness, that's not a problem," Jessica said. "In fact, I'm glad you're working on that. Honestly, I find that to be far more frightening than what's going on here at the inn. That guy is a very real threat to living, breathing people. My...apparition...is just creating wind gusts. And if what you've told me is true—that he's just a child who wants to be buried with the rest of his family—then it turns out it's not even frightening."

"Well, I'd like to spend some time working on that painting this morning," Jenny said, "and trying to get you some answers. Sadly, at this point there's not much more we can do with the murder investigation, so today I'm all yours."

"I do appreciate that," Jessica replied, "but if that changes, don't hesitate to switch gears and focus on the Highway Killer. I recognize how important that other case is."

"Thanks." Jenny smiled as Jessica headed back toward the kitchen.

Zack sat across from Jenny at the table. "Well, while you paint, I'm going to play with Baxter for a while. It'll make up for yesterday when we hardly saw him at all."

Jenny took a bite of her breakfast while she contemplated that Baxter might have been better off living downstairs with Zack when they got back to Tennessee. It also occurred to her that Zack may not turn out to be that bad of a father after all; if he was that concerned about the welfare of a dog, he would probably be excellent with a baby.

At that moment Florence and Roy sat down at a table near Zack and Jenny. "You're still here," Jenny said to them with a smile. "I thought you'd be bouncing that great-grandbaby of yours on your knee by now."

"Well, we're supposed to be," Roy said, "but the little guy is sick. We're waiting for him to get better before we head down there."

Florence looked pleasant as always. "It looks like we're extending our vacation for a few days."

"I can think of worse places to be stranded," Zack said.

"Exactly," Florence agreed. "It's supposed to be pretty out today, and I have plenty of books with me. It should be a good day."

"I'm assuming that since we're the only guests here these days, that painting over there is the work of one of you three," Roy said as he gestured toward Jenny's easel.

With a modest smile Jenny acknowledged the picture was hers.

"Who is that a picture of?" Roy asked.

Unsure of how to answer that question, Jenny glanced at Zack as she spoke. "It's what I imagine a slave woman might have looked like back when this house was a tobacco farm."

"That's very interesting," Roy replied. "Are you planning to sell it?"

"Honestly," Jenny said, "I think I'll leave it here as a present for Jessica."

"Well, that's very sweet of you," Florence noted. "And you're very talented. I realize the painting isn't finished yet, but I can tell it's going to be beautiful when you're done."

Although Jenny had grown in so many ways, she still struggled with compliments. "Thanks," she said softly as she looked at her lap.

"And what about that dog out there?" Roy asked. "Do you know anything about that?"

Zack took over the conversation, the love and pride evident in his voice when he spoke about Baxter. He continued to talk about the dog until long after breakfast was over. Jenny listened politely, but she had to admit she was relieved when his long-winded tale was over and she was able to get back to painting the benevolent slave woman.

As she worked, Florence returned to the lobby with a book, taking a seat in the chair by the window. She looked up at Jenny and posed, "I'm not going to disturb you if I sit here, am I?"

Jenny smiled pleasantly. "Not at all."

For a while the two ladies remained quiet as they each went about their business. Eventually Jenny sat back in her chair and said, "Miss Florence, can I ask you a question?"

Florence set her book face down on her lap and said, "Of course." Then with a laugh she added, "I just hope I'll be able to answer it."

"I think you should be. How long did you say you've been married again?"

"Fifty-two years."

"Fifty-two years," Jenny repeated in a whisper. "That's fantastic." Jenny got up from her chair and sat down next to Florence. "What's your secret?"

"My secret?" Florence put her hand, which was speckled with age spots, to her chin. "I didn't realize I had a secret."

"Well, not everyone has been able to stay in a marriage as long as you have." Jenny lowered her eyes. "Including me. I was actually married before, but it didn't work out."

"I'm sorry to hear that," Florence said sincerely.

Jenny smiled slightly. "Thanks. But I was just wondering what advice you can offer a naïve young woman about how to make a marriage work as long as yours has."

With a giggle she announced, "It's smoke and mirrors, mostly."

"Smoke and mirrors?"

Florence looked around, presumably to make sure Roy was nowhere to be found. "It's all about illusion, see. You give the man the impression that he's in charge, when in reality you are in charge."

Jenny lowered her eyebrows, indicating her confusion.

Florence leaned forward and put her elbows on her knees. "I remember one winter we had a particularly bad snowfall. We were snowed in for days. The kids and I were okay with it; in the summers we were used to being home all day with nowhere to go. But Roy went crazy. He had the worst case of cabin fever I'd ever seen. Like he often does when he's bored, he went into micro-manager mode. He essentially white-glove tested the whole house, loudly complaining about how horrible everything looked." Florence rolled her eyes and shook her head. "So I told him I needed stools."

Jenny wasn't sure if she'd heard that correctly. "You needed *stools?*"

"Yes. I told him that I was too short to reach the tops of the closets and the pantry, and I needed several stools. I mentioned that I was going to buy them at the store the next time I was out." Florence looked around again to make sure the coast was clear. "I knew what his response would be, you see…and I was right. He told me that I shouldn't waste perfectly good money on stools when he could easily make some himself with the tools he had in the garage."

Suddenly Jenny knew where Florence was going with this.

"So he spent the next couple of days out in the garage working on this project, leaving me and the kids alone. But the beauty of it was that he thought it was his idea to make the stools. If I had asked him outright to start this project, then I would have been nagging, or at the very least it would have been clear that I was just trying to get him out of my hair. But this way he believed he was not only the genius in this situation, but also the hero for coming to my rescue. And when he was done, I marveled at how wonderful the stools were. I thanked him many times for making my life so much easier, when in reality I didn't even really need the stools. I could have just used a chair to reach the top shelves; that's what I'd been doing for years. But what I *needed* at that moment was quiet until the snow melted, and I got it." Florence sat back in her chair and interlaced her fingers in front of her chest. "See? Smoke and mirrors."

"And this trip is another example of the smoke and mirrors," Jenny concluded, formulating the thought as she spoke. "You asked him to plan a little vacation, leading him to believe he's in charge of where you go, when you really just needed him to be occupied for a while."

"Bingo," Florence said with a smile. "I don't nag him or tell him that he's bothering me; that would start a fight. Instead I just plant a little seed and let him tend to the tree."

Jenny's voice was distant. "I can plant seeds."

"Indeed you can," Florence replied. Shifting in her seat she added, "So...is this question stemming from the young man you're with on this trip?"

Feeling like Florence might be a safe source to confide in, Jenny said with a sigh, "Yes. We have a baby on the way, and he wants to marry me...but I'm just so afraid to go down that path again. It didn't work out for me the first time, and I don't want to go through another divorce."

"Divorce would be hard, I must agree," Florence said. "Fortunately, I have never had to go through it. But let me ask you a few questions...that young man—Zack, is it?"

"Yes, it's Zack."

"Does he treat you well, this Zack?"

Jenny couldn't help but smile. "Yes, he does."

"Is he faithful?"

"Yes."

"Hardworking?"

She let out a giggle. "Of late."

"Do his actions seem honest or self-serving?"

"Honest."

"Does he love you?"

"Yes."

"Do you love him?"

Jenny's entire relationship with Zack flashed through her mind...the banter, the cuddling, the speeding ticket, the laughter, the clothes on the floor. Ultimately she raised her eyes to look at Florence and simply said, "Yes."

"Let me tell you something, darling." The compassion was evident in Florence's voice. "When you get to be my age, you'll have regrets. You can't possibly live as many years as I have without racking up at least a few of them. But as I look back at my life now, the things I regret the most are the things I didn't do, not the things I did."

The words definitely struck a nerve. With a slight nod Jenny whispered, "That's a very good point."

"If you do get married and things don't work out between you and Zack, you can at least look at your child and tell him—or her—that you tried. You tried to make it work. You tried to be married, but it just wasn't in the cards." Florence held up one bony finger. "But, if you don't agree to marry him, you'll have to look that child in the eye and tell him—or her—that you didn't even try because you were too afraid to fail. Is that really a message you want to send your child?"

Jenny thought back to her first client Elanor, who had left Jenny with some words of wisdom by which she'd vowed to always abide. She found herself whispering, "Fear is not a reason," one of the final messages Elanor had bestowed upon her.

Florence spoke loudly. "I'm sorry. I didn't hear you."

Jenny shook her head as she snapped back into the present. "It was nothing," she said. "Just thinking out loud."

At that moment, Zack came in from outside. He glanced at Jenny's painting as he walked by, announcing, "Looking good. You're almost done."

"Thanks." Jenny smiled at him as he leaned down to kiss her cheek.

"Hi, Miss Florence," Zack said with a quick wave.

"Hello, young man."

"Something funny happened outside, but I feel kind of bad about it," Zack said. "I wanted to see if Baxter could catch, so I threw a tennis ball to him…" He held back his laughter as he added, "and he let it just bounce right off his nose."

Jenny lowered her eyebrows. "Is he okay?"

"Yeah, he's fine. It didn't seem to faze him much at all. But I figured he'd be able to catch it considering he looks like he's got black lab in him."

Jenny glanced at Florence and then back at Zack. "Why would being a lab make him able to catch?"

Zack looked confused. "You mean it doesn't?"

Suddenly Jenny doubted everything she thought she knew about dogs. "They retrieve, don't they? Like, bring back ducks and stuff? But they do that after the duck has hit the water…they don't catch the duck in the air."

"I thought retrievers could catch," Zack said. "A lot of dogs that you see catching Frisbees look like labs or lab mixes."

Jenny turned to Florence. "Do you know the answer to this? Is it in a lab's nature to catch?"

"I'm afraid I don't know," Florence confessed with a smile, "but I can mention it to Roy and he can do a little research for you."

"Yes!" Jenny said emphatically before turning to Zack. "We can mention it to Roy, and he will probably decide to do a little research for us."

Zack, clearly unaware of the inside joke, made a strange face and said, "Okay."

"But what I do know," Jenny said, "is that retrievers can retrieve. Have you thrown the ball across the lawn so he can track it down and bring it back to you?"

"His lead's not long enough," Zack said.

Jenny thought back to the women chained to the wall in the Highway Killer's hideout, and suddenly she felt as if she, too, had taken Baxter against his will. "Well, you can take him off his lead for a while, can't you?"

"What if he runs away?" Zack asked.

She looked at him compassionately. "You've fed him, right? And played with him and petted him and given him a comfortable bed...I doubt very seriously that he'd run away from that, especially considering what he's been through. Besides, you know what they say...if you love something set it free. If it comes back to you, *then* it's yours."

Zack looked sad. "I just don't want to lose him."

"I know," Jenny said, "but I'd like to make sure he actually *wants* to be with us before we take him back to Tennessee." She looked down at her lap. "Otherwise we really are stealing a dog."

"Use food," Florence said. "If you have food in your hand, he won't go too far."

"He *is* a boy," Zack replied quietly, "and we boys do like our food."

"Give it a try," Jenny said encouragingly. "See what happens."

Florence and Jenny watched out the window as Zack went back outside and stuffed his pockets with bite-sized dog bones. Baxter's reaction indicated he could smell the treats; he jumped enthusiastically all around Zack. Once the lead was removed from Baxter's collar, Zack threw the tennis ball about twenty feet. Baxter hardly noticed; he remained fixated on the food in Zack's pockets.

Jenny and Florence found themselves laughing as Zack retrieved the tennis ball himself, throwing it back in the direction he'd come from. The dog stayed by his side like glue, wagging his tail and bouncing all around, completely ignoring the ball. After a few more failed attempts at fetch, Zack eventually threw one of the dog bones; this time Baxter left Zack's side to sniff out his reward. After gulping down the treat, Baxter ran excitedly back to Zack for another round.

This went on a handful of times before Zack put the dog back on his lead. At that point Zack threw the bone in Baxter's direction with a nice, high arc. Once again the dog let the treat bounce off his nose, eating it only after it had hit the ground. "See?" Jenny said to Florence. "Catching is not instinctual for a lab."

"Shhh," Florence replied with a finger to her lips. "We don't know that. I think Roy still needs to spend a good deal of the afternoon investigating it."

At that point Jenny's phone rang. She pulled it out of her pocket and noticed it was Officer Howell calling. She answered with her nerves tingling.

"Jenny," he said instantly, "have you heard the news?"

"No," she replied, "what's happening?"

"It seems our psychopath friend has contacted the press."

Chapter 16

"Oh my God," Jenny said, turning her back to the window and walking to a more secluded part of the lobby. "What did he say?"

"He wrote a letter to a television station in North Carolina, not far from where our latest victim was dropped off. He made a point of saying he isn't done."

Jenny felt as if her blood had frozen in her veins. "He isn't done?"

"That's what he said. He apparently sent this before we found the woman at the gas station. He stated in the letter that he was planning to release the blond because, as he put it, she didn't do it for him. He apparently prefers women with dark hair. He didn't find this blond woman to be worth his time."

"So it was postmarked *before* the blond was released?"

"Yup. He obviously put it in the mail at least twelve hours before he let her go. That's how we know it's legit and not some jackass trying to get attention."

Jenny let out a deep sigh. "What else did the letter say?"

"It taunted the police, essentially," Howell confessed. "He laughed at us, mentioning how long it took us to figure out he even existed. He went on to say that it will be easy for him to keep going because he's smarter than we are. He even gave us a hint, saying that he won't be using the same dumping ground anymore so we can save the taxpayers some money and stop paying a cop to monitor the area."

"How did he know you were doing that? He must have driven by at some point."

"He must have," Howell concluded, "and the cop may have even stopped him. But all he had to do was say he was going to visit a friend who lived back there, and the cop would have had to let him go. You need probable cause to search a vehicle, and driving down a road that passes a killer's dumping ground is not it."

"But there's a chance the cop wouldn't have even stopped him," Howell continued. "The officer's primary purpose for being there is to make sure the killer doesn't come back to ditch more bodies. Cars driving through aren't as much of a concern."

"What if the car had out-of-state tags?" Jenny posed. "Wouldn't that be a bit suspicious?"

"It would," Howell agreed. "So we're inclined to believe the killer is from Virginia, or at least has access to a vehicle with Virginia tags."

"Okay," Jenny began as she formulated more thoughts in her head. "Where was the letter postmarked from?"

"North Carolina," Howell replied. "The same town where the woman was found."

"Does that tell you anything?"

"Only that he travels a lot, which we knew already."

Jenny thought for a moment about the implications of the latest finding. "You know," she confessed, "my grandmother got a funny feeling when we drove past the dump site last night. She was beckoned there while we were heading down route two-fifty-seven. She made me turn around so we could go to the actual site."

"Oh yeah?"

"Yeah. She said that the spirits were upset—that something bad had happened."

"Christ," Howell whispered under his breath. "That's all we need."

"Has anyone new been reported missing?" Jenny posed.

"No, not that I know of. But with his clientele, they don't necessarily get reported missing. Their bodies just get found."

Jenny closed her eyes. "What about the letter itself? Did that give you any information, like fingerprints?"

"It's at the forensics lab right now, being analyzed. Something tells me, though, that this guy is smart enough not to leave any evidence behind. The sad thing is it's going to take them a while to figure out that he's left no trace. I'm sure the letter is littered with fingerprints—the people at the post office, the workers at the television station—who knows how many people have touched the damn thing. All of those people need to get eliminated from our suspect list, one by one, and that will take a long time."

"How about the wording? Did the verbiage give anything away?"

"Not that we can tell. The letter has been made public; if you go online you should be able to read a copy of it for yourself. They're hoping that somebody can recognize the style of writing or something—*anything*—so we can figure out who this jackass is. In fact, the reason I'm calling is because I'd like you to give it a read and see if it inspires anything in your psychic mind."

"I can do that, sure," Jenny replied, "and I'll get my grandmother to do the same."

Ingunn, Jenny and Zack crowded around the computer screen, reading the words that appeared before them.

To the incompetent people who have the nerve to declare they serve and protect,

Congratulations. You finally figured out I exist. Good for you. It's only taken you five years.

I suppose now you think you are closer to catching me. Perhaps you are under the impression that I'll be inclined to stop. I promise that you are no closer to discovering my identity than you were a month ago, and I can assure you that I will not stop. I cannot stop. This is part of who I am. Just like the cheetah must hunt its prey, I must do the same. Your societal rules will not change me. I am a hunter.

I must hunt.

Now that you have found my disposal site, I suppose I must find another way to get rid of these girls when I am done with them. If you think I am stupid enough to bring another body to the same place, you clearly underestimate me. Do the taxpayers a favor and stop paying that officer to sit by the crime scene; it's a colossal waste of money. You will not catch me that way.

I will be leaving you a present, though. I have a blond right now, and I find she does nothing for me. I thought something different might be interesting, but she has proven to be a disappointment. I would receive no joy from watching her die, so I will return her and exchange her for a brunette. Few joys in life rival the exhilaration of seeing a dark-haired woman in captivity, at my mercy, begging for her life as I decide whether she's deserving of another day. The urge to find such a woman is strong; I will need to take one soon. It's hard to function normally when the desire within me reaches this level.

You can go ahead and canvas your truck stops; there are plenty of other places to hunt. You can try to figure out where I'll be, but I guarantee you will always be several paces behind. Remember, I know who you are, but you don't know who I am. You call me the Highway Killer, but that is not me.

I am the Hunter.

Jenny winced as she finished the letter. "What a sicko," she declared.

Zack, who was still reading, posed, "Does that surprise you?"

"No," Jenny replied, "I suppose it doesn't."

"He's intelligent," Ingunn said flatly. "Educated."

"Agreed," Zack said as his eyes left the screen. "He seems quite articulate. But are you ladies getting any divine insight?"

"Nothing new," Ingunn declared, "but this confirms the feeling I got last night. He's already struck again."

Jenny hung her head. "And apparently he's not going for truck stop prostitutes anymore, which is great news for that community…but then who is he after now?"

Zack referred to the article. "Look—it says more." He scrolled down to reveal the police had issued some warnings for women all up and down the east coast. He read out loud, "Prostitutes should still be on high alert, refusing any food or drinks from potential customers. Young women in bars, especially brunettes, should never leave their drinks unattended. Since the perpetrator appears to use Roofies to subdue his victims, women may not be using their proper judgment if they agree to leave with this man; for this reason people should not allow a young woman to go home with anyone other than the person/people she came with."

"These warnings are all well and good," Jenny noted, "but they won't do any good if they came *after* he abducted his next victim."

Pointing to the screen, Zack continued, "They've put up the composite picture and described his car as a dark-colored sedan."

"It's blue," Ingunn announced emphatically.

Jenny spoke much more softly, "With a T." She rubbed her temples. "And personalized plates."

"It doesn't say that in the article," Zack explained.

"It won't," Jenny replied sadly. "Those are our observations, not the blonde's. Our information is just hearsay. The victim is the only one who can give eyewitness testimony."

"Okay then," Zack said as he stood up straight, "now what?"

Jenny glanced at Ingunn. "Do you have anything new to report?"

"There *is* nothing new to report."

With a sigh Jenny conceded, "Then I guess we wait."

The paintbrush made its final strokes on the canvas. Feeling a sense of accomplishment, Jenny sat back in her chair and admired the image of the woman, looking at it for the first time as a complete picture as opposed to the sum of parts. She immediately felt a wave that caused her to close her eyes and relax her body, allowing herself to see the vision this painting had triggered.

A breeze blew through her hair as she appeared outside, close to the building that was once Samuel's home. She saw the woman from the painting walking in the distance, carrying a bucket. Although she was far away, Jenny could still hear the woman's magical voice as she sang. The sound was soothing despite the fact that Jenny felt perfectly healthy; no matter how the listener was feeling, that voice could easily bring anyone within earshot to the next level.

The image was brief, but something about it struck Jenny. Tapping her chin she considered the big picture, wondering if she'd just stumbled onto an answer to a question that hadn't yet been asked.

Getting up from her chair, she headed up the stairs, stopping at Roy and Florence's room. She knocked gently, and after a short moment Florence opened the door with a smile. "Hello, Jenny," she said. "What can I do for you?"

"Well, I was actually hoping I could talk to your husband for a moment."

"Of course. Come on in," Florence said graciously with a sweep of her arm. "He's been quite busy this afternoon; he's looking for answers to your dog question." She flashed Jenny a knowing smile and a wink.

Jenny acted pleasantly surprised. "Thanks, Mr. Roy. That's so kind of you to do!"

He looked away from his computer screen and greeted Jenny with a smile that rivaled his wife's. "I'm still working on it, but I'm under the impression that some labs need to be taught to catch. Strangely enough, some labs need to be taught to retrieve. You would think that a dog with 'retriever' in his name would instinctively know how to bring things back, but it seems that isn't always the case."

Jenny had to giggle. "It appears we may have one of those special cases with Baxter. When Zack threw the ball for him to fetch, Baxter just looked at him like he had no idea why Zack would do such a thing."

Roy let out a hearty laugh. "We had a special dog once. That dog couldn't get out of its own way."

"I think that's what we may have found in Baxter." While Jenny was finding this conversation pleasant, she was eager to get to the matter at hand. "But the reason I knocked on your door was because I actually had a question for you about the Civil War era again. I hope I'm not bothering you too much with these questions."

"No, not at all."

Florence smiled. "He *loves* to talk about the Civil War."

"Well, this has more to do with plantation life than the war itself."

"That's okay," Roy said. "What is your question?"

Jenny sighed as she contemplated how to ask this question without giving away her abilities. "It has to do with wells. I saw a picture of an old plantation, and it looked like there were two wells—one near the house and one far away. In the image a slave woman was walking with a bucket, but it looked like she was coming from the far well. Could that have been a separate water supply just for the slaves?"

"Most likely," Roy said. "Remember how young equal rights are; even in the twentieth century people were required to drink from separate water fountains. Back in the days of slavery they certainly wouldn't have been drinking from the same well."

Excitement grew within Jenny as Roy's words confirmed her theory. "So presumably the slaves would have had to use a well that was far away?"

"I would assume."

Jenny continued, "According to what you told me before, one of the reasons people got deathly ill back then was because their water supply was too close to the outhouse...so is it possible that this segregation could have actually worked in the slaves' favor, then? If their water supply was in an inconvenient spot, might it have been far enough away from contaminants to keep them healthy?"

Roy frowned as he considered the notion. "It's possible, I suppose, as long as the slaves' well was far from the slaves' outhouse."

Jenny could hardly contain her excitement. "Are those illnesses you described before contagious?"

"You mean typhoid and cholera?"

"Yes. Can you catch those from someone else?"

"Not directly," Roy informed her. "A person with one of those bacteria could potentially spread the disease by contaminating the water supply, but as far as catching the disease from casual contact or sneezing or something, no, they are not contagious."

Jenny clasped her hands and said with a genuine smile, "Thank you, Mr. Roy. You have no idea how helpful you are."

Once again he chuckled. "You're welcome, young lady. Is there anything else I can help you with?"

"Not right now," Jenny said as she headed toward the door, "but that may change."

Jenny and Zack walked through the back yard with Baxter on his leash. "It looked like the Davies' well was right about here," Jenny said as she circled her hand over an area that was now part of the professionally-manicured lawn. Closing her eyes to recall the image from her mind, she moved closer to the shed and said, "And I assume the building that was in this vicinity was their outhouse."

Zack glanced back and forth between the two locations. "They do seem awfully close." He curled his lip and shuddered.

"They didn't know," Jenny said. "I'm sure a hundred years from now people are going to be disgusted by some of our practices, but we're none the wiser."

"It's still gross," Zack noted.

Ignoring his comment, she pointed off into the distance. "The other well was way over there, where it's all overgrown now. And I didn't even see another outhouse. Maybe the slaves' latrine was very far away, which may have seemed awful at the time but was actually a blessing in disguise."

They walked with the dog in the direction of the old slaves' well. "I wonder if there's any evidence that the well ever existed," Zack posed. "The Davies' well looks like it got filled in and landscaped, but the area around the other well was allowed to just become natural. Maybe some of the original stones are still out there."

"That would be cool," Jenny replied. "Maybe Jessica can clear the area away and people will enjoy seeing an original well...or at least what's left of it."

A buzzing started within Jenny, causing her to close her eyes and submit to the feeling. She took a sudden right turn toward the trees, feeling drawn, although she didn't know where. She entered the woods that aligned the property, trudging through the brush that littered the forest floor. Led by the pull, she eventually arrived at an inconspicuous location. Pointing toward the ground she said, "Here."

"What's here?" Zack asked.

Jenny looked at the earth and began to inspect for visible evidence. "I'm not sure," she confessed, "but if I had to guess, I would say that we just found Samuel."

Chapter 17

"For real?" Zack asked with wide eyes.

"I don't know," Jenny replied. "There's *something* here, and Samuel's remains would be my best guess." She looked around at the untamed vines and plants that covered the ground. "We'll need some tools to find out for sure."

"There are some tools in Baxter's shed. I can run and grab some. I'll be right back." Zack disappeared with the dog while Jenny stayed in place to mark the spot.

She surveyed the desolate woods, feeling the loneliness. What a sad place for a child to spend over one-hundred-fifty years without his family. Jenny squatted down and touched the soil beneath the plants, compassionately whispering, "It was the best she could do, Samuel. Her heart was in the right place." Feeling as if she was beginning to get choked up, Jenny stood and loudly said, "If you are here, we will move you to where you belong...with the rest of your family." She looked around to see if there were any visible signs that Samuel may have heard her, but nothing happened. It wasn't until Zack returned with the tools that she witnessed any commotion.

"Okay," Zack said, laying various instruments on the ground. "I brought some clippers, a hand trowel and a shovel. I figure that will be good."

Jenny nodded her approval. "I guess step one is to clear out all this brush." Looking at the mess she added, "I wish we had some gloves."

"I'll tell you what," Zack proposed. "You clip, I'll pull."

She glanced at him with love in her eyes, but he was too focused on the ground to notice. She reached down to grab the clippers and began to snip as closely as she could to the surface. As promised, Zack reached his hands into the brush and removed the pieces.

Before long an area was cleared, exposing hard, dark soil. Putting her hand to her chin, Jenny posed, "If Samuel is buried here, how deep do you think he would be?"

"That's a good question," Zack replied. "I would imagine it might have to do with what time of year he passed away. If it was winter, it would be hard to dig very deep."

"As much as I hate to say this, I think we should err on the side of caution and skip the shovel in favor of just the hand trowel."

"Well," Zack countered, "if I use the shovel at the right angle it won't go very deep, but I'll be able to move a lot more dirt at a time than if I used the trowel."

"Okay," Jenny conceded, "just be careful. I wouldn't want to damage anything."

Jenny watched as Zack removed thin layers of dirt. Before long, however, she started to feel queasy. "I think I need to go in and get a snack."

"Go ahead," Zack said without looking up. "I've got this for a while."

After a couple of pieces of toast, Jenny walked back out to the woods to see Zack had made a fair amount of progress. "Well done, chief," she said as she approached. "I assume you haven't found anything yet?"

"Nope, not yet. Are you sure this is the right spot?"

"I'm still feeling a pull," Jenny assured him. "There's *something* about this spot."

Zack wiped the sweat from his forehead. "Okay, then. I'll keep going."

"Do you want me to take a turn?"

"Nah," Zack replied, "I've got it. I don't want you to do anything that might hurt little Steve."

Hearing Zack call the child by name—if, in fact, it was a boy—gave Jenny an undeniable twinge of happiness. There was a human being inside of her...a person whom she would eventually know as her child. Someone she would love more than life itself. She placed her hand on her belly with a distant smile.

As Zack planted the shovel just below the surface, a definite scraping sound emerged. They looked at each other with wide eyes. "What was that?" Jenny asked.

"I don't know," Zack admitted, "but I think it might be time to trade the shovel for the trowel."

After some careful dirt removal, a human skull became visible under the ground. Jenny's emotions ran the spectrum from excited to devastated, but ultimately the logical part of her brain took over. "So who do we call about this?"

"I looked this up earlier, just in case we found something," Zack replied. "We need to call the police first, who will send out a medical examiner. If the medical examiner decides the remains are over seventy-five years old, they will call an archeologist. You and I both know what's going on here, but we have to go through the proper channels. We can't just skip straight to the archeologist."

Jenny thought for a moment. "Is this a job for 9-1-1? Or do we use the non-emergency number?"

"I think finding human remains qualifies as an emergency."

Jenny dialed the police, who were out in force within minutes. Despite Jenny telling them otherwise, they feared the body was related to the missing women discovered off the highway. Car after car arrived on scene, full of uniformed officers who worked furiously to cordon off the area.

The commotion caused Jessica to come running out of the inn. "What's going on out here?" she demanded. "Is everyone okay?"

Jenny felt bad for not having given her fair warning. "Everything's fine, Miss Jessica," she said as she raised her hands in a calming gesture. Once Jessica got closer, Jenny whispered, "I think I just found Samuel; that's all."

Jessica looked over Jenny's shoulder toward the crime scene tape. "He's out there?" she asked with a sad look on her face. "In the woods?"

Jenny nodded. "But hopefully not for much longer. I want to make sure he gets buried with the rest of his family."

Looking concerned, Jessica brought her gaze back to Jenny. "And how do you go about doing that?"

"I have no idea," Jenny replied, "but I know someone who does."

Ingunn responded to the quiet knock on her door. "Come in."

"Hi Amma," Jenny said as she ducked her head through the small opening she made with the door.

Ingunn was looking out the window at the flurry of activity below. "You found Samuel."

With a nod Jenny whispered, "I believe we did."

"That's good." Ingunn let the curtain fall back into place as she stepped toward the bed. Sitting on the edge she added, "Although it will be a while before he can rest."

Jenny sat next to her grandmother. "That's actually what I wanted to talk to you about. If this does turn out to be Samuel—and I can't imagine it won't—how can I make sure he gets buried with his family?"

"Persistence. Patience." Ingunn folded her hands on her lap. "The first step in the process will be conclusively identifying the remains. That in and of itself will take a long time."

Although she had an idea of how it would be done, Jenny asked, "Does that involve DNA?"

"I'm sure these days it would," Ingunn replied. "They were just learning about that when your grandfather died and I quit the mortuary business. It's nice that they now have a way to conclusively identify a body, but from what I understand it's not a quick process. In this case it will be even longer since there are no living relatives to compare his DNA to. To prove he's a Davies, they'll most likely have to exhume his parents."

Jenny put her head in her hands. "Do you think that will be necessary? Can't they just look at the evidence and decide that it must be him?"

"I don't know. That will be up to someone else to decide."

"Okay," Jenny said as she sat up straighter, "after they figure out that it's him, then what?"

"Then you can claim the remains. At that point you can make his final arrangements."

After thinking for a moment, Jenny nodded with understanding. "I still might like to talk to someone from a funeral home around here before we head home; then I can see if I have the ability to bury Samuel in his family plot. If that's going to involve any red tape, I'd like to get that out of the way while his remains are being identified. We might as well have two long processes going on at once. The way I see it, the poor kid has already waited so long; I don't want to postpone this any longer than necessary."

A quiet rap on the open door distracted the women from their conversation. "Hello?" Zack called.

"Hey, we're in here," Jenny said. "What's up?"

"The medical examiner is here."

"Has he said anything?"

"Not yet," Zack explained. "They're still trying to expose more of the remains. They did uncover some of the clothes he was wearing, though, which is a strong indication that this is not a recent burial. People from this century don't wear stuff like that. I imagine it won't be too long before they all leave and a team of archeologists come out."

"That'll be good...for Jessica, I mean," Jenny said. "I'm sure it would look a lot better for her inn to have archeologists in the back as opposed to having a bunch of cops swarming around."

"Yeah," Zack agreed, "that can't be good for business."

"Speaking of Jessica, is she still outside?" Jenny posed. "I want to ask her something."

"Last I saw she was," Zack said.

Jenny excused herself and headed back into the yard, where Jessica was indeed watching all of the activity. Roy and Florence had since joined her.

"You didn't tell us you're a psychic," Florence said immediately upon Jenny's arrival.

Jenny glanced quickly at Jessica before saying with a modest smile, "I generally don't tell people that. I know it's weird."

"It's not weird," Florence assured her. "It's fascinating."

Clearly feeling the need to explain, Jessica said, "I told them what was going on and how this is unrelated to the findings off the highway."

Suddenly Jenny understood why Jessica had disclosed the secret; a haunting from a homesick child was far less disturbing than the notion of a serial killer on the property.

Roy shifted his weight on his cane. "So tell me...that slave woman you painted—she was more than just an image you made up, wasn't she?"

Jenny bit her lip as she looked down. "Yes, sir."

"So, who was she?"

"I believe that woman took care of Samuel when he was dying. I'm under the impression that the rest of his family succumbed before he did, and this woman stayed by his bedside while he was ill."

"And how do you know that?" Florence asked. Her voice reflected awe as opposed to skepticism.

"I saw it," Jenny explained. "I saw *her*, through Samuel's eyes. She was singing to him as he lay in bed, and she had the most *amazing* voice." She smiled lovingly despite her emerging sadness. "It brought him a lot of comfort."

"That's truly beautiful," Florence replied. "I can imagine that poor little boy was frightened." She shook her head with dismay. "No child should have to go through that. It's bad enough that he caught a fatal disease, but to have to face it without his parents...that's just awful."

Perhaps it was the pregnancy, but Jenny could feel the tears fill her eyes. With any luck, her own child would never have to walk in those shoes. "What makes this even more remarkable, in my opinion, is that this woman could have left. If our theory is correct and there were no adults around, the slaves could have easily escaped." Jenny turned to Roy. "Or would they have been free? Did slaves become freed when their...owners died?" She had a difficult time saying the word *owner*.

"No, they wouldn't have been free unless the family specified that in their will," Roy explained. "Slaves were considered property, so they were generally left to surviving family members as part of an inheritance."

"Property," Jenny whispered. That gracious woman with the beautiful voice was anything but property.

Roy continued, "However, it is possible that the family died before any of the heirs would have even known about it."

Jenny raised her eyes to look at him.

"While typhoid would have taken a few weeks to kill the members of the Davies family, the mail could have easily taken longer. And if the Davies family died of cholera instead of typhoid, that would most certainly have been true. Cholera took its toll much more quickly."

Jenny considered all of the possibilities about what could have happened to the slaves after Samuel died, fully realizing she would most likely never know the truth. "Well," she added, "I'm going to operate under the assumption that the slaves were able to find freedom after the Davies family passed away."

"You realize that's a longshot…"

Jenny stuck her fingers in her ears and playfully said, "La la la la la. I can't hear you." She turned to Roy with a smile. "They found freedom. That's my story, and I'm sticking with it."

Taking the hint, Roy remained quiet; he simply nodded with a wink.

"So, Miss Jessica, I wanted to ask you something," Jenny began. "But I don't want to put you on the spot, so I'll wait until later."

"I can assure you, you won't be putting me on the spot," Jessica replied with a smile. "I have no problem saying no to unreasonable requests, believe me."

Jenny briefly pursed her lips, jealous of that ability. She had yet to master that art. Dismissing the notion, she posed, "Well then, if I pay for it, would you be willing to allow a monument to the slaves be built on the property?"

"A monument?"

"Yes, a monument. Something to acknowledge that they lived here too." Jenny looked down. "And something to recognize them as more than just property."

"How big are you thinking?" Jessica asked.

"Nothing huge. I actually have something in mind. I could sketch if it you'd like, and then you can tell me what you think."

"If you want my two cents," Roy said, "I think it's a fabulous idea."

"Oh, I do too," Jessica assured them. "I guess I should have made that clear right away. I was just jumping straight to logistics." She sighed and shook her head before she continued, "This whole episode has made me realize that I've been neglecting a very important part of this house's history. Yes, it was once a Confederate hospital, and that is a big commercial draw, but it had a story before that—and apparently a very rich one. I think it's time I start paying more attention to the years before the war."

"If you'd like," Jenny proposed, "I can also draw what the yard used to look like based on my vision. For instance, there was a well right about here." She pointed to an area not far from the shed. "I think that was the Davies' well, and then back there was the well used by the slaves." She gestured in the direction of the investigation and noticed that a lot of the officers were beginning to walk away from the scene. "Oh," she said with surprise, "it looks like something is happening."

After a moment, one of the police officers approached Jessica and offered an explanation. "The medical examiner has sufficient reason to believe the remains are old enough to warrant a call to the archaeology team. We still want to keep the area cordoned off and have an officer on scene until they can arrive."

Jessica nodded with understanding. "Thank you for letting me know."

"Most of the officers will be heading out of here," the policeman explained. "It appears there's a new development in the Highway Killer case, so we need as many officers as possible to work on that."

Jenny's eyes widened. "A new development?"

"It appears that way, yes ma'am."

He continued to talk to Jessica, but Jenny took several steps away and quickly dialed her phone. "Officer Howell," she said as soon as he answered. "I hear there's something happening in the Highway Killer case."

"Yeah, I'm afraid so."

"What's going on?"

Howell remained silent for what felt like an eternity. "A dark-haired woman was just reported missing in Richmond."

Chapter 18

"Oh God," Jenny said. "Who is she?"

"A twenty-seven year old prostitute named Michelle who works the downtown area."

"A prostitute got reported missing?" she posed. "Isn't that unusual?"

"Yes, under normal circumstances it would be. However, streetwalkers have been told about this man who has been preying on dark-haired prostitutes, and they've been directed to be on high alert. This particular woman reportedly has a best friend that she works with, and the friend hasn't seen her in two days. According to the friend, that's out of character. She and Michelle usually spend their days sleeping in the same motel room."

Jenny rubbed her eyes with her free hand as she spoke on the phone. "Do you have any leads on this case?"

"Unfortunately, no. But I am glad you called. If I give you a picture of this woman, do you think you can try to get a feel for whether she's alive or dead?"

"That's actually not how I operate," she confessed, "but my father might be able to give you some insight on that. If he can get a reading from her picture, that will unfortunately mean she's passed away, but at least it will tell you something."

"Well, let's hope he can't get a reading," Howell said with a disgruntled sigh. "So can I have his contact information? Or might you be willing to pass along the photograph if I send it to you?"

"Honestly, I don't have his number committed to memory; I'd need to look at my phone to give it to you, and I obviously can't do that right now. Maybe you should just send it to me?"

"Absolutely," Howell said. "Give me two minutes and it'll be in your inbox."

After hanging up with Howell, Jenny gave a quick call to Roddan, letting him know that he would be receiving a message that needed immediate attention. As promised, the picture appeared quickly in Jenny's phone, and she sent it on to her father right away.

Once Roddan had the photograph in his possession, Jenny decided to take a look at Michelle's image herself. The picture featured a painfully thin, dark-haired woman with a pleasant smile but distant eyes. Jenny assumed the picture had been taken somewhat recently, perhaps by her prostitute friend, and the glossy eyes were the result of drug use. She shook her head, wondering what could have become of Michelle if she had decided to decline that first offer of drugs. Would she have been a teacher? A businesswoman?

A mom?

Jenny couldn't help but think of Michelle's mother—a woman who rocked this baby to sleep and taught her the ABCs. Jenny was sure that like any parent, Michelle's mother wanted the best for her, only to have her turn out to be a prostitute and the potential victim of a twisted serial killer. Moments like this caused Jenny to second-guess her optimism about becoming a mother. What kind of world was she bringing a baby into? And how would she handle it if her own child went down the wrong path?

Returning to the matter at hand, Jenny focused on Michelle's glossy eyes in the picture, wondering what they were seeing at that very moment. Was she in that horrible soundproof room? Was she looking at the depraved man who kept women as his possessions? Strangely, that would have actually been good news; at least she would have still been alive. The alternative was that Michelle's eyes could see nothing at all. Jenny shuddered at the thought.

Her phone rang, interrupting the silence and breaking her train of thought. Jenny immediately answered when she saw it was Roddan calling. "Hello?"

"Hi Jenny. I got your picture, and I can tell you that one of two things is happening."

Her hands trembled as she waited for the news.

"Either I'm losing my knack," Roddan explained, "or else this woman is still very much alive."

"He didn't get a reading," Jenny said excitedly to Howell.

"No?" He sounded relieved.

"No. So there may still be time."

"Excellent," Howell replied. "So is there any chance you can head up to Richmond to see if you can offer any insight?"

"I could," Jenny said apologetically, "but I don't think there would be a point. If she's still alive, I won't get any information from her. I can only receive messages if she's gone."

"Shit," he whispered under his breath.

"I know. It's frustrating," Jenny agreed. "I can only help solve murders after they've occurred; I can't really prevent them."

Howell's tone remained polite despite his obvious dissatisfaction. "Alright, well, if you get anything let me know."

"You'll be the first person I'll call," Jenny assured him.

"I just feel so helpless," Jenny confessed to Zack as they sat at a table in the lobby. She busied herself with the sketch of the memorial, but Michelle's apparent kidnapping nagged at the back of her mind. "It almost makes me wish I was a cop. At least then I could be investigating. As it stands the only thing I can do is sit here and wait."

"You suck at waiting."

"I know," Jenny said emphatically, unoffended by the remark.

"At least your drawing looks good," Zack noted.

"You think?" Jenny spun the image around so he could see it from the proper angle.

Zack raised his eyebrows and nodded genuinely. "It looks great, actually. Very tasteful."

With a sigh she repositioned the picture so it faced her. "Thanks. I guess I should be grateful that I get to accomplish *something* today. If Jessica gives her approval on this, maybe we can go out and find someone who can actually build it. Who would that be, a stone mason?"

Zack looked at Jenny with a smile. "Not exactly. We'd probably need a sculptor."

"And where, exactly, do you find one of those?"

"Around here? I don't know," Zack confessed, "but back in Georgia there was a guy we used to work with who did good work. A lot of our clients for Larrabee Homes wanted statues either in their mulch beds or flanking their driveways."

Jenny smirked. "Flanking their driveways? You mean like lions?"

"Yes," he replied matter-of-factly, "like lions."

She continued to sketch as she giggled. "That's a bit over-the-top, don't you think?"

"Well, most of the houses we built were over-the-top."

"So," Jenny said, steering the conversation back to the matter at hand, "are you suggesting we use the guy from Georgia to build our monument?"

"No, but I'm suggesting I could probably find somebody similar in the area who could do it." He frowned. "Although, probably not the immediate area. It's not exactly a popular trade."

A gust of wind flew through the lobby, and with it a distinct but fleeting image popped into Jenny's head.

Zack looked at her intently. "What was that about?"

"That," she replied flatly, "was my invitation to go out and talk to the archaeologist."

Jenny didn't elaborate as she headed out into the back yard with Zack following. She approached the area that had been cordoned off by the crime scene tape, finding nothing more than a lone police officer who remained on duty. "Excuse me," she said rather curtly, "do you have any idea when the archaeologist will be here?"

The man shrugged nonchalantly. "It shouldn't be too long. They said they were on their way, and that was twenty minutes ago."

"Okay, thank you." Jenny began to look around the property.

"Do you mind telling me what this is about?" Zack asked impatiently.

"It's about more bodies," she replied as she closed her eyes, trying to equate the scene from her vision to the current landscaping. Determining she needed to walk further out in the property, she continued along.

Zack's strides were long so he could keep up with her. "More bodies?"

"Yes. Or maybe just one." Jenny closed her eyes again for a moment, only to open them and point into the trees. "Over there."

"Okay, seriously, slow down," Zack demanded.

Jenny stopped walking and looked at him.

"Can you please tell me what you're talking about?"

Hanging her head with a smile, Jenny acknowledged she hadn't been acting fair. She sighed deeply and announced, "I saw what looked like a slave burial, somewhere out in that direction. It appeared they were only burying one body, but that's not to say there weren't others before or after that. There may be a whole graveyard full of remains in those trees."

"Dear God," Zack whispered as he gazed in that direction.

She began walking again. "I want to get back there before I forget where I'm supposed to look."

"You're not being pulled?" he asked.

Jenny shook her head. "No, not this time. I'm just relying on memory, based off a very short image. Funny thing…this method is a lot less trustworthy." She walked to the tree line and pointed in. "It's a good ways in there." With a strength-gathering breath she began the journey into the brush; Zack followed closely behind.

Periodically she would close her eyes and try to recreate the scene in her mind; after a while she stood still and proclaimed, "I think this is about where it was." She shrugged and added, "It's so hard to tell, though. It looks a lot different now than it used to."

"I think I'm confused," Zack confessed. "You're not being pulled, but you just saw a visual when the wind blew? From what angle?"

"From near the house. I don't think this is a slave communicating with me; I think it's still Samuel. He appeared to be watching the burial ceremony from a distance. If it had been a slave delivering me the message, I would think it would have come from the viewpoint of the ceremony."

"Yeah, I would have to agree with that," Zack said as he contemplated. "So, *Samuel* is telling you where there are buried slaves? I wonder why he's doing that."

More sadness—which may or may not have been pregnancy-related—washed over Jenny. Blinking to prevent tears from forming, she softly replied, "Compassion...empathy." She looked at Zack as she lost her battle to avoid tears. "Gratitude." She sniffed and dabbed at her eyes with her sleeve. "Samuel, of all people, knows what it's like to be out here, forgotten, for over a hundred years. I guess he doesn't want the slaves to go undiscovered, either. He wants them to be found as well."

Either oblivious to Jenny's tears or choosing to ignore them, Zack noted, "I just wonder why the slave himself—or herself—isn't directing you out here. I would think they'd want to be found just as much as Samuel does."

Jenny shook her head. "I have a theory about that, but I don't want to say it out loud until I talk to Roy, just in case I'm wrong."

Although Zack looked at her funny, he said nothing.

Some commotion from the crime scene area caused Zack and Jenny to focus their attention in that direction. A man who appeared to be the archaeologist had arrived on scene, carrying a tool kit. "Perfect," Jenny said as her sadness dissipated. "I want to go and talk to him."

"I can stay here if you want," Zack proposed. "That way we won't lose the location."

Jenny smiled at him. "You're a doll, you know that?" She took a moment to determine her best approach to leaving this overgrown area and heading to the other one. She could have either walked through the overgrown woods directly to the other spot, or else she could have schlepped her way back out of the trees, only to re-enter them later on. "The shortest path between two points is a straight line," she muttered under her breath. Although she was less than thrilled about the trek, she began making her way through the thick brush to the archaeologist.

The man looked at her strangely as she approached; she realized she must have appeared to be an insane woman wandering through the woods. She didn't let that notion faze her. "Hello," she said from a short distance. "You must be the archaeologist."

"Yes," he replied, "and you are…"

She finally reached the crime scene tape. "Jenny Watkins. I was the one to find the remains."

"Well, that was a good find." His older features had a kindness to them which shone through his curious look and curt question. "Are you looking for more?"

"Yes, actually, I am…and I think I may have found some."

He looked at her incredulously.

"I'm a psychic," Jenny explained, "and I was led to this boy's remains." She pointed to Samuel's half-exposed body. "I've also been advised about an area over there, although it's not as clearly defined. I can't help but think that at least one more person is buried over there."

"Advised?"

Jenny decided this was clearly going to be a hard sell. "I get visions," she explained, still a little out of breath from climbing through the woods. "And I saw a distinct image of a slave burial happening in that area."

He still looked unimpressed.

After letting out a frustrated exhale, she continued, "I was hired by the owner of this inn to investigate some strange occurrences that have been going on here. I think what's happening is that some people have been buried on the property and forgotten about. They want a better final resting place." She pointed to Samuel's body. "Or at least this boy does."

The archaeologist remained pleasant-looking as he said, "Lady, I've heard a lot of interesting stories over the years, but this one takes the cake."

"Well, there's got to be an element of truth to it, no?" She smiled knowingly. "I found his body, didn't I?"

Jenny imagined he was having a mental debate as he remained quiet. "Yes, I guess you did," he eventually said. "So, do you think this whole area is an unmarked grave yard?"

"Not necessarily the whole area, although I can't say for sure. I do think there's a body over there where my friend is standing." She pointed through the trees as Zack.

The archaeologist reached into his tool kit and handed Jenny a bright orange rag. "Here. Tie this around the tree closest to where you think the body is located. That way your friend doesn't have to keep standing out there. I'll go over and take a look when I'm done with this scene."

Jenny took the rag and smiled. "Thank you, sir...although I do have to admit it would be more fun if he had to just stand there."

"I just got Jessica's blessing," Jenny told Zack as she walked into the Statesman room. "She seemed to love the monument."

"No surprise there," Zack replied as he typed on his computer. "I told you it was great."

Jenny blushed modestly.

"I was also able to find a guy online who could potentially build it." He pulled out his phone and noted the time. "It's far, but if we leave now we have time to make it there before he closes."

With a shrug Jenny said, "We might as well."

Before long the couple was in the car, sketch in hand. Zack had typed the directions into his phone; the path took them across the highway to the eastern side, an area they had never driven before. About twenty minutes after passing the truck stops, Jenny felt a sudden urge to bring the car down a side road.

Zack remained quiet as they took their unforeseen detour. Jenny's pulse raced, which would ordinarily have threatened her ability to receive the message, but fortunately for her the pull was strong. Jenny felt an overwhelming sense of fear, the source of which was calling her closer.

She eventually stopped the car in front of a white house on a wooded lot. The stone driveway was long and curved through the trees, but Jenny was able to make out a lone vehicle sitting up by the garage.

A small blue passenger car.

"Holy shit," Zack proclaimed. "Could that be the car Ingunn was talking about?"

"I'm thinking it is," Jenny replied. Parked along the side of a narrow, windy road, she glanced in her rearview mirror to make sure nobody was coming. She put on her hazard lights.

"So what do we do?" Zack asked.

Jenny inspected the property for signs of life before pulling into the end of his driveway.

"What are you doing?" Zack seemed both confused and angry.

"Checking something." Jenny left her car running as she scurried up the driveway and inspected the car more closely. With the same speed she rushed back and climbed into the driver's seat.

"Are you out of your fucking mind?" Zack said as soon she closed the door.

"Sorry. I just had to verify something."

"You could have sent me to do it. Dark-haired women are his favorite targets, remember?"

"I know," she said quickly, backing out of the driveway and returning the way they had come. "It wasn't the smartest thing in the world, but I did get some information."

Zack shook his head. "What did you get?"

"See for yourself," Jenny said, handing him her phone. She had snapped a picture of the back of the car, which was complete with an orange T decal and a license plate that read TENICVOLS. "Correct me if I'm wrong, but that's a customized plate."

"It sure is," he confirmed.

Jenny's nerves began to subside the further away they drove. "I understand the Tennessee part," she began, "but what's the VOLS?"

"It's their team name," Zack said as he forwarded the picture on to Howell.

Jenny furrowed her brow, contemplating what a bizarre name that was for a team. Dismissing that quickly, she said, "Can you call Howell and let him know we may have just found our man?"

"One step ahead of you. I'm texting him the picture now, and I'll call him in just a second."

A thought occurred to Jenny. "Shit," she proclaimed. "I didn't look at the address. I have no idea where that house was."

"Well, that's what your partner is for." He spoke slowly; his focus was on sending the text.

"Oh my God, you did that?"

"Well, I was paying attention to the street signs as we went there. Then while you were risking your life looking at that car, I was watching the front door to make sure he didn't come out. The house number was right next to the door."

At that point Zack dialed the phone and put it on speaker. Jenny could hear it ring. The officer answered with a very gruff, "Howell."

"Officer Howell," Jenny said excitedly. "I think we may have found the Highway Killer."

"What do you mean *you may have found the Highway Killer*?"

"I got pulled to a house where there was a blue car with an orange T sticker on it and customized plates. We just sent you the picture."

"Holy shit," Howell muttered. "You say this car was at a house?"

"Yes," Zack replied, "5402 Forest View Lane."

"The house was absolutely brimming with fear," Jenny said. "I can't help but think it has to be involved somehow."

Howell remained quiet for a moment, presumably as he wrote that information down. "Okay, well, I'll get on this right away. I'll let you know if anything comes of it."

"Thanks," Jenny said with a great deal of satisfaction. Zack concluded the call as Jenny let out a deep breath of relief. "Now that the official business has been taken care of, can I just tell you how scary that was?"

"What," Zack retorted, "you mean watching your girlfriend approach the house of a kidnapper and murderer?"

While Jenny didn't appreciate the dig, deep down inside she knew she deserved it. "No, I mean the feeling I had back there. There's some pretty serious fear surrounding that place."

"All the more reason you should have stayed away from it."

"Well, now I can. Hopefully the police will be able to find what they need and this case will be over."

After a short silence Zack posed, "Wow. Wouldn't it be amazing if it was really that simple?"

Jenny smiled. "It would absolutely be amazing." She felt herself beaming with pride.

"Although," Zack added, "you do realize we just jinxed it by saying that."

Chapter 19

Jessica and Ingunn both joined Zack and Jenny for their late dinner. "The sculptor's name was Stuart Brisbane," Jenny explained, "and he does amazing work. You should have seen some of the sculptures he had on his property."

Zack grunted in affirmation as he swallowed his food. "It was impressive."

"Anyway," Jenny went on, "he said he'd be able to make the monument, although it may take a while. He's got a waiting list."

"That's fine," Jessica assured her. "I've got time."

"I also asked if he could make little monuments for Samuel and the slave buried in the back—provided there is one—and he said he could."

"Okay," Jessica replied thoughtfully, "if there is a slave graveyard back there, what should I do about it? I know you want to put Samuel with the rest of his family, but we don't know anything about the others. Where would be the most respectful place for them to rest?"

"Well, I wanted to talk to Roy about that," Jenny confessed. "I have a theory, but I'd like to verify it."

"You'll need to speak to him soon," Jessica said. "He and Florence are checking out in the morning. It seems the baby they're planning to visit is better now, so they're headed out of town at sunrise."

"I can get them if you want," Zack offered.

Jenny smiled at him. "Thanks. That'd be great."

Moments later Zack returned with the couple, who joined the rest of the crowd by pulling up chairs from another table. Roy leaned forward on his cane and said, "I hear you've got a question for me, young lady."

"Indeed I do...again," Jenny replied with a smile. "I recently saw a vision of a slave burial, and it appeared that the people in attendance were...*happy*. It looked more like a party than a funeral."

"That was probably true," Roy said.

Everyone waited silently for an elaboration.

"The slaves were a very religious group of people," Roy continued. "They strongly believed that when they left this earth, they got to live in paradise with the Lord. And if you think about the poor quality of the life they endured in this world, having it come to an end wasn't necessarily a bad thing. When a slave passed, the others gathered to celebrate rather than mourn. The deceased was fortunate enough to go to a better place, and despite the feeling of personal loss they had, friends and family regarded that as a good thing."

Jenny turned to Zack. "I think that answers your question from before. You wondered why Samuel was the one leading me to the slave burial site instead of the slave himself. My theory is that the slave isn't contacting me because he has already crossed. According to what Roy is saying, it sounds like the slaves would have wasted no time crossing over. They knew something beautiful was on the other side, and they would have wanted to get there as quickly as possible."

"A slave certainly wouldn't want to linger," Ingunn added as she continued to eat.

"Precisely," Jenny said.

"But I still don't know what to do if they find people back there," Jessica declared with a worried look on her face.

"My suggestion would be to clean up the area, give them nice headstones, and leave them there," Jenny replied. "Maybe plant some grass and put a fence around the area. It's my understanding that they aren't unhappy where they are. Their burials were joyous, and I'm not sure they'd want to be moved, but I think we would all agree they need to be treated with a little more dignity than what's currently going on."

Jessica turned to Roy. "Do you concur with that? Should we just turn that area into a graveyard? Is that respectful enough?"

Roy nodded. "I believe so. And then history buffs like me can come pay respect to them, just like we do the soldiers."

Jessica seemed to be absorbing the words. Turning to Jenny she added, "And you said the sculptor was willing to make little memorials for them?"

"Yes, ma'am. He said he'd make as many as turned out to be necessary."

At that moment Jenny's phone vibrated in her pocket. Glancing down at the screen, she saw that Howell was the caller. "Oh, if you'll excuse me," she said, "I've got to take this." Stepping away from the table she eagerly answered.

"Hi, Jenny," Officer Howell began. "I just wanted to let you know we paid a visit to your friend on Forest View Lane."

"And?"

"And, unfortunately, he appears to be a regular, law-abiding citizen."

"What?" Jenny exclaimed. "You mean he's not the guy?"

"I'm not saying that. However," Howell added, "we really don't have anything on him. Nothing concrete, anyway. I know the car matches the description of the one you'd seen in your visions, and he did resemble the composite sketch, but our only true witness—the surviving victim—didn't choose his photo from a line up. She fingered someone else when showed several options."

Jenny wiped her face with her hand. "Is the fact that she's a detoxing meth addict being taken into account?"

"Yes, it is," Howell assured her, "and so is the fact that eyewitness testimony is often unreliable. However, even if you take that out of the equation, the fact remains that we've got nothing on this guy."

"Did you go to his house?"

"We just got back," he replied. "We went there under the guise that we were canvassing the neighborhood, just looking for information. We even went to several of his neighbor's houses to perpetuate that claim. But this guy didn't act the least bit suspicious; he invited us in and allowed us to look around, in fact. Nothing seemed out of the ordinary; we didn't see anything that would cause us to officially put him on the suspect list. Couple that with the fact that he's got no criminal record, and there's really no reason for us to pursue him."

"But that house screamed with fear when I went there."

"I understand that," Howell said, "but our resources are limited, and we have to follow the more tangible leads. I'm sorry, but the boss would never approve of using funds and manpower to investigate an individual who has already been cleared, simply because a psychic directed him to."

Jenny's heart was in her feet. "Okay," she said helplessly, "but can you at least promise me that you will keep his name in mind?"

"I'll do that," Howell assured her. "I, personally, will keep tabs on him."

Jenny politely concluded the phone call before she returned to the table with her shoulders sagging. Resuming her seat she announced, "You know that guy who lives on Forest View Lane? The one I got led to and had the blue car with the T? Well, they cleared him."

"They cleared him?" Zack also seemed shocked.

Jenny nodded reluctantly. "Afraid so. They searched his house and found nothing, and the drug-addicted witness couldn't identify him in a line up."

"Bring me there," Ingunn directed.

"What?" Jenny asked.

"Bring me there. Let me get a feel for that house."

Glancing at Zack for affirmation, Jenny replied, "Okay, Amma, we can bring you there. I'd rather wait until morning, though, if you don't mind. I don't want to be anywhere near his place in the dark."

With one single nod, Amma said, "We'll go in the morning. If this is your guy, I'll know it." She pointed at Jenny. "And I'll make sure they get him."

Jenny looked over Zack's shoulder as he typed the address in the county's real estate website. With a click of a button, Zack was able to conclude, "If he owns the house, it looks like his name is Hunter Tate."

Jenny stood up straight with a gasp. "That was how he signed his letter, remember? He insisted he wasn't the *Highway*

Killer but rather *The Hunter*." She placed her hands on her head. "I guess he was taunting the police more than anyone realized."

"Well, we don't know for sure that this is our guy. The person driving the car may have just been visiting, or our killer might be renting from this Tate character."

"How can we find out if it's him?" Jenny posed.

"Give me a minute." Zack's fingers pressed more buttons as he accessed the white pages website. He typed in Hunter Tate's name, and the address on Forest View Lane appeared on the screen. "It appears he lives there. Whether or not that was his car remains to be seen."

"Scroll down," Jenny commanded.

Zack obliged but then posed, "What do you want me to look for."

"I want to see if there are any Mrs. Tates on here."

Suddenly understanding, Zack clicked on a few women that were close in age to Hunter, and none of them had the same address. "Provided this is a complete list, he appears to live alone." He paused a moment and added, "In fact, I think I can verify that." He used the reverse look up feature to type in the address, which revealed only one resident.

Jenny curled her lip. "Do you find this a little disturbing? We're total strangers and we're able to find out all of this information about him."

"Hell, yes, it's disturbing," Zack agreed. "But in this case I'm grateful for it."

Scratching her head, Jenny asked, "So how can we tie him to the car? Is that public knowledge, too?"

"I don't know. Let me check that out." He tried several avenues to connect Hunter Tate to the blue sedan with the personalized plates, but he had no luck. "I think that might actually be private," he eventually concluded.

"That's good, at least," Jenny noted. "Not for us right now, but I'm glad at least some things are sacred in this day and age. I guess we have to leave it to Officer Howell to run the tags."

"Okay." Zack released a breath and returned his focus to his laptop. "Now to see what Mr. Hunter Tate looks like."

"How are you going to do that?"

"Social media. Hopefully he has an account somewhere and his face is on his profile picture. Even if his settings are private, we should at least be able to see what he looks like." Jenny took a moment and stretched while Zack searched. She was surprised by how quickly he said, "Bingo."

She looked at the screen, expecting to see a face that resembled the composite sketch she'd seen at the truck stop. However, she saw something entirely different.

An orange T.

Jenny deliberately didn't say anything as she drove her car past Hunter Tate's house. It turned out she didn't need to.

"It's that one," Ingunn announced as she pointed. "It's engulfed in fear."

"That's what I said yesterday," Jenny agreed. "Unfortunately, the police can't feel that."

"Turn the car back around. And drive slowly when you go by."

Jenny did as her grandmother said.

"There's no car there," Ingunn announced. "He's not home."

"It could be in the garage," Jenny noted.

Ingunn responded quickly. "It wasn't yesterday, right? He may not use his garage."

"But he may." Although Jenny wasn't sure what Ingunn was thinking, she was already wary of it.

"Pull into his driveway."

Somehow Jenny knew that was coming. "I'm not sure that's a good idea."

"I'm an old woman," Ingunn declared. "If he's there and he questions me, I can just tell him I'm lost. He won't suspect me, and I'm not his type." She folded her arms. "Being old has its advantages."

Zack chimed in from the back seat. "She did hold her own against the pimp." He paused a moment before adding, "Although, I do think I agree with Jenny on this one. It's a little too risky."

"So then what?" Ingunn demanded. "We just let him keep going?"

Both Zack and Jenny remained quiet.

"I just want to get closer," Ingunn added.

With a sigh Jenny reluctantly turned around yet again, driving slowly to the house. She turned up his driveway and kept the car running.

Ingunn quickly exited the car and marched with purpose to the garage.

"What is she doing?" Jenny said with both urgency and annoyance in her voice.

"Now you know how helpless it feels to sit here and watch that," Zack remarked.

Jenny wasn't amused by the poorly-timed dig. Fear was surging through her body, consuming her. She knew the fear was only half her own, but the anxiety was physically painful.

Ingunn cupped her face as she peered through the glass of the garage door. Her face remained expressionless as she walked back toward the car, leading Jenny to wonder what she had discovered.

She approached the driver's side door, prompting Jenny to roll down her window. "He's not home," Ingunn announced before turning back around and returning to the garage.

"Oh my God," Jenny exclaimed. "What the hell is she doing?"

"I don't know," Zack said as he opened his door, "but I'm not letting her do it alone." He got out of the car and also walked toward the garage.

Jenny shook her head before turning off the car and doing the same. When she arrived, Ingunn was pulling on the garage door handle. "Locked," she announced. Undeterred, she walked around the back of the garage and jiggled the handle of the pedestrian door. It, too, appeared to be locked.

"Are you seriously trying to get into his house?" Jenny asked with dismay.

"Trying," Ingunn replied, "but not getting anywhere." She began to scour the ground.

"Amma," Jenny argued, "I can't let you do that. It's crazy, not to mention illegal."

"Illegal..." Ingunn raised her finger and looked Jenny in the eye. "But not wrong."

Jenny hated how much her own actions were being held against her at this moment.

Ingunn seemed to find what she was looking for. "You," she said, pointing at Zack. "Come pick up this rock."

Jenny was stunned. "You are *not* planning to break a window."

"I'm not," Ingunn said, "but he is."

"We can't do this," Jenny implored.

Ingunn looked her in the eye again. "You think we should leave?"

"Yes," Jenny said emphatically, feeling like she finally may have gotten her point across. "I absolutely think we should leave."

Ingunn approached her granddaughter and lowered her voice to a whisper. "Do you feel that fear?"

Jenny didn't reply; she didn't want to admit the answer was yes.

Ingunn continued to whisper, "Can you really walk away from that? Can you face Michelle's mother and tell her that you came this close and turned around?"

Jenny only swallowed.

"That's what I thought," Ingunn declared as she continued to look Jenny in the eye. "And right now, we're wasting time."

The sound of shattering glass caused both women to look toward the garage. Zack poked his head around the corner. "I guess he doesn't have an alarm system."

"I can't believe we're breaking into his house," Jenny said as Zack reached inside the hole in the glass.

He stuck out his tongue as he concentrated, eventually opening the door from the inside. "We've done this before," he reminded her.

"But we had a distinct purpose in mind," Jenny argued, "*and* the guy wasn't a serial killer."

"True," he conceded as he walked through the open door, being careful not to step on the glass. "But we did get away with it."

Deciding to throw Zack's own words back at *him* she added, "and now you've totally just jinxed it."

Unlike the last time she found herself in a house where she didn't belong, Jenny didn't have a clear idea of the floor plan, nor did she have particular destination in mind. She felt horribly vulnerable as they crept through the garage, which she noted had been converted into a wood shop. She was struck by the organization...wrenches hung on a pegboard, arranged by size; cabinets adorned the walls, seemingly hiding everything that would make the garage look untidy. She noted there wasn't even any sawdust on the floor. She deduced he was either was very neat or else he didn't use his workshop.

Feeling like she was having an out-of-body experience, Jenny followed Zack and Amma as they walked up a few steps and into the door that led them into the kitchen. As soon as she walked through the doorway she felt her lungs tighten. "Shit," she whispered, "he has a cat." Her nose immediately filled and her eyes became teary.

Her comment went unanswered. Instead Ingunn said, "We're definitely on to something. Do you feel that?"

In addition to the allergies, the fear was also choking Jenny. "Yes," she agreed softly, "I do."

She looked around the kitchen, which definitely lacked the feminine touch. The window had no curtains, and the decorations were basic. Jenny did note, however, how incredibly neat and clean everything was. The counters were so clutter-free they were almost bare—there wasn't even a pile of junk mail and important papers, something Jenny had always regarded as a staple in every home. She noted the pots and pans that hung from a rack above the island; they were so shiny they looked unused. Strangely, it almost looked like no one lived in the house at all.

"Are you getting anything?" Zack asked.

"Not anything specific," Ingunn replied bluntly.

Jenny blinked and sniffed away an impending sneeze. "Me neither."

They walked through an opening which led them into the dining room; once again Jenny was struck by both the neatness and simplicity of the room. She looked for trinkets—items he may have taken from the girls as trophies—but she found no such things. Everything seemed to appear perfectly normal for an obsessive-compulsive bachelor.

Ingunn entered the living room first, followed by Jenny and then Zack. The source of Jenny's discomfort made itself known; a slender orange tabby cat was sitting on the top of an elaborate cat tower, looking out the front window. Jenny also took advantage of the view, noting that Tate's car hadn't appeared in the driveway. Still, she felt a desperate need to be quick. She didn't want to find out what would happen if he came home to find them there.

The cat hopped down from the tower, walking silently toward Jenny. With a purr that grew increasingly more audible, the cat weaved its way through and around Jenny's legs. "Every friggin time," she whispered, referring to her incredible knack of attracting the very creatures she desperately tried to avoid. Despite her effort to thwart it, a sneeze made its way to the surface.

"I don't see anything unusual," Zack noted. "Do you?"

As Jenny agreed that nothing stood out, Ingunn made her way silently down the hallway. Zack watched her walk away but said to Jenny, "I was actually hoping to look in the basement next."

She looked at him with a puzzled expression. "How do you know there's a basement?"

"Do you forget what I used to do for a living? I can tell by the outside that it's got to have a basement." He walked back into the kitchen and opened a door that led to the pantry, where Jenny noted an excessive amount of gourmet cat food stacked neatly, by flavor, with the labels facing outward. It looked like a grocery store. Soon after, Zack opened a second door that was situated near the opening to the living room; indeed, it did have steps that led downward.

"Good call," Jenny said, legitimately impressed. As she broke through the threshold of the doorway she felt overcome by a wave of fear that was nearly forceful enough to bring her to her knees.

Zack sensed her weakness and held her up by her arm. "Whoa. Are you okay?"

Jenny nodded but didn't reply to him; instead she called to her grandmother, "Amma! Over here!"

Ingunn reappeared from down the hallway and headed straight for the basement door. "Indeed," she said as she started down the steps, passing Jenny and walking with purpose into the cellar.

Jenny followed her grandmother down the steps, where she was forced to make an immediate U-turn through an extremely narrow hallway into a finished basement that was completely decorated in University of Tennessee memorabilia. Jenny noticed there was no door to the outside; if Tate decided to make an appearance, they would have been cornered. She tried to dismiss that thought, although she recognized the need for rapidity.

Despite the urgent screams in Jenny's head, everything seemed perfectly normal upon inspection. The room looked like a typical man-cave: comfy-looking couch, big-screen TV, coffee table. Autographed pictures hung on the walls in various places, including the one wall that was made of ugly vertical wood paneling. She searched around for any evidence that would have suggested the girls had been there, or at least that they had been in contact with Tate. Sadly, she was unable to find such a thing.

Fear gripped her body, but she wasn't sure if that was her own or the victims'. Assuming it was the former, she reluctantly announced, "I think we should leave." Her voice was beginning to sound scratchy.

"I don't see anything, either," Ingunn said, "but the horror is tangible."

Jenny looked at Zack, who stood motionlessly as he stared at the wood-paneled wall adjacent to the hall that led to the room. He looked as if he was having a vision.

"What is it?" Jenny asked him.

He remained quiet for what seemed like an eternity; eventually he announced, "This can't be code."

Jenny wasn't sure if she'd heard him correctly. "It isn't *code*?"

Still looking deep in thought, Zack pointed to the hallway they'd walked through in order to enter the room. "The entryway. It wouldn't be code in any state. It's too narrow. A builder would have never gotten away with that."

Jenny and Ingunn remained silent.

"And look," Zack continued, pointing back to the furniture in the room. "This couch would have never fit through that opening. Neither would that coffee table." He once again looked toward the wood-paneled wall. "This had to have been put in afterward."

Suddenly Jenny knew what Zack was getting at. She inspected the dimensions of the square area encompassed with the wood-paneled wall—this very well could have been the outside of the soundproof room she'd seen in her vision.

"How do you get in?" Jenny asked quickly, looking for a doorway. She was unable to find one.

Zack didn't answer at first. He simply looked at the wall, studying it. Taking a few steps forward, he reached out and touched the seams between the panels, tracing his fingers up and down the lines. He glanced back and forth between two hanging autographed photos, stepping forward to look even more closely at the paneled wall. He reached up and removed one of the pictures, revealing a handle imbedded in a recession that was hidden behind the photo.

"Holy shit," Jenny said breathlessly.

Without hesitation Ingunn removed the other photo from the wall, revealing a second handle.

"Turn it," Zack immediately directed to Ingunn, who did as she was told. With the release of both handles, a seal seemed to break and the section of the wall between them loosened. Zack used his handle to pull on the hidden door and slide it off to the side, revealing a horrified, dark-haired woman chained to the wall.

Jenny rushed through the opening to the woman, who had been beaten to the point of being unidentifiable. Her cheekbones were swollen so badly that her eyes were nearly forced shut, and bruises tainted the rest of her face. Kneeling in front of her, Jenny said, "It's okay. We're here to help you. What's your name?"

The woman could barely speak through her injuries. With a whisper she replied, "Erin Stottlemeyer."

Jenny looked back at Zack and Ingunn with wide eyes. That was not the name of the woman who had been reported missing from Richmond. Then a thought occurred to her. Returning her attention to the victim she added, "Erin, what's your street name?"

"Michelle."

Chapter 20

Jenny immediately dialed 9-1-1 while Ingunn and Zack ran upstairs for reasons unbeknownst to Jenny.

"9-1-1, what is your emergency?"

Although her nerves were tingling, Jenny remained focused. "I'm at 5402 Forest View Lane. We need the police here as fast as possible. We found the missing woman from Richmond; she's being held here against her will."

The woman on the other end of the line sounded as if she couldn't believe what she was hearing. "The missing woman from Richmond who is the suspected victim of the Highway Killer?"

"Yes ma'am. She's chained to a wall in the basement of this house."

"She's *chained* to a *wall?*"

"Yes ma'am."

"Are you in the house now?"

"Yes, I'm in the basement with her."

"Do you live in the house?"

"No, ma'am."

"Are you also a hostage?"

"No ma'am."

Ingunn returned with a glass of water, rushing quickly to the imprisoned woman. Jenny left the small chamber to give her grandmother more room to comfort Erin.

The operator continued, "What are you doing in the house?"

"We came in when we heard screams," Jenny found herself saying.

"Is the resident home?"

Zack came rushing in with a pair of long-handled pruners. "It's the best I could find," he explained as he quickly went to work at cutting the chains.

"No, ma'am," Jenny said to the operator, "the resident isn't home."

"How did you get in?"

Jenny saw no sense in lying. "We broke in."

"You *broke* in?"

Zack grunted as he strained to bring the handles together. "Come on, you little fucker. Break, dammit!"

"Yes, ma'am. We broke in." Jenny noticed how eagerly Erin drank from the water glass.

"Who is with you?"

"My boyfriend and my grandmother."

Zack continued to curse as the chains held strong.

"You all need to leave that house right away," the operator said. "You could be in danger. The police are on their way; they'll handle it from here."

Jenny sneezed into the crook of her arm. "The operator wants us to leave," she announced to her cohorts.

Zack's voice reflected his exertion. "I don't want to leave without Erin."

Jenny spoke into the phone. "My boyfriend is trying to free the hostage."

"The police can do that," the operator said with urgency. "You need to get out of that house now."

"Zack, we need to leave now."

"You two go," he replied, referring to Jenny and Ingunn. "I want to stay with her."

"I don't want to leave without you," Jenny said adamantly before succumbing to another sneeze.

"I'll be fine." Zack continued to struggle with the clippers. "But you should go. Make yourselves safe."

Jenny recognized the level of danger, and her allergies were about to do her in. While part of her wished Zack would leave with them, another part of her was glad he wanted staying with Erin. That poor woman had been through too much already; the last thing she needed was to be left all alone, still chained helplessly to the wall.

"Come on, Amma," Jenny said. "Let's get out of here. We can wait for the police outside."

Ingunn lowered the glass from Erin's mouth and patted her leg gently. "Don't worry," she said. "The police are coming."

Erin nodded subtly with understanding.

"Stay on the phone with me," the operator said to Jenny. "Don't hang up until the police get there."

Jenny and Ingunn made their way up the basement stairs, heading back the way they came through the house. As they walked past the picture window, which was once again admired by the cat, Jenny froze.

"Amma," she said with urgency, "his car just pulled in the driveway."

Ingunn looked out the window and without a moment's hesitation replied, "Go out the back door. I got this."

"I can't leave you alone," Jenny insisted.

The 9-1-1 operator spoke urgently. "He's there? Is there a way you can get out without being detected?"

Jenny saw there was indeed a back door, but she was unwilling to use it without her family.

Ingunn shook her head and held up her hand. "I'm an old woman. I'll pretend I'm confused and I thought this was my house. You, on the other hand, are just the type of woman he likes to hurt. You need to get out of here."

While she didn't like the idea, she glanced outside to see Hunter Tate exiting his car and walking quickly toward the house. She knew she didn't have time to argue. "Be careful," she said as she looked her grandmother in the eye.

Ingunn flashed a rare smile. "Always."

"Are you leaving?" the operator demanded.

Jenny looked at the back door that led to freedom and instead raced down the basement steps. "Zack," she said quickly, "he's here. Tate is here."

The voice on the phone sounded distraught. *"You have to leave that house now."*

Zack looked concerned. "Where's Amma?"

"She's staying upstairs. She's going to pretend she's a confused old woman. But we need to hide."

"Come on," he said. "Let's put this door back and make it seem like we were never here." He looked at Erin. "Don't worry. We won't let anything happen to you."

The fear in Erin's eyes made Jenny feel like a monster as she helped Zack put the door back in place and twist the handles. Quickly she and Zack reached down and placed the pictures back on the wall, looking around for a place to hide.

"The couch," Zack said quickly.

"Are you leaving?" the operator asked again.

"I'm sorry," Jenny whispered into the phone as she and Zack slid the sofa a little further from the wall. "I have to hang up on you now." As the two of them worked their way behind the couch, Jenny ended the phone call and lowered the volume to silent.

She could hear some commotion upstairs, but she couldn't make out what it was. *Dear God, please don't let anything happen to Amma,* she thought as she began a text to Howell.

In Forest View house. Found Michelle. Tate came home. Ingunn is with him. Zack and I are hiding.

In an attempt to be able to hear better, Jenny closed her eyes and focused on what was going on upstairs. She could detect footsteps and faint, indiscernible bits of conversation, but little else. Eventually Ingunn's voice was loud and clear. "But I don't want to go downstairs."

Jenny forced her breathing to become shallow, although she still felt like the wheeze that accompanied each exhale was loud enough to be heard from a mile away.

"I just want you to get comfortable," Tate said in a compassionate tone that grew louder as they descended the steps. "Then we can figure out where you belong."

"But I want to stay upstairs," Ingunn said even louder, although she made her voice sound fragile. Jenny knew this was her grandmother's way of warning them; she only hoped that after all of this was over she'd be able express her gratitude for that.

"Well," Tate replied sweetly, "you can have a seat down here for now."

Jenny's phone lit up; it was a text from Howell that read, *police are almost there. We'll proceed with caution. Stay safe.* She closed her eyes as she desperately tried to suppress the urge to sneeze.

For some reason Tate's demeanor changed dramatically. "That's what I thought," he yelled angrily. "Just who the fuck are you?"

Ingunn continued to have confusion in her voice. "What do you mean?"

"Those pictures!" Tate shouted. Jenny could only imagine he was pointing to the photographs they had re-hung. "They're not in the right spot. Don't even tell me you don't know what's going on."

Ingunn's voice reflected genuine fear. "I-I-I...I don't know what you mean."

"Like hell you don't!"

At that moment a sneeze crept up on Jenny; despite her efforts to keep it silent, she knew she had made a noticeable amount of noise.

"Who's there?" Tate called angrily.

Every muscle in Jenny's body tightened; she hoped she could remain silent enough that the sound would be dismissed. However before she knew it, Zack stood up from behind the couch. "I'm here."

Ingunn let out a shriek that led Jenny to wonder what had just happened.

"Let go of her," Zack commanded as he climbed over the back of the couch.

"You just stay over there and she won't get hurt," Tate ordered.

"It's not her you want," Zack said calmly. "It's me. She doesn't know what's going on."

Jenny's phone lit up again. *Police are there.*

Almost simultaneously, the home phone started ringing. The silence between the rings was deafening, seeming to take an eternity.

The phone eventually stopped ringing.

Then it started again. The sound was unnerving.

"I think that's the police calling," Zack said quietly.

More quiet followed, interrupted only by the disturbing ring of the phone. Jenny's mind raced. What possibly could have been going on in there?

Finally Jenny heard some commotion, including what seemed to be weak whimpers from her grandmother. Jenny squeezed her eyes closed, overwhelmed with both fear and guilt over what Ingunn was going through. She eventually heard a beep that signaled the phone had been answered. "Hello?" Tate's voice said.

A long pause.

"Well, I've got hostages in here. Two of them. So you just keep your distance."

Two? Jenny thought. By her account there were three. Then a thought occurred to her. Her thumbs pressed the keyboard on her phone.

Torture chamber is behind paneled wall in basement. Remove pictures for handles. Michelle is there. Real name Erin Stottlemeyer.

As she pressed the send button, she took satisfaction in knowing that, at the very least, Erin would be found and properly identified at the end of all of this. She only hoped Erin would be found alive.

Tate's voice interrupted Jenny's thought. "Let me think about this." Another beep signaled he hung up the phone. "Alright, up the stairs," he commanded. "And don't try anything. Your grandma's life depends on it."

Jenny heard the sound of footsteps going up the stairs, followed by eerie silence. She let out a deep, wheezy breath and allowed her body to loosen.

What to do? She thought. Her presence had gone unnoticed; perhaps she'd be able to maneuver through the house undetected and do something that would help Zack and Ingunn.

But what?

Whatever it was, she knew she wouldn't be able to accomplish it from behind the sofa. Slowly creeping out into the open, she kept her ears alert for any indication that Tate may be on his way back downstairs. She heard nothing of the sort.

She tiptoed across the room to the hall that led to the stairwell, flattening her back against the wall once she arrived. A thought occurred to her; she used the phone that was still in her hand to send another silent text to Howell.

Are you outside? Can you see in the window?

As soon as she finished her message, the home phone rang again, causing Jenny to nearly jump out of her own skin. She prepared to run back for the safety of the couch if Tate planned to return downstairs, but then she realized that wouldn't be necessary. The phone had been ringing from upstairs.

The ringing stopped, and Jenny heard Tate's angry voice, although she couldn't make out exactly what he was saying. Her own phone began to glow, causing her to read the screen. *Am outside. Can see in living room.*

Hearing that Tate was still arguing upstairs, Jenny replied, *Do you see Tate?*

The reply seemed to take forever. *Yes. In window. Has grandmother.*

Jenny thought for a moment. If she snuck up the stairs now—while Tate was near the picture window—she could possibly maneuver into the kitchen without being seen. She wanted to take some time to gather herself before she headed up there, but she knew that was time she didn't have. As quietly as she could, she rounded the corner; a stairwell had never looked so long. One step at a time she crept silently, desperately hoping she wouldn't get caught. After much too long, she reached the top of the stairs and took an immediate left, taking shelter on the floor behind the kitchen island.

Once she accepted the fact that she had made it safely, she finally zeroed in on Tate's words. "I'll let the guy go, but you won't get the woman."

Jenny looked around for something to arm herself with. She saw the knife block sitting on the counter in front of her, but she noticed it was already missing a knife. Perhaps Tate had it at Ingunn's throat. She dismissed the thought before it crippled her.

Quickly she decided against wielding a knife. She doubted she'd be able to win a knife fight against Tate, nor did she think she could actually plunge a blade into a man's skin if it came down to it. She'd need to come up with something else.

Tate continued, "And I want to be assured I won't get the death penalty."

Jenny felt sickened by the irony of that statement. For a man who was so quick to impose death on others, he sure was acting like a coward when the tables had turned.

At that moment the cat discovered Jenny in the kitchen. It rounded the corner, approaching Jenny without hesitation. For a moment Jenny considered the elaborate cat tower, the gourmet cat food all in a row and the profiler's description of Tate as being *socially awkward.* Perhaps this cat was his life. Maybe she should appear in the living room holding the cat, threatening it with harm if he was to hurt Ingunn. She looked at the cat's adorable face and thought better of that plan. She'd be bluffing, and there was a good chance Tate wasn't. Besides, if she actually touched the cat there'd be a distinct possibility that she'd have a full-fledged asthma attack, so she knew she needed to reconsider. Pushing the cat away with her foot, she tried to come up with better options.

"There are more, you know," Tate said, "and if you don't meet my demands, you'll never find out where they are."

Jenny covered her face with her hands. Was *that* a bluff? She certainly hoped so.

Feeling the need to stay focused, she looked up at the ceiling for some divine intervention, hoping his previous victims could provide her with some guidance. And there she saw it, as if presented to her by the women themselves.

Her weapon of choice.

Slowly she stood, determined not to make any noise. Once upright she reached up and carefully began to remove a heavy iron skillet from the rack that hung from the ceiling. The process took forever—one misstep threatened to be very loud and very costly. With surgical precision she freed the handle from the hook, bringing the pan slowly down to her side.

And now all she needed was the right moment.

"I'll think about it," Tate muttered before hanging up the phone. "You," he continued, "I don't like your presence here. You go outside."

"I'm not leaving without her," Zack replied.

"Well," Tate explained, "you either leave and she stays alive, or you stay and she ends up dead. Your choice."

"She's your leverage," Zack argued. "You wouldn't kill her."

"I have other leverage," Tate replied. "There are six other bodies they don't know about. That's all the leverage I need."

"Go ahead and be safe," Ingunn said. "You're young. You have your whole life ahead of you."

Jenny began to tiptoe toward the living room.

"So what's it gonna be?" Tate posed. "Do I have to kill her or what?"

Slowly Jenny approached the doorway, pressing her body against the wall, peeking around as much as she could without compromising her position. She was able to see Zack with his back toward her, which presumably meant that Tate would have been facing her. At a snail's pace she withdrew, making sure she couldn't be seen from anywhere in the living room.

"Go," she heard Ingunn say. "Please."

Jenny looked down at the phone that remained in her left hand. Silently tucking the skillet under her arm, she shot Howell a text. *Get Tate to look out the window for a long time.*

Zack let out a frustrated sigh. "I'll go, but if you do anything to hurt her, I swear to God I'll find you and kill you myself."

Tate laughed. "Yeah, that's a viable threat."

The phone rang again, once again causing Jenny to jump.

Tate answered by saying, "What now?" After a long pause he said, "The man is on his way out, and if he doesn't hurry, the woman's going to pay for that."

Jenny heard the front door open and close again.

Her thumbs worked the keyboard. *Is he looking out the window?*

Another eternity passed before Howell responded. *Yes.*

Jenny wriggled her fingers around the handle of the skillet as she peeked around the corner, this time noticing Tate's back was toward her. He had his arm wrapped around Ingunn, who stood in front of him as he looked out the window.

Knowing there was no time to waste, Jenny stepped quietly into the room where she saw the back of Tate's twisted and arrogant head. She could feel the anger and hatred of thirteen different women filling her body as she raised the skillet overhead. This was the man. This was the man that the others couldn't fight. This was the man who had rendered the others helpless and did as he pleased. This was the man who squeezed the life out of the other women as they lay chained to a wall. Drawing strength from every one of those women, Jenny threw her arm downward, landing the pan squarely on the back of Tate's head. She distinctly heard the disturbing crunch of metal hitting bone.

Tate and Ingunn both screamed as they fell together to the floor. Jenny immediately noticed the pool of blood forming around Tate's head; she was unsure if she had killed him.

Policemen in full body armor came bursting through the front door as others filled the room from the direction of the kitchen. Before Jenny knew it she was being swept away by two men who had each grabbed an arm. "My grandmother," she said to them. "I need to know if my grandmother is okay."

The men said nothing as they carried her off.

Jenny was immediately ushered outside into the bright sunlight, down the front yard and beyond her car to the awaiting emergency vehicles on the street. Only then did they let go of her.

Zack rushed over and threw his arms around her. "Are you okay?" he asked.

"Yeah. I'm fine." Jenny felt herself shaking all over. "I'm just not sure about Amma."

He held her close as they both turned their faces toward the front door, trying to grasp what was going on. Officers swarmed from every direction, but for the longest time there was no sign of Ingunn. Finally, two policemen rounded the corner with Ingunn between them, escorting her slowly and gently out the front door.

Jenny began to run toward the house, but Zack held her back. "We're not allowed up there," he explained. "We need to wait for her to come to us."

Looking her grandmother up and down as she walked, Jenny tried to determine the extent of Ingunn's injuries. She appeared to be unharmed, although she was walking slower than Jenny had ever seen. Eventually Ingunn came within earshot.

"Are you okay, Amma?" Jenny shouted to her.

"I'm okay," Ingunn replied. "I already told you; I'm a tough old bird."

Jenny hung her head with relief as tears made their way to the surface. For the first time since they entered the house she could fully relax, and the flood of emotion was overwhelming.

Ingunn soon was close enough for Jenny to hug her, and she wasted no time in doing so. "I'm so glad you're okay," Jenny said in near-sobs. "I would have felt horrible if anything happened to you."

"It wouldn't have been your fault," Ingunn assured her. "It was that lunatic." Ingunn initiated the release of their embrace. "And by the way, what exactly did you do to him?"

Jenny laughed through her tears as she remembered her past conversation with her grandmother. "I hit him over the head with a frying pan."

"Did you now?" Ingunn said with pride in her eyes. "Well I'll be damned."

The wait outside was painful as Jenny watched the flurry of activity without knowing the well-being of the people involved. She was still unsure if she had killed Tate, a concept she could intellectually accept but would inevitably bother her emotionally. Running her hands up and down her arms, she considered his comment that there had been other victims. If that had really been the case, Tate's death would have been horribly unfortunate for those families who would never know the fates of their loved ones. Jenny shook her head to clear the thought; speculation would get her nowhere.

Two paramedics carried a stretcher down the front steps, lowering the wheels once they reached the bottom. Jenny noted the victim had long curly hair and a battered face, but her condition was not immediately obvious as she lay motionless on the platform. Curiosity got the better of Jenny, who walked over to the paramedics as they rolled the stretcher toward the back of one of two ambulances that had arrived at the scene. "Excuse me," Jenny interjected. "How is she doing?"

"Vitals are fine," one of the paramedics replied, "but they'll have to do a full work-up on her at the hospital."

Jenny looked at Erin, who met her gaze. Erin reached out her hand, despite the IV injected into the back of it, and Jenny gently touched her fingers. Although she said nothing, Erin had spoken a million words with that single gesture. They put her into the back of the ambulance and closed the door behind her.

Jenny turned to the paramedic. "What about the other guy?"

The paramedic shrugged. "I didn't work on him. They were trying to stabilize him when we left."

With that he disappeared into the ambulance.

Jenny jumped when she felt a hand rest on the back of her shoulder. "Whoa," a familiar voice said. "Sorry about that. I didn't mean to scare you."

Laughing with relief when she realized it was only Howell, Jenny replied, "I'm just a little edgy, that's all."

"Well, that's understandable considering everything you've been through," Howell noted. He pointed to the ambulance as it started to drive away. "Rumor has it she's going to be okay."

Tears once again rose to the surface, but Jenny blinked them away. "I'm glad." She braced herself as she posed, "What about Tate?"

"Haven't heard," Howell replied. "But speaking of Tate, I'd like to have a word with you about what went on in there. Just what the hell were you doing in his house?"

Jenny bit her lip as she recognized how similar this question was to one she had heard in the past. Somehow she kept getting herself into jams that were way over her head. With a sigh she admitted, "There was just too much fear emanating from this house. Bad things had to have happened there. My grandmother felt it, too." She hung her head. "I guess we both kind of knew Erin...or Michelle...was in there, and we had to do something about it."

"You're just lucky she was. You'd have a lot of explaining to do if you broke into an innocent man's house. You could have gone to jail for that."

Feeling emotionally drained, Jenny said, "It wasn't luck. We were directed there."

"All the more reason it was crazy of you to break in like that," Howell replied.

"Well, we tried the proper channels first." She looked up at him. "And it didn't work."

Apparently her point had been taken; Howell said nothing more about it.

After an awkward silence, a second stretcher emerged from the house. Jenny's heart skipped a beat as she looked to see if Tate's head had been covered, indicating he was deceased. She was relieved to see that his head was exposed, although it was wrapped with bloody bandages. At the very least, he appeared to be alive.

The paramedics wheeled the stretcher toward Jenny, who still stood next to where the ambulances had been parked. She looked at Tate as he grew closer; she had nearly taken his life, a concept which she found impossible to believe. All of the friends he'd ever had, all of his family members, all of his co-workers...they'd all come very close to losing someone from their lives, and it would have been because of her.

She wondered if that was the type of power that sick bastards like Tate craved. Perhaps he felt God-like when he took a life—like he had just done something that mattered to people. Something people would remember. She shook her head as she contemplated the demented train of thought. No one should be motivated to do such a thing, for any reason.

The paramedics wheeled Tate past Jenny. "Is he going to be okay?" she posed.

One of the ambulance workers flashed a sly smile. "If you were trying to kill him, you would have needed to hit him a little bit harder."

Relief washed over Jenny. Feeling immediately lighter, she was able to return the smile. "So I guess I'm a lousy murderer?"

He lifted the stretcher into the back of the ambulance. "Yes," he said with a strain, "but you make one hell of a mean housewife."

The sound of the ambulance door shutting almost sounded like music to her ears. As horrifying as the last hour had been, this scenario had worked out in the best possible way. Jenny glanced up at the sky, wondering if the victims had anything to do with the way the events had unfolded. Had they kept Jenny safe? Did they make sure she felt inclined to go upstairs in time to see Tate's car pull in the driveway? She couldn't help but feel that they did.

She closed her eyes and felt the sun on her face, taking a deep breath, enjoying the sensation of being alive. She felt the silent approval of the women who had lost their lives at this house; the fear was gone, replaced by a delightful sense of serenity that was long overdue. Opening her eyes Jenny smiled at the clouds, knowing the victims were now free to go and enjoy the wonders that awaited them on the other side. She knew that one day she would meet them, and when she did they would be beautiful and free—not imprisoned and tormented like they had been here on earth. In a strange way she looked forward to that day, although she knew she had more to accomplish before that happened. More souls needed resolution. More killers like Tate needed to be exposed.

And she had a baby to raise.

Chapter 21

Jenny's allergy symptoms were starting to subside as she sat at the table in the lobby of the Heritage Inn, although she still longed for a pill. The tall glass of water in front of her was her only source of relief, and it was minimal at best.

"Here's one that leaves tomorrow, but it's pretty early," Zack said as he referred to his computer. "Although, it's a direct flight."

"Book it," Ingunn said. "I hate those landings. I only want one."

With a few more keystrokes, Zack said, "...and, done."

Jenny smiled at her grandmother. "Are you sure you don't want to go to the hospital? Or at least to a doctor?"

"Nah," she said gruffly with a wave of her hand. "Nothing hurts."

Jenny had to admit she would miss her grandmother's curtness. "Okay," she conceded, "but be aware that sometimes injuries don't make themselves known until the next day."

"Then I'll go to the doctor tomorrow, but right now I don't need one."

At that point Jessica approached the trio. "Do you mind if I sit down?"

Zack used his foot under the table to push out a chair, silently inviting her to take a seat. She obliged, folding her hands on the table. "I just spoke to the archaeologist; he said he was able to remove Samuel's remains...well, I assume they're Samuel's remains. He said they belonged to a child, roughly between seven and ten years old. I can't imagine who else it would be."

"Did he say how long it would take for him to get a positive identification?" Jenny asked before letting out a wheezy cough.

"He didn't say," Jessica admitted. "But then again, I didn't ask either." She looked at Jenny with a raised eyebrow. "However, what I do know is that he took some soil samples from the area you had pointed out to him. There does appear to be a disturbance which would indicate there could be something beneath the surface." She smiled at Jenny. "Although, he did say you were about fifteen feet off."

Jenny remained expressionless. "That man thinks I'm a lunatic."

"I don't think he does anymore. But, I can promise you that if you come back next year at this time, that area will be well-manicured and fenced off, complete with as many headstones and memorials as necessary. *And*," she added with emphasis, "both the slave painting and the painting of the Davies family will be proudly on display above the fireplace."

With as much of a smile as Jenny's allergies would permit, she said, "I'm glad."

"Well, this whole episode has taught me that I've been neglecting a very important part of the inn's history. I can assure you that will be different going forward."

Zack leaned back in his chair. "That's because of us meddling kids."

Jenny playfully smacked her forehead. "Speaking of the dog," she said, turning to Zack, "how's he doing?"

"I've got his vet appointment rescheduled for later this afternoon. I should be able to tell you more later, but he seems to be fine." Zack beamed with pride.

Jenny's phone rang, and with a quick glance she saw it was her father calling. "Ooh," she said, "this should be good." She stepped away from the table and put the phone to her ear. "Hey, Pop."

"Are you okay?" he demanded immediately. Jenny had left a message giving a brief overview of the day's events, which admittedly would have been a frightening thing to hear.

"Yes, we're fine," she assured him. "Although, Amma refuses to go to a doctor. I do wish she'd at least get checked out."

"What happened to her?"

"Tate was holding her when I hit him with the frying pan. She fell to the ground with him, but she claims to have landed softly."

"My God," Rod replied. "She's in her seventies."

"I know," Jenny said. "She could have been very hurt, and I've tried to convince her to get checked out. But have you ever tried to convince your mother to do something she didn't want to do?"

"Yeah, you're right," Rod said with defeat. "It's wasted breath."

Jenny filled him in on the details of the afternoon, defending herself when he scolded her for breaking into the house. "Um...are you really getting on my case about that?"

"I know," he replied. "I don't have a leg to stand on there. I'm just glad you're okay. I hate the thought of you putting your life in danger."

"I understand," Jenny said. "I hated putting Amma's life in danger, so I get it. *But,*" she added, "were you able to get that reading I asked for?" Jenny hadn't informed him about the discovery in the woods, but she did send him a picture of Samuel's image on the painting in hopes that Rod would be able to get an idea of what he was feeling.

"Yes, I was able to get a reading," he told her, "and I think you'll find the news to be good. The child is definitely happy. I'm not entirely sure what's going on over there, but that young man is pleased by whatever it is."

Jenny didn't need a DNA analysis; this provided her with all the confirmation she needed. "We found his remains, and now he can be buried with the rest of his family."

"That's fantastic," Rod said genuinely. "No child deserves to be all alone."

"Agreed. Now I'd just like to find out about the young woman we rescued. I certainly hope she finds her way home to her family and her life takes a turn for the better."

"I imagine it would," Rod replied. "Something like this should be quite an eye-opener."

For a moment, Jenny considered the thirteen women who didn't have the chance to learn from their experience—as well as the six others that Tate claimed to have victimized. With a shudder she hoped he was just bluffing and the death toll would remain at thirteen.

She eventually concluded her phone call with her father and informed the others of Samuel's newfound happiness. As expected, they all rejoiced in the news.

Zack excused himself so he could bring the dog to the vet; Jenny and Amma decided they needed to start packing up for the trip home. Jenny made sure she packed up everything that wasn't on the floor; the clothes that littered the ground would need to be cleaned by the creator of that mess. She resolved to have a conversation with him about that once he returned from the Baxter's appointment.

Jenny tapped the pin of the hinge into place while Zack held the door steady. Once she was finished with the third hinge Zack let go; the door behaved like it should. He stood back and admired it for a moment. "Good," he eventually concluded. "Now Baxter can go outside whenever he needs."

She also smiled at the new door to the fenced-in yard, complete with a flap large enough for the dog to fit through. "That'll definitely help if we need to leave quickly."

Her phone rang as soon as the words came out of her mouth. "Ooh," she said, "it's Howell. I wonder what he has to say." She answered eagerly.

"We were able to talk to Tate today," Howell said after the typical pleasantries.

"So I guess that means he's doing okay," Jenny replied with a touch of relief.

"Yeah, he'll be fine. He's still in the hospital, but he's going straight to a jail cell when he gets out."

That notion made Jenny smile.

"He still insists he has six other victims, and unfortunately he may be speaking the truth. With the way he obtained his victims, who knows how many he's taken?"

The smile faded from her lips.

"He's trying to strike a deal. While he can't tell us the names of his other victims, he's saying he'll disclose the whereabouts of their remains if he doesn't get the death penalty."

Jenny was disgusted. "For a man who was so quick to impose death on other people, he's awfully afraid to face it himself."

"I'm pretty sure he knows he's going to hell," Howell grumbled. "I'm sure he wants to postpone that as long as possible."

For a brief moment Jenny wondered if all spirits went to the same place after this life. Would she end up seeing Tate again once they'd both passed? Would his victims see him again? How cruel that would have been for those girls.

Howell continued, distancing Jenny from her thoughts. "We're most likely going to take the deal. I'm sure the missing girls' families want answers, and this is probably the only way we will get them."

She closed her eyes and silently prayed for strength for the families who were about to receive the worst news imaginable.

"Anyway," Howell went on, "I just wanted to let you know that so you can understand the magnitude of your accomplishment. If it wasn't for you, who knows how many women he would have killed?"

A compliment. Jenny felt the need to change the subject. "What about Erin? How is she doing?"

"She's going to be released from the hospital tomorrow. Her parents are there, and she has agreed to go home with them. Not only that, but her friend—the prostitute who had reported her missing—agreed to go with them, too. It seems this was a rude awakening for both girls."

"That's good," Jenny said with a genuine smile.

"But there is another matter I should make you aware of. I doubt it will become an issue, but Tate is asking to press charges against the three of you for breaking and entering and you, specifically, for aggravated assault."

Jenny placed her hand on her pregnant belly as panic started to set in. "Do you think I can go to jail for that?"

"Under the circumstances I don't think the charges will stick," Howell explained. "Based on what you said on the 9-1-1 tape, you went into the house because you heard screams."

"Well, I didn't hear screams, per se. I felt the nervous energy."

Howell spoke firmly and loudly. "I said, *you went into the house because you heard screams*."

Suddenly his message clicked into place. "Oh, yes, I *did* hear the screams. We never would have gone into the house if we hadn't heard them."

"That's what I thought," Howell said. "And under those circumstances, it wouldn't be considered breaking and entering."

Jenny felt relieved as she ended the conversation with Howell and informed Zack of the latest developments. He agreed that the likelihood of Jenny facing jail time was slim.

Returning to the matter at hand, Zack remarked, "Okay, all we need to do is find a dog door for the basement and Baxter will be all set."

"Are all basement doors the same size?" Jenny asked.

"Most doors are a standard size," Zack noted, looking at Jenny with curiosity. "Why? Do you know of someone who is looking to get rid of an interior door with a dog flap?"

"No," she said as she approached him, sliding her arm around his waist and kissing him on the cheek. "I was just thinking my mother's basement door—you know, the one with all the kids' heights on it—could be installed there instead."

Zack furrowed his brow. "I think I might know what you're saying, but then again I may not."

With a giggle Jenny replied, "What I'm *saying* is that my mother will probably want to take the sentimental door with her when she moves here." She hugged him tighter. "And I'm saying that, yes, I will marry you."

To be continued in Vindicated.